Death of an Irish Mummy

CATIE MURPHY

KENSINGTON
PUBLISHING CORP.

www.kensingtonbooks.com

KENSINGTON BOOKS are published by

Kensington Publishing Corp.
119 West 40th Street
New York, NY 10018

All Kensington titles, imprints, and distributed lines are available at special quantity discounts for bulk purchases for sales promotion, premiums, fund-raising, educational, or institutional use.

Special book excerpts or customized printings can also be created to fit specific needs. For details, write or phone the office of the Kensington Sales Manager: Attn.: Sales Department. Kensington Publishing Corp., 119 West 40th Street, New York, NY 10018. Phone: 1-800-221-2647.

The K logo is a trademark of Kensington Publishing Corp.

First Printing: July 2021
ISBN-13: 978-1-4967-2422-9
ISBN-10: 1-4967-2422-4

ISBN-13: 978-1-4967-2423-6 (ebook)
ISBN-10: 1-4967-2423-2 (ebook)

10 9 8 7 6 5 4 3 2 1

Printed in the United States of America

Praise for the Dublin Driver Mysteries by Catie Murphy

DEATH ON THE GREEN

"There is so much to like about the cozy perfection that is Catie Murphy's *Death on the Green* from the lush Irish travelogue to the precise balance between comic relief and crime. Megan's friendships and romantic life—dating a woman but also crushing on a male detective—give the story a lived-in feel. And while murder is nasty business, there are cuddle sessions with the Jack Russell pups that Megan keeps telling herself she's fostering, not adopting. All this plus seeing justice done? Megan (which is to say, Murphy) makes it look easy."

—*Bookpage,* STARRED REVIEW

"A Texas transplant can't stop tripping over bodies in Ireland. Cleverly blends rivalries on and off the golf course with colorful characters as a plucky limo driver takes the wheel again."

—*Publishers Weekly*

DEAD IN DUBLIN

"Murphy's Dublin feels immersive and authentic, and even minor characters add depth and detail . . . This is an auspicious series debut, and hopefully the luck of the Irish will hold for many more stories to come."

—*Bookpage* STARRED REVIEW

"[Murphy's] irrepressible debut provides a lively entry in the Dublin Driver Mysteries. A bad review can kill a restaurant—but what if a restaurant kills a reviewer?"

—*Kirkus Reviews*

"*Dead in Dublin* serves up an interesting whodunit story as it helps push the cozy mystery genre forward into the new decade. One cannot help but be curious to see how this new series unfolds."

—*Criminal Element*

The Dublin Driver Mysteries by Catie Murphy

Dead in Dublin

Death on the Green

Death of an Irish Mummy

ACKNOWLEDGMENTS

The Dublin Driver books are great fun to write, and about 85 percent of the time I'm confident of my use of Hibernian English in them. The other 15 percent of the time I spend texting "would you say this or that" to my Irish-born friends and getting a consensus on my phrasing. In that light, thanks are due to Brian Nisbet, Fionnuala Murphy, Kate Sheehy, my Lady Writers Ruth, Sarah, and Susan, and probably about eleventy other people I'm forgetting.

Thanks are also due to my editor, Elizabeth May, and to artist Anne Wertheim, along with the Kensington art department for guiding the cover art for these books along such charming lines.

And I couldn't write these books (or any others!) without a family who makes sure I can hide away to write, so as always, all my love to Ted, Henry, and my dad.

CHAPTER 1

The body lay in a coffin eighteen inches too small, its legs broken and folded under so it would fit.

Megan stood on her tiptoes, peering down at it in fascinated horror. Dust-gray and naturally mummified, the body in the box, nicknamed "the Crusader," must have been a giant—especially for his era—while he lived, some eight hundred years ago. How he'd come to rest in the crypt at St. Michan's Church in Dublin was beyond Megan's ken.

Next to him, in a better-fitted coffin, lay someone missing both feet and his right hand. Megan didn't quite dare ask if he'd gone into the grave that way or if his parts had been . . . *misplaced* . . . over the centuries. Given that there was a tiny woman called "the Nun" lying beside them both, Megan assumed nobody in ancient, Catholic Ireland would have had the nerve to liberate the fellow of his limbs under her supervision. The fact that he was buried here, in the church, suggested he'd been a decent sort of fellow in life, although he was known, according to both the tour guide and the plaques in the crypt, as "the Thief." The final body, a woman, was referred to only as "the Unknown," which, Megan felt, just figured.

"Are any of these the earl?" A brash American voice bounced off the crypt's limestone walls and echoed unpleasantly in the small bones of Megan's ears. She, being Texas-born and not quite three years in Ireland, knew from brash Americans. Cherise Williams fell squarely into that bracket. Megan had been driving Mrs. Williams around Dublin for two days, and recognized the brief, teeth-baring grimace the young tour guide exhibited after only knowing the woman for ten minutes.

Like Megan had done dozens of times herself, the guide turned his grimace into a smile as he shook his head. "No, ma'am, the earls are interred, but not among the mummies on display. As you can imagine, the church can hardly condone breaking open coffins to admire the mummies, so those we see here are . . ."

He hesitated just briefly, and Megan, unable to help herself, suggested, "Free-range?"

The poor kid, who was probably twenty years Megan's junior, gave her a startled glance backed by horror. As he struggled to control his expression, Megan realized the horror was at the fear he might burst out laughing, although he managed to keep his voice mostly under control as he said, "Em . . . well, yes. Free-range would . . . yes, you could say that. *I* wouldn't," he said, like he was trying to convince himself, "but you could. Their coffins have slipped, decayed, or been damaged over the centuries, and in those cases we've chosen not to . . ." He shot Megan another moderately appalled look, but went along with her analogy. "Not to re-cage them, as it were."

"But I need the *earl's* DNA," Mrs. Williams said in stentorian tones.

"Yes, ma'am, but you understand I can't just open a coffin at the behest of every visitor to the vault—"

"Well, what about one of these?" Mrs. Williams made an impatient gesture at the wall, where nooks and vaults held crumbling coffins of various sizes, and the floor, where a variety of wooden coffins had succumbed enough to age that mummified legs and arms poked out here or there.

"Yes, ma'am, some of these *are* the earls of Leitrim, but—"

"Well, let me have one, then! I only need a sample. It's not as if I'm going to carry an entire skeleton out of here in my handbag, young man; don't be absurd."

The kid cast Megan a despairing glance. She responded with a sigh, taking one step closer to Cherise Williams. "We'd better be leaving soon to get to your two p.m. appointment, Mrs. Williams. The one you're meant to be speaking with officials about this, instead of a tour guide. You know how difficult it is for young men to say no to the ladies. We wouldn't want to get him in trouble." She *wanted* to say it was difficult for young men to say no to women who reminded them of their mothers, but Cherise Adelaide Williams wore her sixty-three years like a well-bandaged wound and seemed like the sort who could imagine no one thought her old enough to be a twenty-year-old's mom.

Just like that, the guide's gaze softened into a sparkle and he bestowed an absolutely winsome smile on Mrs.

Williams. His voice dropped into a confiding murmur as he offered her his arm, which she took without hesitation. "Sure and she's right, though, ma'am. It's breaking me own heart to see the distress in yer lovely blue eyes, but if I lose this job it's me whole future gone, yis know how it is. It's true university's not as dear in Ireland as I hear it is back in the States, but when you're a lad all alone, making his own way in the world, it's dear enough so. I'd be desperate altogether without the good faith of the brothers at St. Michan's and I know a darling woman like yourself would never want to see a lad lost at sea like." He escorted her toward and up the stairway, both of them ducking under the stone arch that led to the graveyard. He laid the Irish on so thick as they mounted the rough stone stairs that Megan lifted her feet unnecessarily high as she followed them, like she might otherwise get some of the flattery stuck on her feet.

By the time she'd exited the steel cellar doors that led underground, the guide had jollied Mrs. Williams into smiles and fluttering eyelashes. "We have a minute, don't we?" she cooed at Megan. "Peter here wants to show me the church's interior. Maybe I can convince the pastor"— The tour guide bit his tongue to stop himself correcting Mrs. Williams on the topic of priests versus pastors, an act of restraint Megan commended him for—"to let me have a finger bone or something, instead of going through all this bothersome legal nonsense."

"Of course, Mrs. Williams." Megan could imagine no scenario in which that would happen, but she followed the flutterer and the flatterer into the church.

Parts of St. Michan's Church looked magnificently old from the exterior. Its foundation dated from Dublin's Viking era, and a tower and partial nave had survived since the seventeenth century. They looked like it, too, all irregular grey stones and thick mortar. The rest of the nave had been repaired with concrete blocks that, to Megan's eye, could have been as recent as the 1970s, although apparently they were actually from the early 1800s. She expected the interior to be equally old-fashioned, but its clean, cream walls and dark pews looked as modern as any church she'd ever seen. Arched stained glass windows let light spill in, and a pipe organ—one that Handel, composer of the *Messiah*, had evidently played on—dominated one end of the nave. Megan shook her head, astonished at the contrast with the narrow halls and sunken nooks of the crypts below.

But Dublin was like that, as she'd slowly discovered over the years she'd lived there. Modern constructions sat on top of ancient sites, and builders were forever digging up the remains of Viking settlements when they started new projects. Even this church, well over three hundred years old, was predated by the original chapel, built a thousand years ago. According to the literature, the ground had been consecrated five hundred years before *that*.

Any temples or building sites that old in the States had been razed to the ground, and all the people who'd used them, murdered, around about the same time St. Michan's had been built.

"Cheerful," Megan told herself, under her breath. Peter the tour guide had introduced Mrs. Williams to the priest, who currently had the look of a man weathering a storm. He actually leaned toward Mrs. Williams a little, as if bracing himself against the onslaught of her determination, and if he'd had more hair, Megan would have imagined she could see it waving in Mrs. Williams's breeze. He had to be in his seventies, with a slim build that had long ago gone wiry, and a short beard on a strong jaw that looked like it had held a line in many arguments more important than this one.

"—grandfather, the Earl of Leitrim—" Cherise Williams persisted in saying *Lye-trum*, though the Irish county was pronounced *Leetrim*. Megan—a fellow Texan—couldn't tell if Williams didn't know how it was said, or if her accent simply did things to the word that weren't meant to be done. Everyone who had encountered the *Lye-trum* pronunciation had repeated *Leetrim* back with increasing firmness and volume, while also somehow being slightly too polite to directly correct the error. So far the attempted corrections hadn't taken, leaving Megan to suspect the other Texan didn't hear a difference in what she said and what everyone else did.

The priest had interrupted with a genuinely startled, "Your *great-grandfather*?" and Mrs. Williams simpered, putting her hand out like she expected it to be kissed.

"That's right. I'm the heir to the Earldom of Lyetrum."

The tour guide and the priest both shot Megan glances of desperate incredulity while Mrs. Williams batted her eyelashes. Megan widened her eyes and shrugged in response. A week earlier she hadn't known Leitrim (or anywhere else in Ireland, for that matter) had ever had any earls. Then Mrs. Williams, styling herself *Countess* Williams, had called to book a car with Leprechaun Limos, the driving service Megan worked for. Megan's boss, who was perhaps the least gullible person Megan had ever met, had taken the self-styled countess at her word and charged her three times the usual going rate for a driver. Megan had looked up the earls of Leitrim, and been subjected to Mrs. Williams's explanation more than once since she'd collected her up at the airport. In fact, Mrs. Williams had launched into it again, spinning a fairy tale that drew the priest and Peter's attention back to her.

"—never knew my great-grandfather, of course, and my granddaddy died in the war, but his wife, my granny Elsie, she used to tell a few stories about Great-Granddaddy, because she knew him before he died. She said he always did sound Irish as the day was long, and how he used to tell tall tales about being a nobleman's son. We'd play at being princesses and knights, when we were little, because we believed we had the blood of kings." Mrs. Williams dipped a hand into a purse large enough to contain the Alamo and extracted a small book, its yellowed pages thick with age and a faded blue-floral print fabric cover held shut with a tarnished gold lock. The key dangled from a thin, pale red ribbon tucked between the pages, and Mrs. Williams deftly slid it around to open the book with. She opened it to well-worn pages and displayed it to a priest and a tour guide who clearly had no idea of, and less genuine interest in, what they were looking at.

"Granny Elsie never seemed to take it at all seriously, but after she died we found this in her belongings. It's all the stories Great-Granddaddy Patrick used to tell her, right down to the place he was the earl of, Lyetrum. She said he never wanted to go back because of all the troubles there, but that was then and this is now, isn't it! So all I need is a bit of one of the old earls' bones, so I can prove I'm the heir, you see?"

As if against his will, the priest said, "What about your father?"

Creases fell into Cherise Williams's face, deep lines that cut through her makeup and drew the corners of her mouth down. "Daddy died a long time ago, and the Edge-worth name went with him. If I'd only known it meant something, of course, I'd have kept it, but when I got married I changed my name. Everyone did in those days. But my girls and I, we're the last of the Edgeworth blood. My middle daughter, Raquel, is coming in this afternoon to be with me for all of this. We meant to fly together, but there was an emergency at work." She turned a tragic, blue-eyed gaze on Megan, who was surprised to be re-membered. "Ms. Malone is going to get her at the airport while I speak with the people at vital statistics about get-ting a DNA sample from the mummies here, aren't you, Ms. Malone?"

"I am, ma'am." Megan was reasonably certain the Irish version of vital statistics was called something else, but neither she nor the two Irish-born men in the church seemed inclined to correct Cherise on the matter. "And I don't mean to pressure you, Mrs. Williams, but we really should be going. I'd hate to be late collecting Ms. Williams."

Cherise Williams gave the priest one last fluttering glance of shy hope, but he, sensing rescue, remained res-olute. "I do dearly hope you find what you need at the Central Statistics Office, Mrs. Williams."

"I'm sure I shall." Mrs. Williams sniffed and tossed her artistically graying hair. "I'm told the Irish love to be accommodating, and no one can resist the Williams charm." She swept out of the church, leaving Megan to exchange a weak, wry glance with two Irish people who had proven neither accommodating nor susceptible to the Williams charm. Then she hastened out in Mrs. Williams's wake, scurrying to reach the car quickly enough to open the door for her client. "I can't imagine why they couldn't just—" Mrs. Williams waved a hand as she settled into the vehicle. "Surely a little finger bone wouldn't be missed."

"Well," Megan said as gently as she could, as she got into the Lincoln's front seat, "I suppose we'd have to think about how *we* would feel if someone wanted to just take a finger bone from *our* grandfather's hand."

"That's just it!" Mrs. Williams proclaimed. "He *is* my grandfather! Or one of them is. The last earl was my great-granduncle, so it's his father who was my direct ancestor."

"But your immediate grandpa. The one who was married to Grandma Elsie." Megan pulled out into traffic, albeit not much of it. The River Liffey lay off to their right, beyond the light-rail Luas tracks, and she forbore to mention that Mrs. Williams would probably get to Rathmines, where her appointment with the vital statistics office was, faster on the tram than in Megan's car.

"No one would want Granddaddy's finger!" Mrs. Williams replied, shocked. "What a horrible idea, Ms. Malone. What on earth could you be thinking, suggesting somebody go and steal Granddaddy's finger!"

"My apologies, Mrs. Williams," Megan said, straight-faced. "I can't imagine what got into me." She drove them across the tracks and pulled onto the quays (a word she still had trouble saying *keys*), offering bits of information about the scenery when Cherise Williams had to pause for breath while scolding her for the imaginary sin of violating the sanctity of her poor sainted grandfather's body. "Here's Ha'penny Bridge. It was the first bridge across the Liffey, and cost a ha'penny to cross—up there is Trinity College, I suppose it's possible the earls of Leitrim were educated there—entering the old Georgian

center of Dublin, made popular when the Duke of Lein-
ster moved to the unfashionable southern side of the
city—"

"To be a duchess," Mrs. Williams sighed. "Now
wouldn't that be something?"

"Countess is more than most of us can hope to aspire
to." Megan smiled at the woman in the rearview mirror,
and Mrs. Williams, evidently assuaged, listened to the
rest of Megan's tour-guide spiel in comparative silence.
Half a block from the clunky-looking statistics office
building, Megan broke off to say, "Now, I just want to
verify, Mrs. Williams, that I'll be bringing Ms. Williams
back to your hotel, and you'll be meeting us there?
You're certain you don't need me to collect you here at
the office?"

"I'm sure, honey. You go get Raquel and I'll see you
tomorrow morning when we drive up to *Lye*trum."

Megan, wincing, said, "Leitrim," under her breath and
pulled in under the ugly statistics building to let Mrs.
Williams out. "You have the company's number if you
decide you need a lift. Don't be afraid to use it."

"Thanks, honey. Oh! And you take my extra room key,
so Ray-ray can go right in." Mrs. Williams handed the
key over, despite Megan's protestations, and disappeared
inside the building. Megan, letting out a breath of relief,
drove out to the airport in blissful silence, not even turning the radio on. Raquel Williams's flight was almost an
hour late, so Megan got a passingly decent coffee and a
truly terrible croissant from one of the airport cafés, and
sat beside arrivals to wait for her client.

She would have known Raquel as Cherise's daughter
even if Raquel hadn't waved when she saw Megan's
placard. She was taller than her mother, with rich auburn

hair that didn't match her eyebrows, but with the same strong facial shape that Cherise had. Her hair was worn in a much looser, more modern style than Cherise's hair-sprayed football helmet, but otherwise she was her mother's younger doppelgänger, down to the pronunciation of Leitrim. She swept up to Megan, said, "Hi, I'm Raquel Williams, the heir apparent to Lyetrum, and I just can't wait to see this whole darn gorgeous Emerald Isle."

"Megan Malone. It's nice to meet you, Ms. Williams. I've dropped your mother off at—"

"Oh my gosh, you're American too! Are you from Texas?" Raquel leaned across the barrier to hug Megan, who stiffened in surprise and found an awkward smile for the other woman.

"I am, yes. From Austin. And here's your room key, from your mother."

"Oh, wasn't that nice of her? And woo-hoo! Keep Austin weird, honey! I live there now myself, but Mama's from El Paso. Who'd have ever thought an earl would settle in Texas, huh?" Raquel Williams tucked the key in a pocket and came around the barrier rolling a suitcase large enough to pack three-quarters of a household into and wrangling a huge purse along with a carry-on. "Not that he did right away, of course. It was New York first, but when his son died in the war, he took sick and Gigi Elsie—that's his daughter-in-law, our great-great-grandma Elsie—took him down to El Paso, where she'd always wanted to live, and heck fire, here we are. How's Mama?"

Megan smiled. "She's just fine. Visiting the statistics office now in hopes of getting permission to get a DNA test done on one of the mummies. I'll take this, if you like, ma'am." She nodded toward the enormous suitcase.

"Oh heck fire, sure thing, but you'd better call me Raquel or you'll have me feeling old as sin." Raquel swung the suitcase Megan's way and smiled. "I've never been out of Texas before, this is all a big old adventure for me. How did you end up here?"

"I had citizenship through my grandfather, so they couldn't keep me out." Megan smiled again and gestured for Raquel to walk along with her as they headed for the hired cars parking lot. "Not quite as fancy as a connection to the earls of Leitrim, but it's worked for me."

"*Leetrim*? Oh my gosh, is that how they say it here? We've had it all wrong all this time! Won't Mama have a laugh!" Raquel chattered merrily, her Texan accent washing over Megan in a more familiar, friendly way than her mother's did, as they reached the car and drove back to Dublin. Raquel peppered her with questions about the scenery, Leitrim's history—Megan wasn't much help there—and whether the Irish were really as superstitious as she'd heard.

"It's not that they're superstitious," Megan said with a smile. "It's that you wouldn't *really* want to build a road through a fairy ring, would you?"

Laughter pealed from the back seat. "Gotcha, right. Look, I don't mean to be rude, but are we almost there? I forgot to use the ladies' before I left the airport."

"Just a few more minutes, and you can run right in to use the toilets in the lobby while I get your luggage," Megan promised.

Raquel breathed, "Thank goodness," and, a few minutes later when they arrived, did just that. She met Megan at the hotel's front doors, an apologetic smile in place, afterward. "Thank goodness for public restrooms. Would you mind helping me bring the luggage up? I hate to bother—" She nodded at the bustling lobby, full of people already doing jobs.

"I don't mind at all. It's room four-oh-three." They took the lifts up, Raquel in the lead as they entered a narrow hall with dark blue carpeting.

"Oh, isn't this terrific, it's so *atmospheric*, isn't it?"

"A lot of Dublin is. Old buildings, lots of history. It's one of the reasons I love it."

"I can see why." Raquel slipped the key in the door, and, pushing it open, smashed the corner into her dead mother's hip.

CHAPTER 2

Raquel screamed, the sound bouncing off concrete wall to come back at her full-force. She dropped to her knees, grabbing Cherise Williams's body, and Megan swayed as the screams' echoes bounced around the small bones of her ears. There were a few words in Raquel's cries—*Mama? Mama? Mama, wake up! Mama, no!*—but mostly they were heart-wrenching sounds of loss.

Megan, cool with shock, stepped over both the Williamses, knelt on Cherise's far side, and felt for a pulse. The woman's skin had lost enough heat to be noticeable, and Megan could find no sign of a heartbeat, or breath. She whispered, "I'm sorry," and rose to walk to the other side of the room, where windows overlooked O'Connell Street. A group of teenagers were horsing around four floors below, and people in everything from business-wear to sweatpants made their way along the thoroughfare. A child had just dropped their ice cream cone and was rigid with horror, while their distressed father fluttered beside them helplessly. Everything was absolutely normal down there, while up here in Cherise Williams's hotel room, tragedy had struck. Raquel's screams had brought hotel staff to the room and babbling sound filled smallish space.

Megan took her phone from inside her uniform's inner pocket. With hands so cold she had to try several times for the phone's sensors to recognize her fingers, she called Detective Paul Bourke of An Garda Síochána, the Irish police force. He picked up with a rather cheery, "Megan? What's the story? You always text unless you've found a body." His self-satisfied chuckle faded into worried silence when she didn't respond, and when he spoke again all trace of humor had fled from his voice. "*Megan?*"

"I'm okay." Megan cleared her throat, trying to sound less like she'd swallowed a frog. "I mean . . . I'm okay. But my client is dead."

"*Jayzu—*" Bourke seized the curse back by the skin of his teeth and lowered his volume considerably. "What in *hell*, Megan?"

"I don't know. I don't know! I dropped her off at vital stat—uh, no, sorry, I mean the Central Statistics Office—about three hours ago and got her daughter at the airport and we just got back to the hotel and she's—" Megan swallowed her own volume as hotel staff noticed her. One, a brisk woman in managerial clothing, strode over and thrust a hand out, obviously expecting Megan to hand over the phone.

"I'm sorry, ma'am, I'm going to have to ask you not to discuss the particulars of occurrences at the hotel with—"

Megan snapped, "I'm talking to the police," and the woman altered between pale and flushed beneath the dark gold of her skin tones.

"I'm sure that's not necess—"

"Believe me," Megan said grimly, "it is."

Detective Bourke was talking in her other ear, the short breaks in his speech sounding like a man pulling on his suit jacket, his coat, finding his hat, heading out the garda station door. He would be there in ten minutes; Pearse Street garda station was just across the Liffey from the hotel, and most days walking was faster than trying to get a car through Dublin's congested streets.

The hotel manager still had her hand out, as if expecting Megan to give in like a toddler suddenly too tired to fight anymore. Megan turned toward the window, looking down at the bright, cold January afternoon. The abandoned ice cream wasn't even melting on the sidewalk, and Megan, seeking them with her gaze, found the defeated father hurrying after the child, whose skip and hop suggested they'd been promised a new ice cream to replace the fallen soldier. Raquel's sobs had taken on the harsh, throat-grating sounds of worn-down screams. Megan, who might have normally related the Williams story to Bourke with a laugh over a pint, reported what she knew of their visit to Ireland while he crossed the river in the Luas. She could hear the tram's imperious *bing bing!* in the background, and its prerecorded, RTÉ-Irish-accent customer service voice telling people what to do, as if nothing untoward had happened anywhere in the city. She thought she kept her voice quiet enough that the hotel manager couldn't hear what she had to say, much less Raquel Williams.

She watched Bourke exit the Luas just outside the hotel at the O'Connell Street Upper stop. He glanced at oncoming traffic and sprinted across the road ahead of it, narrowly missing stepping in the bereft blob of ice cream. He still had his phone to his ear, hearing the last of the details Megan could share, when he arrived in the Williamses' hotel room door. She looked at the duration of the call—seven and a half minutes, faster than she'd thought he would get there—and hung up as Bourke's gaze went from Cherise Williams's body, down the length of the room to her, and back again. Then, all professionalism, he crouched at Raquel's side, not quite touching her shoulder to gain her attention. "Forgive me, ma'am. I'm Detective Paul Bourke. Can you tell me what happened here?"

The hotel manager rallied, shooing her employees out ahead of her as she tried to make her way down to the detective without intruding on Raquel's grief. "Detective, I appreciate your coming so quickly, but it is not . . . unprecedented . . . for a guest to die on the premises, only very unfortunate. We do not require—"

"Mama was *fine*!" Raquel burst out. "This can't be natural! She's just been in for her checkup, right before she came here, the doctor said she's healthy as a horse. Detective, I want a—I want a—" The passion dumped out of her as quickly as it had come, leaving her in tears again.

Bourke looked up, meeting Megan's eyes. He looked tired, she thought, ginger hair in disarray and his blue eyes dismayed. As well they might be, when she kept dragging murders, or at least unexpected bodies, into his life. Not, she supposed, that there were often *expected* bodies in his line of work. Unexpected ones were presumably more common.

"We'll do whatever is necessary to learn what happened to your mother," he promised Raquel. "My forensics team is on its way. In the meantime, Ms. Williams, would you step out into the hall with me? I'm afraid I've some questions to ask you."

Raquel stood at his prompting, looking rather small and bewildered beside Bourke's tall, slender self. The room door, which had been held open by Raquel kneeling in front of it, finally began to swing closed as Bourke guided her out into the hall. Megan made her way forward to catch the door, ostensibly to hold the door so Raquel would be able to enter again, but, more honestly, so she could listen in. A sharp-jawed young man in a suit came bustling up and the hotel manager said, "Doctor," in relief, ushering him into the room. Megan ended up stepping out to make way, because Cherise Williams's body sat propped against the bathroom doorframe, which was barely an arm's length from the room door. So far at least six people, including Megan, had stepped over her.

A glitter in Bourke's eye said he knew she'd come out after them, though he didn't actually look at her as she moved an unobtrusive distance down the hall, where, she admitted to herself, *unobtrusive* meant "just far enough to be polite, but close enough to overhear." Raquel Williams was in bewildered tears, shaking her auburn head. "Of course Mama doesn't have any enemies. Not unless you count Peggy Ann Smithers, who always hated her."

"And why did Ms. Smithers hate your mother?"

"Well, she thought she would have been prom queen if

Mama hadn't stolen her boyfriend, but Daddy says he wasn't her boyfriend to begin with and that nobody was going to put a crown on that bottle-blond head anyway after the way she treated Cliff Johnson at the rodeo after the car crash—"

Bourke cast a slightly wide-eyed glance at Megan, who sucked her cheeks in and focused hard on a carpet seam as she fought a troubled smile. She could have told half-a-dozen stories like that about her own high school years, and they would have all sounded as fraught and overwrought to a stranger's ears, even if they'd been the height of importance in her teen life. She imagined Bourke had similar tales of his own, although probably none of his featured a rodeo. He returned his attention to Raquel, noting down her commentary as if it might be relevant to her mother's death while she said, "But I don't think Peggy Ann has talked to Mama in fifteen years, and I don't know why she'd come to Ireland to hurt her."

"It seems unlikely," Bourke agreed, "but we'll look into it. And it could be it was just the excitement of being here that put a strain on her heart, ma'am. An autopsy will hopefully tell us more. But it's quite a story, the one that brought you here. Who knew about that? About your family's belief that you're heirs to an Irish title?"

"Oh, gosh, I guess we told everybody," Raquel said miserably. "Wouldn't you? Mama might have put on a few airs, but that was all back home. Why would anything follow her here? She hasn't even been here long enough to meet anyone!"

Megan thinned her lips on a response to that, thinking of the number of people *she* knew Cherise Williams had spoken to about her noble connections in the past two days. Dublin was a small town, for a big city, and Megan could imagine word spreading about an American thinking she could lay claim to a British title on Irish soil. She couldn't push that far enough to imagine it could end in murder, but Mrs. Williams had introduced herself at Leprechaun Limos as *Countess* Williams. Word would have gotten around.

The doctor exited the Williamses' hotel room and Raquel surged forward, seizing his hand. "What did you learn? Anything? Oh, God, what happened to my mommy?"

Regret spilled across the young man's face. "I'm afraid I can't tell anything from a cursory investigation, ma'am. There are no obvious signs of violence, which initially suggests cardiac arrest, but more information might emerge from a more thorough look. I'm sorry. I wish I could give you an answer now." He hesitated. "I can offer you a prescription for something to help you sleep for the next few nights, if you want. I imagine these next days will be hard."

"Oh, God, please, yes." Raquel seized the prescription paper he offered—Megan wondered if on-call physicians for hotels carried prescription pads as a matter of course—and he, with his apologies, left as Bourke's forensics team arrived. Megan, glancing at her phone, was surprised to find it had barely been half an hour since they'd found Cherise's body.

The lead forensics person, a solid woman in her midfifties, began speaking with the hotel manager about who had been in and out of the room. Megan, dismayed, realized she could count at least eight—Bourke, herself, Raquel, four members of the hotel staff, and the doctor—

which had to contaminate the crime scene, if that's what it was. At this news, the forensics leader nodded grimly and put her team to work. Megan wondered if she should introduce herself, given this was the third body she'd come across in eight months, but it had been a different forensics team every time. Bourke had only been the lead detective on all the cases because she knew him, and even so she wondered what his superiors had to say about the American who kept finding dead people.

Bourke had gotten everything he could out of Raquel, whose grief had mounted toward hysteria again. The details of what needed doing—not least, calling her family back home to break the terrible news—were starting to come to her. With one breath she would be making calm decisions, and with the next, clawing the wall in helpless despair. Megan approached and asked, quietly, if Raquel would like her to go get that prescription filled, and the mourning woman thrust the paper at her without hesitation. Bourke caught her eye and walked her to the lifts, although left on her own Megan would have taken the stairs. "What's your take on the whole story?"

"I really don't know. Raquel's wrong about how many people here might know about the earldom connection, because Mrs. Williams was telling everyone who would listen and plenty of people who wouldn't. I can't imagine why anybody would kill her over it, though. It's not like it's a hundred years ago and Ireland's fresh with scars from its separation from Britain. There are probably a few people who still feel strongly about old titles, but I don't think there are many of them hanging around the Leprechaun Limos offices or anything." Megan took a deep breath. "Look, there's something else I should probably mention. It's probably not a big deal, because the hotel lobby and airport cameras, and my vehicle's GPS tracker provide an alibi, but—"

Bourke's peachy-gold colouration drained to an unhealthy pallor that made faint freckles stand out across his cheeks. "But *what?*"

Megan sighed. "I had a key to Cherise Williams's room."

CHAPTER 3

Paul Bourke sagged less like a stringless marionette and more, Megan thought, like a balloon losing its air. His clothes—a slim-cut dark blue suit and his ubiquitous tan trench—which normally fit perfectly, suddenly looked too big for him as his shoulders caved and his head dropped. "Jesus, Megan."

"I know." She made a fluttering motion with one hand. "Mrs. Williams gave it to me, so I could let Raquel right in to the room, and she wouldn't take no for an answer. Honestly, between the airport and the car and everything I don't think there's five minutes of unaccounted time over the past few hours, but I . . . well, I thought I should mention it."

"My superiors are going to have a field day."

Megan grimaced. "I'd just been wondering if they had any . . . opinions about me."

Bourke, still slumped, gave her a grim look from under his eyebrows. "Absolute fecking loads. The captain wants to take away your commercial license."

"But I haven't *done* anything!" Megan felt like an eight-year-old, stating the truth so emphatically it sounded like a lie.

"I know. *They* know. But all these deaths in half a year, Megan—"

She muttered, "Eight months," defensively.

This time Bourke's glance was dangerously warning, before he rallied and pulled himself straight and tall again. The elevator doors *dinged* and slid open. A crisp-looking woman in her thirties exited, forcing Megan and Bourke to both step back and make way for her. Neither of them entered the lift, and after a moment the doors slid shut again. "Eight months or half a year, you're a civilian and you're not meant to be wandering in and out of situations where suspicious deaths occur."

"Oh really. I thought it was de rigueur. All the best limo drivers are doing it."

"Megan."

She lifted a hand in apology. "Yeah. Sorry. You don't need snide on top of the rest of this. Maybe Mrs. Williams *did* just die of a heart attack."

"Even if she did, you being on scene to find the body . . ." Bourke sighed from the bottom of his soul and pressed the lift button again. The doors opened immediately and this time he gestured for Megan to precede him into it. She did, leaning against the handrail on the back wall and catching infinite glimpses of herself and Bourke in the sidewalls' mirrors. "Tell me what else you know."

"I told you everything on the phone. Our schedule—Orla will kill me if I tell you our schedule. Client confidentiality."

"Orla Keegan may be little and fierce and have the whole lot of you who work for her cowed, but she'll hand over the keys to the kingdom if the guards tell her to."

Megan, offended, said, "I'm not afraid of Orla," and Bourke snorted.

"Sure and you're only keen to not rock the boat where she's concerned."

"She's my boss, Paul, and at this point I don't know that I could get another job driving in Dublin if I lost this one."

"Not if my chief had anything to say about it," Bourke admitted. The lift rebounded gently as it reached the ground floor and opened its doors to release them into a corner of the Gresham's melodramatically spacious lobby. Chandelier light bounced off hard, polished white floors with darker stone inset in labyrinthian lines. Megan could imagine walking them meditatively, as long as she didn't look up at the field of large, blown-glass flowers that hung from the ceiling near the reception desk, and as long as she wasn't interrupted by the surprisingly (by Irish standards) helpful floor staff. Megan's soft-soled black driving shoes were silent on the marble floors, but Paul's hard-soled leather Oxfords clicked like a pair of high heels as they headed for the doors.

"I'll claim you used police pressure if Orla goes on a tear," Megan warned. "Anyway, the itinerary includes driving up to Leitrim for a couple of days so they can see what they imagine are their old stomping grounds, and spending as much time nagging St. Michan's or the CSO as necessary to get the DNA samples they want. Or that was the itinerary, anyway. I don't know what'll happen now."

"They can't really imagine someone's going to let them drill a hole in an old finger bone for a DNA sample, can they?" Paul trotted down the shallow hotel steps outdoors ahead of Megan, glancing back at her as she caught up.

"I dunno. Um, where's the nearest pharmacy?" Most of the afternoon sunlight had faded, leaving O'Connell Street blue and gold with twilight and streetlamps. A green pharmacy cross glowed from a building down the street toward the river, and she headed that way. "I read up on it and it said the last Earl of Leitrim spent thousands of dollars trying to find his missing brother. Thousands back then would have been tens of thousands, maybe even hundreds of thousands, in today's money, so even if there's not anything left of the title now, it was worth a lot to somebody once upon a time. Someone might be willing to see whether it's true, at the very least. Everybody likes a good lost-heir story. Look at Anastasia."

"Anastasia was over a century ago, Megan."

Megan shrugged her eyebrows. "So was the missing heir to Leitrim. Are you supposed to have followed me out of the hotel, or did you just forget what you were doing?"

Bourke laughed, glancing back toward the hotel as they went into the pharmacy. "I probably shouldn't have, now that you mention it. There's staff to question and security tapes to review. Grand, now it's me you're getting in trouble, Megan."

"I'd hate to be the only one your superiors are mad at."

A few minutes later, the pharmacist asked Megan if the medication was for her. Megan said, "It is," and nodded along at the woman's instructions for taking it, then paid and left again, Bourke in tow.

"You just lied to a pharmacist in front of a police detective, Ms. Malone."

Megan blew a raspberry. "I tried to get migraine medicine for a friend once and told the truth and they wouldn't sell it to me, so I'm not doing *that* again. Besides, you've got bigger fish to fry than me." They reached the hotel again within a couple of minutes, Bourke jogging up to hold the door for her in a very gentlemanly fashion. "I'm going to bring this up to Raquel and call Orla, because God forbid she hear this on Six One." She said the last couple of words carefully, trying not to sound like an American, because her instinct was still to call it "the six o'clock news," which just wasn't how the Irish referred to their evening newscast.

"I'd tell you to stay out of trouble, but it wouldn't take." Bourke split off and went to reception, where the hotel manager had a small group of employees huddled around her. Megan thought they were all the staff who had been in and out of the room, and suspected the manager was doing her best to teach them the hotel's party line on the topic of Cherise Williams's death. She veered toward the stairs, preferring them over the lift, and took most of the four flights two steps at a time. Her thighs ached by the time she reached the fourth floor, but at least it had gotten her blood moving.

Raquel Williams sat alone on one of the beds, her back to the windows, in her mother's hotel room. The door had been left open, but Megan tapped on it anyway; a warning, at least, that she meant to come in. Raquel barely lifted her head. She held her phone in both hands, on her lap, and her rounded shoulders spoke of defeat. Megan put the pharmacy bag on the desk and went to sit silently beside the bereaved woman.

"I have two sisters," Raquel said after a while. She sounded drugged already, her voice heavy and slow. "I don't know how to tell them. I don't even know what to tell them. They're going to want to know how, why, and I don't have an answer. But I can't wait, either. What do I do?" When Megan didn't answer, she lifted her gaze to stare at the opposite wall and said, "No, you don't have to say it. I know. I call them. I tell them." She turned her head, not quite enough to meet Megan's eyes. "I'd like to be alone, please, but could you wait for me? In the hall?"

"Sure." Megan rose and left the room, closing the door behind her and just as grateful to not have to witness Raquel sharing terrible news with her sisters. She had her own version of it to share already, and, with a sigh, rang her boss, who picked up with an acerbic, "Whaddaya? Traffic keep you from getting the Williams girl?"

"No, I got her, but when we got back to the hotel room, Mrs. Williams was dead."

Orla Keegan's silence went on so long Megan pulled the phone away from her ear to make sure the connection was still active. "Orla?"

"You're fired and I want you out of the apartment by the weekend."

"Orla!"

"No, I won't hear it. You've got a curse on you and I won't have it in my business, not a minute longer."

"*Orla!*"

"Bring the car back. I'll have your last paycheck waiting for you when you get here." Orla hung up and Megan flinched as if she'd had a receiver slammed down in her ear. Her hands had gone cold again, at odds with her heart's beat, so ferocious she felt dizzy. She backed up to the wall opposite Raquel's room and leaned against it, afraid she'd fall otherwise, and waited for anger to start burning the shock away.

Incredulity rose instead, a laughing disbelief that clutched her chest. Orla couldn't possibly mean it, except she obviously *could*. Megan turned her phone over and fumbled a search query on whether Orla was allowed to just fire her like that under Irish employment law. The internet suggested she couldn't, and that Megan could sue if she wanted to. Orla was too savvy a businesswoman to risk that, so Megan reckoned *something* could be done. But part of her mind ran through contingency plans— where she could live, whether she could live on her military retirement, whether a competing driving service would hire her, or whether she could get a taxi of her own—while the rest of her focused on making a phone call with shaking hands.

Her friend Brian picked up with the same cheery, "Hi, Megan, what's the story?" that Bourke had used earlier. He'd acquired the phrase, though: Brian, like Megan, was an American immigrant. His day job, running a small publishing business, allowed him to dog-sit her puppies more often than Megan thought she should ask, and as a sort of masochistic hobby, he'd developed a well-honed outrage about Irish tenancy agreements after nearly twenty years in the country. Concern filtered into his voice when she didn't speak for a moment. "Megan? Are you okay?"

"What . . . ah." Megan's voice cracked and she swallowed, trying again. "Uh . . . how much notice does a landlord have to give you before they throw you out, if you've lived someplace for about two and a half years?"

"Fifty-six days, why? Oh, crap, did Orla finally lose her shit over the dogs?"

"Oh, God, I hadn't even thought of them, but I bet they'll be her excuse." Megan had rescued newborn puppies and their mother months earlier, and somehow, although more than half a year had passed, she still had all three of them. "No, she fired me and told me to move out because another client just died."

"*What?* I mean, what a cow, but—*what?*"

"She thinks I'm cursed. She might be right. I shouldn't be telling you, but yeah, my client today—I don't know. A heart attack, maybe. I hope."

"Well, she can't fire you for that. You're not the one killing people." Measured anger filled Brian's voice. "Are you okay?"

"That," Megan said grimly, "is logic talking, and if Orla thinks I'm cursed, we're not trucking with logic. I don't know. I was okay a few minutes ago, but I called Detective Bourke when we found the body and he almost had an aneurysm on the phone." Across the hall, Raquel's door handle jostled. Megan groaned. "I think I have to go. My client—her daughter—asked me to stay."

"Okay, look." Brian spoke rapidly. "She can't kick you out without almost two months' notice, and even then only for failing to fulfill the terms of the tenancy or if she's going to sell or a family member is going to use it and we know none of that is true. You come over after work tonight. We'll get this sorted. It's going to be fine."

Megan took a deep breath. "Thank you. I think I just needed to hear somebody say that. I was starting to melt down."

"That's what friends are for. I'll get the paperwork you need to prove your point, just in case she decides to push it."

"You're a star, Brian. Okay. I've got to go." Raquel's door opened as Megan hung up, the younger woman looking smaller and more fragile than she'd been a few hours earlier.

"My sisters are flying over tonight," she whispered. "Could you get them at the airport in the morning? I'll text you their flight information."

Megan smiled as best she could. "Leprechaun Limos will be there to help you. Is there anything else I can do?"

Raquel shook her head. "I think I'm going to take one of those sleeping pills and try to rest. I can't do anything else tonight and my head is full of fog." All her Texan bluster had disappeared; Megan, off-kilter herself, empathized.

"If I may make a suggestion?" At Raquel's nod, Megan said, "Order a bowl of soup before you sleep. It's going to be hard enough without being hungry, even if you're not consciously hungry."

"Oh." Raquel looked around, gaze vague. "I was hungry before—before. Maybe I sh—do you know where they've taken her?" Her voice broke. "They told me when they took her away, but I forgot. A hospital."

"The Mater is closest. Your sisters will want to see her?"

"I don't know." Raquel's facade of calm was breaking. Megan stepped forward, offering a hand.

"I'll ask the detective if he knows, and text you the details so you'll know, and the service will drive you and your sisters wherever you need to go tomorrow."

Raquel squeezed Megan's hand with cold fingers. "Thank you. I don't know what I'd do without you."

"I'm glad to help." Megan let her go and took the stairs down to the lobby again. Bourke was in an alcove, talking to one of the staff members, and Megan caught his eye as she passed by. She tipped her head toward another set of chairs and he gave a minute nod in return, so she sat down to wait, thumbing through web pages about unlawful termination and looking for apartments to rent. Not that anyone would rent to her if she didn't have a job, but she would burn that bridge when she got to it.

"What's the story?" Bourke appeared and sat across from her, his long legs splayed with an undignified lack of professionalism.

"Raquel wanted to know where they'd taken Mrs. Williams's body, in case her sisters want to see her when they fly in tomorrow. She thought they'd said it was a hospital, and the Mater's closest, but I told her I'd check and see if you knew for sure." Megan sounded mechanical even to her own ears, and from the curious upward sweep of Bourke's pale eyebrows, to his too.

"Yeah, the Mater. Are you all right?"

"Orla fired me and told me to find a new place to live. I knew I was stupid to rent from my employer."

Bourke's jaw went long with surprise. "She never!"

"Oh, but she did. Said she'd have my last paycheck waiting for me when I got back with the car."

Distress and anger turned Bourke's light eyes a darker blue. "That check had better have two weeks' severance attached to it. What the hell is she thinking?"

"That I'm cursed."

For the space of a heartbeat Megan saw Bourke genuinely consider the possibility before shaking it off. "I see her point, but, I don't know. Maybe you could get an exorcism."

Megan stared at him a moment. "I wonder if that would work. I mean, if it would satisfy her." She shook herself, then sighed. "Yeah. I spent eight years as a medic in the army and I came across fewer random dead people than I have in this job. I see her point too."

"I assume you came across considerably more *not*-random dead people, though."

"We tried pretty hard to make sure they didn't actually die, but yeah." Megan sighed. "Look, I'd better get the car back and see whether there really is a final paycheck waiting for me or if she was just blowing off steam. Boy, I'm going to be good fun tonight."

Despite the circumstances, Bourke's eyebrows rose with interest. "Got a date?"

"No, although I should probably call Jelena and tell her I might need to crash on her couch while I find a new place to live."

"On her *couch*?"

Megan breathed a laugh, glad for at least a moment of humor. "We're nowhere near 'move in together' status, so I wouldn't want to presume. No, I'm going over to my friend Brian's so he can talk me off the panic cliff I'm standing at the edge of. He says it's going to be fine. Or, I don't know, how late are you on tonight? Maybe we should all get together to keep me from losing my mind."

"I'm going to be busy until late, but we should all go out for pizza next weekend when Nee is back in town. She's only here a few days before she flies to New York to—" Bourke waved his hand. "Be famous."

Megan's humor improved a little bit more. "She does that. Okay, next weekend at Gotham Café, maybe."

Bourke rose, offering Megan a hand up. "That sounds like a game of Cluedo."

"Next weekend at Gotham Café with a pizza cutter? Yeah, except there's no suspect." Megan made a face as she headed for the Gresham's double doors. "Of course, with me around, that could change in an instant."

CHAPTER 4

Megan usually loved the drive through Dublin's city center, even during the worst of its traffic. Crawling through the streets let her gaze linger on the landmarks—the General Post Office on O'Connell Street, which held a place in Irish history as being the headquarters for the 1916 Easter Rising, still bore wounds from that rebellion. A critical client, examining the pits and holes in the massive Georgian pillars, had once said, "Why don't they fix those?" then exclaimed, "Oh, they're *historical* holes!" at her explanation. She smiled every time she went by, remembering that. And just beyond the GPO lay O'Connell Bridge over the River Liffey, where a glance to the east showed off the white cast-iron arch of Ha'penny Bridge, two hundred years old and counting, now. In the other direction lay the gorgeous Georgian-era Custom House on the riverfront, and beyond it, the modern build of a glass-fronted convention center and the sweeping, harp-like curve of the Samuel Beckett Bridge. She'd seen so many gold and flame sunrises over those bridges in the almost three years since she'd moved to Ireland, and every one of them had settled a little more contentedness into her soul.

None of it gave her any peace just then. Not the shadows of Temple Bar's cobbled streets and neon lights, not the Pride flag flying over The George, almost across the street from the 130-year-old arcade that was Dublin's oldest—and in Megan's opinion, coolest—shopping centre, and not the green copper dome of a Rathmines church that served as an orientation point for a kilometre in any direction. She saw it all with a blind gaze, her conscious thoughts on driving while everything below it was a kind of tumultuous blur of static. Orla couldn't have fired her, couldn't have told her to move out of her apartment, couldn't have taken her off the client who was now relying not just on Leprechaun Limos, but on Megan herself, in the wake of a personal disaster.

Traffic moved smoothly enough that Megan approached the garage before she felt prepared to face Orla. She pulled into a convenience-store car park a few blocks before the garage and sat with her hands on the steering wheel, watching kids run into the shop and come out again a minute later with energy drinks and cheap candy. They knocked into each other, laughing uproariously with the unashamed enthusiasm of youth and friendship. Megan, smiling a little, reached for her phone, slumped deep into the seat, and checked the local signal for enough strength to put in a video phone call. *Vone call*, if her friend Niamh was to have her way. The signal came through and she dialed California, doing the time-change calculation in her head. Six pm in Ireland meant ten am in San Francisco. Raf would probably be awake, if he wasn't working nights, or sleeping from a long shift, or—

A black woman with close-cropped curls and the greatest cheekbones Megan had ever seen opened the video phone app on the other end, a smile already in place. "Megan, hi! Rafael is on shift. You're stuck with the interloping wife."

An unexpected laugh burst from deep in Megan's chest. She'd missed Rafael—her best friend—and Sarah's wedding, thanks to being stationed overseas and unable to get leave to go home. When she'd finally made it home after retiring, Sarah had been on tour with her ballet company, and then Megan moved to Ireland, so even now, years later, they hadn't met in person. Megan still felt nearly as close to the glamorous dancer as she did to Rafael, and her laugh turned into a watery smile. "You're so not an interloper. If anybody is, it's me, because, um, hi, look, I know I'm over forty and definitely a grown-up who doesn't fall apart when things go wrong, but if my boss has really fired me forever and I can't get a new job, can I come live on your couch for a week to get myself together?"

"Oh, no, Megan!" Sarah folded herself into their computer chair, long legs crossed and knees poking at elegant angles as she leaned toward the screen. "What's happened?"

"Let me essplain." Megan hid half her face with one hand, managing another watery smile as Sarah laughed, putting on her own Inigo Montoya accent as she quoted *The Princess Bride* back at Megan.

"'No, there is too much, let me sum up'? What happened?"

"Another client died, and my boss fired me and wants to kick me out of my apartment."

Sarah's brown eyes widened. "Wow. That's a lot of summing up. Yes, of course you can come here if you need to. Are you okay?"

"No." Megan dragged in a deep breath and tilted her chin up, staring at the Lincoln's caffe-latte upholstery. "I will be," she said to the ceiling. "I think I really just needed to hear a friend say they had my back."

"We've got your back," Sarah promised.

Megan reversed the tilt of her head to smile at the other woman. "Thank you. I've got friends here who do, too. People who have told me they do, and who are help-ing. I don't know. Maybe I just needed . . ."

"Raf," Sarah said easily. "The person who's had your back since you were eleven years old and your bra strap snapped in class and he lent you his jacket so nobody would notice."

Tears stung Megan's nose. "Yeah. Yeah, I guess so."

"Well, I'll have him call you when he gets off shift, but you don't worry, okay? You can crash here for a lot longer than a week, if it comes to it."

Megan gave a little giggle. "I think you should proba-bly meet me in person before you make rash promises like that. I might be a terrible houseguest."

"I know for a fact you do dishes, because Rafael's mom told me at least eighty times when Raf and I were dating. She was trying to chase me off because she be-lieved her son was meant to marry you."

"Oh my god. That ship sailed in like eleventh grade. I don't think she ever even knew we *dated*, that's how little time it lasted."

"But you went to prom together!" Sarah's voice trilled into an absolutely flawless imitation of Rafael's mother. Megan burst out laughing as Sarah waggled a telling finger at her and launched into a scold that caught Mrs. Silva's inflections perfectly.

"Stop, stop. Raf's mom is the best." Megan wiped tears of amusement away as Sarah, smiling, reined it in.

"Yeah, she is. And I bet you still do dishes."

"I have to, or they just pile up. Perils of living alone. Boy. Thank you. I really needed somebody to make me laugh. I owe you one."

"Well, you can play tour guide when Raf and I come visit next summer, okay? How's that sound for payment?"

Megan straightened in her seat, a smile blossoming. "Really? You're coming to visit for real?"

"I'm booking the tickets as soon as Raf gets the days off confirmed."

"Yay!" Megan hugged her phone, sending Sarah into gales of laughter.

"Thank god you weren't wearing a cleavage shirt when you did that. Boobs, then blackness. It would've been the last thing I ever saw."

"There are worse ways to go out. Oh, great, I'm so looking forward to you visiting. And hey." Megan made a sour face. "If I get kicked out of my apartment, maybe I can find a two-bedroom place so you don't have to pay outrageous Dublin hotel prices."

"Oh, you think we're not sleeping on your couch as it is?"

"I think *I'd* be sleeping on my couch, since it's a single that doesn't fold out."

"That works for me too," Sarah assured her serenely. Megan laughed again and the dancer smiled. "You okay now?"

"Yeah, I think so. Thanks."

"No worries. I'll have Raf ping you when he gets home." Sarah glanced away, presumably toward a clock. "Or not, since it'll be about two in the morning your time. Tomorrow, though."

"You're a star."

"It's true, I am!" Sarah waved and disconnected the call, leaving Megan with an afterimage of her smile. She took a couple of deep breaths, then rang Jelena, whose voice mail picked up.

"Hey, babe, it's Megan. I've had kind of a day that involves getting fired and kicked out of my apartment unless I can convince Orla otherwise, so . . . give me a call? I'll see you later." She hung up, took another deep breath, and then, feeling a little more prepared, drove the remaining few blocks to the garage.

It was bustling for a Tuesday evening, with most of the drivers there and the whole support staff scurrying around, cleaning vehicles, slotting them into spaces in the parking lot behind the main garage, and yelling good-naturedly at each other as they tried to get things done. Megan parked and got out of the car, feeling stiff and unnatural. One of the newer hires, Dayo, shouted a Yoruba greeting at her. Megan was trying to get a leg up on the language so if Rafael and Sarah, whose mother had taught her Yoruba, had kids, she wouldn't be left out in the cold while they spoke together. Dayo was as delighted to tutor her as she was to learn, and usually her bad accent made her wince and smile. This time her voice only cracked as she answered.

Orla wasn't in the garage, and from the casual nods and waves Megan got as she crossed toward the office door, she hadn't told anybody about firing Megan, either. Megan's hands were still cold with nerves and her face hot with anticipation when she went into the office.

A glance told her the front door had been locked, the shades drawn over the big picture window, and most of the lights turned off, all to signal the outside world that Leprechaun Limos was closed for business. With all that preparation, Megan expected Orla Keegan—small, leathery, ruthless—to be waiting for her with a tongue-lashing, but instead an envelope with Megan's name on it sat alone on the front desk. Incredulous, Megan opened it to find a severance check and a short, signed letter stating that Megan had been released from employment effective that day. A second sheet of paper turned out to be an eviction notice.

Megan laughed, a short, explosive sound of disbelief, and put the paperwork back where she'd found it. Neither *passive-aggressive* nor *conflict-averse* were phrases she would typically assign to Orla Keegan, but it sure looked like the short-tempered Irishwoman was making every effort to avoid actually talking to her.

To hell with that. If Orla couldn't fortify herself to talk to Megan in person, then she could at least spend the eight quid to send a letter registered mail in order to ensure Megan got the message. Megan certainly wasn't going to do the work for her. She turned around and stalked back out of the office into the garage, momentarily determined to tell everybody the kind of crap Orla was trying to pull.

A last-second sting of wisdom made her snap her teeth shut on her outrage as she caught the eye of one of the other drivers, Cillian Walsh. His eyebrows quirked at her expression and she twisted her anger into a tight smile. "Gas. Shouldn't have eaten all that popcorn at the movies earlier this week."

Cillian, who was seventeen years her junior and had the twentysomething metabolism to go with it, looked baffled but sympathetic. "You all right?"

"Probably, but if Orla calls you to do my morning drive you'll know why." Megan pulled her face into another uncomfortable smile, waved her goodbyes, and left the garage with her hands fisted.

She had every damn reason to burn Orla with the rest of the staff, but if Orla hadn't admitted to firing Megan yet, then Megan would probably only make things worse by snarling about it. There was a chance, if everybody didn't know, that Orla could find a way to back down gracefully, but if Megan blew up about it, the company owner would double down. Not giving her a reason to was the mature, rational choice.

Sometimes being an adult *sucked*. Megan, with all the strength she could muster, kicked an empty water bottle someone had thrown on the sidewalk and watched it spin and clatter into the gutter. Then, because being a grown-up sucked and because she wasn't personally a horrible human being, she went and picked the stupid bottle up and threw it away in one of the bruscar bins and stomped all the way home.

Two puppies, still gloriously wiggly at seven months of age, greeted her at the door to her first-floor flat. Megan started to say, "Not until I've changed clothes," then remembered she'd been fired and that it didn't, presumably, matter whether she got dog hair on her uniform anymore. She sank down to the floor and let the two little dogs crawl over her, all short, stubby wagging tails and quick pink licking tongues. Thong, whose white coat with brown patches had in no way earned her the name, stood on her hind legs, put her front paws on Megan's shoulder, and stuck her nose in Megan's ear to snoofle and lick. Megan said, "Augh," at having a wet ear, and carefully snuggled the little dog.

She hadn't meant to keep the puppies after she'd rescued them and their mother from the commercial kitchen they'd been born in. Her friend Fionnuala had taken the boy, Dip, for several weeks, until it was clear that her partner's allergies were just too terrible for them to keep a dog. A little to her embarrassment, Megan had been overwhelmingly glad to get Dip back, as both she and Thong had both missed him terribly. Mama Dog, who had enjoyed the relative quiet of only one six-month-old puppy, had been less delighted, and after Dip's return, had flirted outrageously with Detective Bourke until he made good on his promise and adopted her. Megan and Bourke got together about once a week to walk the whole family of dogs together, which seemed to satisfy everyone.

After a couple of minutes of happy squirming, the puppies began to whine and cast hopeful brown-eyed looks at the door. Megan, chuckling, put them all down and rubbed their heads as she got to her feet. "I do need to change clothes," she told them. "Give me two minutes and then we'll go for our walk."

At the magic word *walk*, they sat by the door, ears alert and tails thumping, while Megan went into the flat's single bedroom and changed from her uniform—which she hung up out of habit—into warm running gear. January weather in Dublin ranged from glorious to inclement, and while it had been dry for weeks, Megan had lived in Ireland long enough now to not trust it. She pulled on a pair of runners, a lightweight, waterproof jacket, and put harness leashes on all the dogs before they headed out. The puppies were so excited that, without the harnesses, they would tumble head over heels down the stairs leading to the street-side door.

Megan's phone buzzed as they reached Belgrave Square, a pretty little park about a kilometre up the road from Megan's flat. The puppies strained at their leads, but there were no fenced-in spaces safe enough to let them run free in. Megan wrapped the leashes around her wrist, muttering, "Hang on a second" to them, and checked her phone. A text from Jelena said, **Call me now?!** and Megan did, saying, "Hi," with a degree of embarrassment when the other woman picked up.

"Megan, what on earth happened? Are you all right? Do you need somewhere to stay? You can stay with me, of course."

"Thank you." Megan's voice softened with gratitude. "I'm on my way over to Brian's to figure out what's going to happen next, but I really appreciate that." She started walking, trying to keep warm, as she summarized the day to Jelena's increasing sounds of dismay.

"How does this keep happening to you?" Jelena asked as Megan's explanation came to an end. "Do you need me to come over to Brian's too?"

Megan sighed. "I don't think so, but thank you. He's got all those tenancy expert friends, so he'll have some good ideas. If I can't stand being alone later tonight I'll ring, okay?"

"You'd better." Jelena sounded both affectionate and serious. "Otherwise I'll see you at the gym tomorrow?"

"Well, I guess I'm not going to work early, so yeah, I should work out my aggressions. I'll see you then." Megan's phone buzzed again as she hung up, with a text from Brian saying **have you eaten?**

She texted back **noooo**, and he said **yeah, didn't think so. I'll order Indian. ETA?**

IDK, 30 minutes if you don't mind me bringing the dogs?

I don't mind, he wrote back. **Ms. Kettle, however . . .** Ms. Kettle, a long-haired Angora who outweighed the puppies put together, had thoroughly cowed the little dogs within minutes of their first introduction. Brian, satisfied that his cat was the boss of them, never objected to Megan visiting with the dogs.

30 minutes, then, Megan said. **Maybe 45**. She put the phone back in her pocket and unwound the leads from her wrist. "All right, pups. Let's go."

The dogs charged off down the track that encircled the park, pulling Megan along with them. A couple of Indian guys who often jogged there waved a greeting as they passed her going the opposite direction, and they all grinned at each other when they met up again halfway around the park. A kid of seven or eight ran up toward her, calling, "Excuse me, are your doggies friendly?" with his mom a few metres behind shouting, "She's exercising, honey, please leave her alone!"

Megan stopped, though, and the kid shrieked happily as the puppies came over to say hello. The beleaguered mother sent Megan an apologetic glance that Megan waved off with a smile. After a moment they moved on and Megan resumed her run, taking the track around the park twice before the puppies started to look properly exhausted. The walk to Brian's house took the rest of their energy, and Ms. Kettle didn't even have to glare at them in order to establish her dominance. They just went inside and fell asleep on the shoe rack as soon as Brian opened the door.

He watched them with amusement and pulled Megan into a hug. "You okay?" His American accent had softened in the decades he'd been in Ireland, but to Megan it still had a touch of home.

"Orla tried leaving me a letter saying I'd been fired instead of actually facing me, so I decided I hadn't seen it and went home. The nerve on her! Oh, is that the new book?" Megan elbowed her way past him and went to pick up a beautiful slim hardback volume sitting on top of a box in the hallway. "It's gorgeous. Lynda E. Rucker. I met her, didn't I? Another one of us expats."

"Yeah, but she lives on the continent now. It's pretty, isn't it?" Brian, tall and black-haired, with green eyes and an affectation for tweed, smiled. "I like to think the team's outdone itself."

"You always do." Brian's small press specialized in Irish Gothic and horror fiction, and Megan thought herself rather fancy, having a publisher friend. She put the book down, smiling and sighing all at once, and suddenly realized the house smelled great. "Dinner got here before I did?"

"Benefits of being a loyal customer close enough for them to walk a takeaway order down to you. All right. Come on in, we're going to sort this out. I think leaving the letter where you found it was a good idea."

"Yeah, me too." Several minutes later, sitting at the blue-topped table in Brian's galley kitchen with her mouth stuffed full of samosas and lamb koftas, Megan groaned and mumbled, "Maybe I just needed food. Nothing seems quite so awful now."

"Good. That's a better place to start figuring things out from."

Megan's phone buzzed as Brian spoke. She raised a finger, digging it out of her pocket to find it ringing with a call from Paul Bourke instead of just notifying her of a text. Eyebrows elevated, she answered with a muffled, "What's the story?"

"Megan." Bourke sounded incredibly grim. "I shouldn't be telling you this, but the coroner found a puncture wound in Cherise Williams's upper arm, and my supervisor is on the warpath about your involvement in her death."

CHAPTER 5

"But I wasn't involved in her death!" Megan's appetite evaporated and she pushed the takeaway cartons across the table toward Brian. He set the lids back on them and, with a tilt of his head, asked if he should leave Megan alone with her phone call. She shook her head no and put the phone down, speaker turned on, in order to save herself the time of repeating it all back to Brian in five minutes' time.

"I know that," Bourke was saying wearily. "My supe does too, for that matter, but she's still madder than hell and wants to know how you keep getting into these messes."

"I don't know, Paul, just call me Miss Marple. Besides," Megan said with a bit of asperity, "I did say I wouldn't promise not to get involved in any more murders. Wait. It is a murder, then? What's the story with the puncture wound? Was she poisoned? Who would do that?"

"Who's listening in?" At Megan's startled silence, Bourke made an exasperated sound. "I can hear the speaker echo and you never put the phone on speaker unless you're either with somebody or cooking. I don't hear any fans, pans, or boiling, so you're not cooking."

"It's as if he's a detective," Brian said to Megan, and—as if Bourke hadn't heard that—added, "It's Brian, Paul."

"Brilliant. They'll have my badge for letting multiple civilians in on the workings of an ongoing investigation."

"I can leave," Brian offered.

"Megan would only tell you anyway. To answer your question, Megan, there were no signs of poison in her system. People don't understand how hard it is to poison somebody without it being pretty bloody obvious. It's not the nineteenth century, when people just had kilos of arsenic lying around to kill rats with, anymore. You can't just pop down to the chemist to buy a load of cyanide."

"I take it Cherise didn't have a false tooth loaded with it, either," Megan said, hoping to head off what she thought could turn into a lengthy lecture on modern poisons. Another time she'd be fascinated to hear it, but not when a police superintendent was mad at *her* for being in the vicinity of a suspected murder.

"What? Oh." Bourke gave a reluctant chuckle. "No, not that the coroner mentioned. The only evidence of a suspicious death is the bruise. He suspects an air embolism."

"Like . . ." Megan sat in bewildered silence for a second or two. "Like somebody shot a syringe full of air into her arm and gave her a heart attack? Wouldn't there be some kind of evidence of that?"

"Not if an autopsy is performed," Bourke said with another sigh. "The evidence disappears when the body is opened up."

"That sounds like a really good way to get away with murder. How come everybody doesn't do it?"

"I'm going to pretend you didn't say that, but the easiest kind of syringe to buy is for insulin, and they don't hold enough air to kill somebody with, generally speaking. And it works best if you—" Bourke broke off. "You don't need to know this. Especially under the circumstances."

Megan curled her lip at the phone, but didn't argue. "It can't take very long to kill somebody with an air embolism, though, right? Just however long it takes for the air to circulate to the heart or brain? That's only a minute or two, isn't it? So if I'd killed her she'd have died at the vital statistics office."

"Central Statistics," Paul said half under his breath, as if he recognized it wasn't important but still couldn't keep from correcting her. "Yes, probably so."

"Great! So it was probably somebody at her hotel. That lets me off the hook." Megan hesitated. "That kind of came out wrong."

"You think? Captain Long knows that, but she still feels like there's something fishy going on."

"Oh, crap," Megan said brightly. "I bet it's my new perfume. Eau de Murder. I'll get rid of that right away."

Brian clapped a hand over his mouth, muffling a laugh, while Bourke choked one off and said, not very convincingly, "This isn't a laughing matter, Ms. Malone."

"I think we're into laugh-so-I-don't-cry territory." As Megan spoke, Ms. Kettle hopped up on the table and put her face in the closed food cartons, then turned a look of disgust on the humans before sitting with her back to them and her fluffy tail lashing in scolding commentary. Megan rubbed the big cat's head just in front of her ears and she settled down, ears flattening with pleasure. "Look, would it help if I came in and talked to Captain Long?"

"I'm torn between thinking it would sort everything out and that it would precipitate the heat death of the universe."

"Wow, that good, huh? Okay. Tell me what I can do, then."

"Stay away from the Williamses."

"Since I seem to still be fired, that seems easy enough, so okay."

"Megan, I've met you."

Megan, offended, said, "What's that supposed to mean?" and Brian, helpfully, said, "Orla tried to take you off the last two clients that things went badly with and somehow you stayed right there in the thick of it. You could have restraining orders and you'd still find a way into the heart of the mystery."

"I would not! Restraining orders are serious business!"

"Very well," Bourke said dryly. "Anything short of a restraining order, though."

Megan squinted between the phone and Brian. "Are you two ganging up on me?"

"No, just calling it like we see it," Brian said.

"Just please do me a favor and stay away from Raquel Williams," Bourke said.

"Okay, okay." Megan paused. "I did kind of promise I'd check up on her."

Bourke exploded, "This is exactly what I mean!" and Brian began to laugh again. Megan threw her hands in the air and rose from her chair, sending it backward sharply enough that it scraped the floor, startling Ms. Kettle. The cat lurched forward, back paws scrambling for purchase on the tile-topped table, and kicked the loosely lidded food cartons over. Rice and sauce-laden vegetables splattered all over the table, all over Brian, and all over Megan's phone. Both humans yelped in surprise and Brian lurched to his feet, arms and hands spread wide as hot lamb *saag* dripped from his chest and lap toward the floor. Ms. Kettle landed neatly on the counter and started licking herself as if nothing untoward had happened. Bourke, on the phone, said, "What the *hell?*" as the dogs, awakened by the ruckus, burst into the kitchen to see what they were missing. Thong sniffed the *saag* and made a delicate face of revulsion while Dip, less picky, began lapping it up eagerly.

"Oh, god, no, the spices in that will give you the runs." Megan picked up both the puppies, who weighed less than ten pounds between them, and wrangled them while they first tried to squirm back to the floor, then gave that up as a bad job and squirmed the other direction to try licking Megan's face. She lowered her head toward them, happy until Dip accidentally caught the edge of her nostril with the tip of a sharp tooth. Megan wailed, narrowly avoided dropping the dogs, and instead dropped to the floor herself, scraping her back on the front edge of the chair she'd forgotten about. Tears rushed down her cheeks to be washed away by two worried puppies.

Bourke's concerned voice rang out in the comparative silence of the aftermath. "Megan? Brian? What happened? Is everyone all right?"

"That," Brian said with a degree of awe, "was worthy of Laurel and Hardy. Someone should have been filming that."

"No." Megan sniffled and wiped her nose. A smear of blood came away on the back of her wrist and she wiped it again. "If it had been Laurel-and-Hardy-worthy it would have involved a broomstick and a hat."

"Fair point."

"What *happened*?" Bourke asked again.

"Chaos theory in action." Megan looked over the edge of the table at the sauce slowly separating on her phone's tempered glass screen protector and put the dogs down to clean it off. "It's not worth explaining."

"It *is* worth explaining," Brian disagreed. "Later, over drinks, at enough distance for it to be funny."

Bourke, tentatively, said, "Is anyone hurt?"

"Not enough to worry about." Megan prodded her nostril gingerly, then lifted her eyebrows at Brian to see if he agreed. He examined her with a glance and shrugged.

"Probably no permanent disfigurement. That's going to hurt like hell while it heals, though."

"Thank you for giving me that to look forward to while the rest of my life is falling apart."

"I'm going to hang up," Bourke announced cautiously. "Megan, just . . . try to stay away from the Williamses, okay?"

"I guess."

Bourke made a sound like he wanted to argue the worthiness of that promise, but hung up instead. Megan spent a couple of minutes helping Brian clean up, surprised to find that, despite the extensive mess, they'd lost very little food to the pandemonium. Ms. Kettle wandered away, satisfied with the disaster she'd sown, and the dogs, concluding they weren't getting anything nice to eat out of it, went back to the hall to sleep on the entryway rug. As they sat down again to eat, Brian said, "I'd ask what else could possibly go wrong, but . . ."

Megan pointed her fork at him. "Do not tempt fate."

"Exactly. All right," he said between bites of food, "I called a friend who's a tenancy expert, and she knows somebody who works in employment law, so you're going to have a meeting with both of them tomorrow to find out how much trouble Orla is in. Unless she decides to pretend the whole thing never happened, anyway, in which case what do you want to do?"

"Find another job and somewhere else to live ASAP? Not that anybody is going to hire me when they realize I'm the driver that murders follow around. People I don't know still stop me sometimes because they saw me on the news after the last one. 'Oh my god, you're the one who was on the news with Aibhilín Ní Gallachóir, did you really find a body, was it scary,' yadda yadda yadda. And actually I like driving for this company. Orla's the only real pain in the ass."

"Too bad she's the owner," Brian said dryly. "Okay, well, I think a new place to live is a good idea, anyway. Living somewhere your boss owns is just a recipe for nineteenth-century slumlord treatment."

"Dublin's just so frickin' expensive, though. Did you know that before I decided on Dublin I was looking around Cork and with the exchange rate, the prices down there for a commuter town were about equal to what you'd pay for the same amount of house and land in a San Francisco commuter town? Except you're only living outside of Cork here, not San-Fran-freaking-cisco. Don't get me wrong, I liked Cork a *lot*, but if you're gonna pay three quarters of a million dollars for a postage-stamp house and land . . . !"

"But it's okay," Brian said, straight-faced. "It's gotten worse since then."

"Right." Megan squinted at him. "How exactly is that 'okay'?" They rolled their eyes at the entire situation and ate their way through most of the food before Brian said, "So are you still just looking for a one-bedroom place in Rathmines?"

"Being across the street from the only gym in Dublin that opens at six am is amazing, so yeah, if I can stay in the area that'd be great."

Brian laughed. "I think more than one gym opens at six."

"I've had a hell of a day, Bri. Leave me my hyperbole."

He waved a hand graciously. "Hyper-bowl granted. And you want a place of your own?"

"Ideally, although rent being what it is . . ." Megan shook her head. "No, I want a place of my own. I might have to move to Spain to get one, but yeah."

"How's your Spanish?"

"*Muy bueno, actualmente. No crecer en Texas con un mejor amigo quien hables espanol a casa sin aprendizaje una a dos cosas.*"

"The only word of that I understood was *Texas*."

"I said my Spanish is actually very good because you

don't grow up in Texas with a best friend who speaks it at home without learning a thing or two. More or less."

Brian eyed her. "A 'yes' would have been sufficient. Anyway, I'll ask around to see if anybody I know is renting. Did you check your lease to see if you had a tenancies board number on it, or a letter from them? Because if your place isn't listed with them you'll have all the power. The tenancies board loves finding landlords who are renting illegally."

"I didn't look. I was only home for a few minutes before I headed over here. But she's so tight with money I assume she wouldn't risk having to pay extra for getting caught with her hand in the cookie jar." Megan shoved a piece of naan laden with leftover *saag* into her mouth and chewed thoughtfully. "Unless she figures she'd never get caught. I'll check when I get back."

"All right, so we have a plan of attack. It's gonna be okay, Meg. You know that, right?"

"Yeah." Megan pushed the food away and pressed her fingertips into the corners of her eyes. "Yeah, you know the legal stuff here and are helping me; and my friend Raf back at home, his wife says I can sleep on their couch until the end of time if necessary, and Nee and Fionn and Paul will have my back and I've barely even *talked* to Jelena yet—"

"Paul, huh?"

Megan glanced up to see Brian's eyes sparkling, and looked around the kitchen like she'd find a reason for the sparkle in it. "Sure? We're friends? We hang out and he calls and tells me I'm in trouble with the cops, of whom he is one, so I think we're friends?"

"Mmm-*hmmm*."

Megan balled up a paper napkin and threw it half-heartedly at Brian. He batted it away and Ms. Kettle appeared out of nowhere and jumped at it, crashing into the kitchen door with her enthusiasm. She shook herself, sending fur everywhere, and trotted out the door as if her dignity remained intact.

Both Brian and Megan blinked after her for a moment, then burst out laughing as she came rushing back in to throw herself on the napkin, flip it into the air, catch it, and eviscerate it into a blizzard of paper shreds. The puppies, awakened once more by the noise, came tearing in after her. She jumped to the table and sat there, tail lashing with disapproval as they finished shredding her napkin and then attacked Brian and Megan's feet with the same reckless abandon.

Brian tried moving his feet out of the way, but the puppies carried on savaging them with whines and yelps of excitement. "I guess they showed that napkin."

"Apparently so. Okay. What time am I meeting the lawyer and tenancy person?"

"Ten and eleven, respectively. I assume that's not too early."

"Not for me, but if they're Irish you may be applying cruel and unusual punishment."

"I'm not sure that's constitutionally against the law here."

"Brian! Ow." She pushed a puppy away with her foot, which only made the dog think she wanted to play more. The attacks resumed, until a sudden contented sigh rose from beneath the table and when she looked, both puppies were napping.

Brian chortled as she peered under the table. "No, they're both Irish-born but also only had morning appointments left for tomorrow. Ruth, the employment expert, is roving and wanted to know if there's a city center café you wanted to meet at. I'll text you her details."

"Oh good, I'll ask her to meet me at Accents so I can see my café boyfriend."

Brian's eyebrows shot up. "Your who?"

Megan laughed. "There's a cute guy who works there. I recognized his geeky T-shirt a while ago and now we smile every time we see each other, so I call him my café boyfriend. Shh, he doesn't know."

"Were you like this when you were fifteen?"

"Pretty much, yeah. All right, look, I—" Megan's phone rang, the Leprechaun Limos number coming up on it. Hairs rose on her arms and a pit opened in her stomach. "Wow. I really don't want to answer that."

"You could let it go to voice mail."

"Who checks voice mail?" Megan took a deep breath and slid the call bar to *answer* as she lifted the phone to her ear. It still smelled faintly of onions and mustard from the *saag*. "This is Megan."

"Megan." Orla Keegan's artificially pleasant voice came over the line. "I've Raquel Williams down here at the office and she'd like to speak to you in person."

CHAPTER 6

"Are you—" Cords stood out in Megan's throat as she squelched the first several ways she wanted to end that question.

"I know it's late, but I'd really appreciate it," Orla went on in the same falsely gracious tone. "Could you come down?"

Megan, aware she sounded like a recording, said, "One moment, please," and put the phone against her chest as she met Brian's anticipatory gaze. "Orla wants me to come down and meet the client whose mother died this afternoon."

"Oh, this should be great. Let me get my coat, I'm coming with you."

"I'm going, am I?"

"Oh yeah. You're going because I want to see what's about to happen."

"Are you living voyeuristically through me now?"

"Megan, you've been eyeball-deep in three murders in the past year. Everybody you know is living voyeuristically through you now."

Megan muttered, "Yeah, okay, legit," and brought the phone back to her face. "I'll be down in a few minutes. While I'm on my way you can think about how you'd like to express your gratitude, given the circumstances." She hung up and followed Brian out to the hall to put the dogs on their leashes and get her own coat. "This should be good."

"This should be *epic*." Brian held the door for her, hissing Ms. Kettles away from it, and followed in her wake as Megan walked the dogs home and left them there before continuing down the block to the garage.

Its office blinds were now half open, blocking the view inside, but allowing yellow light to fall in slats onto the pavement and street in front of its street-facing window. Within the light's square, shadows marked the etched-glass *Leprechaun Limousine Services* logo. The garage doors, painted with the same logo, were closed, with no spill of light leaking from beneath its lower edge. There were always people in the garage, and the lack of light both worried and intrigued Megan. If everybody had been sent home, there was a bigger storm brewing than she could imagine. The only other reason she could imagine all the lights being off was that the on-duty staff hoped Orla would forget about them if they were very quiet and hid in the dark while listening to whatever was happening in the office.

They clearly had something to listen to, too. Even from outside, Megan could hear shouting. She pushed the door open, its jangling bells silencing the women inside.

They were both on the street side of the desk, with Orla standing closer to the door but with her back to it. Raquel Williams, wearing what looked like a long coat over her pyjamas, heaved a sob and rushed into Megan's arms, nearly knocking her into Brian, who grunted and fumbled both the door and an attempt to keep Megan from falling into him. She caught herself and Raquel, got the other woman propped onto her own feet, and stared between her erstwhile boss and client. "What's wrong?"

"She says you don't want to d—d—d*riiiiive* for me anymore! I thought we were *friends*, Megan. I don't understand, you p—p—p—p*romised* you'd *be* there for me—" Raquel's eyes were dilated and her stance unsteady, even when she reached out to lean on Megan again. Tears smeared her face and her hair was a rat's nest, making her look haggard and older than her years. "Y—y—you said to *call* if I needed anything and I couldn't *sleep* and the *pills* made me *sick*—"

"Oh, god, you poor thing." Megan guided Raquel to the couch and sat her down, checking her pulse and eyes again. "Had you ever taken Ambien before?" Raquel shook her head and Megan groaned sympathetically. "Usually it really does just knock people out, but sometimes it's kind of a bad trip. And sometimes it's both. There are whole Reddit boards about people doing things they don't remember on Ambien. You—"

"Why won't you drive me?" Raquel wailed. "Did I say something wrong? I know it's awful and everything, but you're the only person I even know in Dublin and my sisters are coming and we just need a friend—"

Megan fixed Orla with the most vicious smile she had available. "I swear to you, Raquel, I never said I wouldn't drive you. That kind of decision is above my pay grade."

"Then it's *your* fault!" Raquel swiveled her gaze toward Orla, her voice rising to a shriek. "I *knew* it, I knew I couldn't trust you with the way you *cheated* Mama on the cost of the driving service, don't think I didn't *check* the rates on the website and your competitors, you bleach-blond *bitch*, but Mama just loved the idea of the leprechauns and *insisted*!" Raquel surged to her feet, approaching Orla with what she probably meant as a threatening stalk, but which in fact was more of a wobbling weave.

"I don't have to take this kind of abuse from a client," Orla began, but Megan lifted her voice, overriding her.

"Ms. Williams is having a bad reaction to a prescribed drug and while I'm sure she's sincere in her sentiments, I'm also sure that under normal circumstances she would never express herself so . . . robustly. Given—" Megan raised her voice again as Orla began a protest—"*Given* that it appears the only reason she's even here is due to an *executive decision* to remove me as her driver, and the extenuating circumstances of grief combined with a prescription reaction, I'm sure that Leprechaun Limos will be forgiving in this particular case and allow me to drive this poor woman home."

"I don't want you to drive me home," Raquel cried. "I want you to drive us everywhere! You're my *friend*! We're both from Texas! Go, Longhorns! If Megan doesn't drive me and my sisters I'll—I'll—" She swung her attention back to Megan. "Is there a Better Business Bureau here?" At Megan's nod, she bellowed, "I'll report you!" at Orla. "I'll *report* you for doing that thing you're not supposed to! With the money! Overcharging! Overcharging *my dead mama*!"

"You can't blame me for charging what the market

will bear," Orla began, and Brian, whom even Megan had nearly forgotten, murmured, "No, of course not, but it certainly won't play well on social media, especially combined with the circumstances under which Megan isn't driving the Williamses."

Raquel shrieked, "What circumstances?" and collapsed back onto the couch, suddenly wracked with sobs. Sympathy twisted Megan's heart and she sat, putting an arm around the grieving woman's shoulders.

Orla stared at Brian like he'd turned up a viper. "What social media?"

"All of it." He met her gaze flatly. "The Six One news, for that matter. Aibhilín Ní Gallachóir may be a sportscaster, but I bet she'd *love* to have another story with Megan Malone, after the whole thing last September. I bet we can have the whole country talking about Leprechaun Limos by tomorrow afternoon." He took his phone out, making a show of opening an app.

Orla nearly slapped the phone out of his hands. "You wouldn't dare!"

"Why not? I'm just a casual observer, noticing how badly your clients and employees are being treated."

"When Mama is *dead*!" Raquel wailed.

"Indeed, when Mrs. Williams is dead. How many is tha—"

"All right! *Fine*, have it your way, you will anyway. Megan, drive this woman home—"

"*Excuse* me? Last I checked I didn't even wo—"

Impotent fury flushed Orla's cheeks bright red. "Fine, you're rehired—"

"For half again my former salary."

Orla's eyes bulged. "That's highway robbery so!"

"And no more yanking Tymon and the others around,

making them work shifts with no overtime. Oh, please," Megan said as Orla's eyes bugged again. "Like we all don't know you take advantage of the kids and the immigrants whose first language isn't English."

"I will pay you a contractor's rate to finish the Williams contract," Orla snarled. "That's it."

"Wait, she *fired* you? Because Mama died?" Raquel swept a goggling gaze between Megan and Orla. "That's why you wouldn't drive me? It's not because we're not friends?"

"It's not because we're not friends," Megan promised. She hoped, for Raquel's sake, that this was one of those drug-induced episodes that she wouldn't remember.

"I'd suggest not agreeing to anything until you've spoken with your employment lawyer tomorrow, Megan," Brian said from the corner, as if a Greek tragedy—or perhaps a vaudeville farce—wasn't playing out in front of him as he spoke.

Orla's face went so white her bleached hair looked dark in comparison. "You're talking to a solicitor, you treacherous cu—"

Megan bellowed an incredulous, "*You fired me!*" over Orla's accusations of disloyalty. "What did you *expect* me to do?"

The door between the office and the garage flew open, a full half-dozen staff suddenly framed in it. Cillian, whom Megan had thought out driving a client, stood in the middle of them, his handsome face drawn with shock. "You *fired* Megan?"

Orla snarled, "This is none of your business," at the lot of them, but none of them, whether Irish-born or new to the country, looked even faintly cowed. A part of Megan that was neither seething at Orla nor worried about Raquel wanted to cheer for the strength they found in numbers, but it didn't seem like the time for that, either. Cillian stepped into the office, the rest of them crowding around him. Megan saw a couple of others even farther back, hardly more than shadows in the light cast from the office.

"I'd say it is our business," Cillian replied. "If you think you can fire one of us without warning, you must think you can do the same to any of us. What's the story here, Megan? Why'd she fire you?"

"The woman is cursed!" Orla shouted. "The dead follow her!"

Megan could see them all consider that as a real possibility, just as Bourke had done. Most of them shook it off as he'd done, although one of the older drivers had the look of a man carefully and deliberately choosing sense over superstition. All things considered, Megan couldn't even really blame him.

Raquel whispered, "Megan?" and when Megan turned to her, gazed at her with wide-pupiled astonishment. "Megan, do you see dead people?"

"Aw, honey." Megan sat beside Raquel, pulling her into a hug. "No, I don't. Look, I'll call a taxi and we'll get you home, all right? And I'll stay with you until you're actually asleep."

"N—n—no. No! No! I want Megan to drive me and my sisters." Raquel fixed what was obviously the most gimlet gaze she had available on Orla. Megan had seen more threatening marshmallows, but she admired Raquel for trying.

Orla, at the center of many other much more effective glares, curled her lip in frustrated rage and snapped, "Then take our conversation this afternoon as notice that your employment with Leprechaun Limousines will end in two weeks' time."

A glint of satisfaction lit Orla's pale eyes and Megan realized she'd found a way out of the legal problems a no-notification firing would cause her. Megan still intended to push it on the no-justification front, but not just then. Right then, she only slipped an arm around Raquel's waist and helped her stand. "Guys, could you get the Lincoln ready for me so I can drive Ms. Williams back to her hotel? And Brian . . ." She sent a guilty look at her friend, not wanting to mention the puppies in Orla's presence. "Could you . . . ?"

"No problem."

"Thank you." Raquel overpronounced the words. "I knew you were my friend." She wobbled with Megan to the front door. By the time they got there, the garage doors were opening and Cillian was bringing Megan's favorite car, a new-model black Lincoln Continental, to them. He waited in the vehicle while Megan poured Raquel into the back seat and made sure she was buckled in, then got out and held the door for Megan himself, murmuring, "Are you all right, Megan? What's going on? Do you need—" He clearly didn't know how to finish the sentence, but just as clearly meant the nebulous offer of help. Megan resisted the sudden impulse to hug him.

"I think I'm okay right now. You lads all being at the door helped, I think. It helped me, anyway."

A tiny smile crept across his face. "We were all listening like mad, but we could only hear the half of it until you shouted about being fired. I didn't mean to open the door. It just happened."

"Pretty good timing, if you ask me." Megan gave him a ghost of a smile in return and glanced down at her running gear. "God, she'll have my skin for driving out of uniform too."

"She didn't when you wore that gold number."

Megan surprised herself with a real laugh and, fortified by it, took her place in the driver's seat. "No, but Carmen was paying for that too. Are you on late tonight?"

"I am."

"Okay, great. I'll text if I need anything, okay?"

"Grand so." Cillian closed the door for her and Raquel trilled, "He's very nice," from the back seat in a voice that indicated she was a few breaths from asleep.

"Yeah, he is. I mean, yes, ma'am, he is. It's just a few minutes back to the hotel at this time of night, Ms. Williams. We'll get you home safe and sound."

"My mama's dead," Raquel whispered. "I'll never be safe and sound again."

The drive back through Rathmines to Dublin's city center really did only take a few minutes in ten pm traffic, but Raquel wasn't quite conscious when they arrived. Megan parked in front of the hotel and helped her client out of the vehicle, guiding her to her room ushered by loads of sympathetic looks from the hotel staff. Megan got her into bed and Raquel, bleary with grief and drugs, mumbled, "You don't have to stay. 'Mmokay. 'Mm*not* okay but 'mmokay."

Megan sighed. "I'm worried about you going for another Ambien walk. Is it all right if I ask the staff to . . ." She trailed off, looking for a polite way to phrase it, then cautiously said, "To not let you leave the hotel again?"

"That's a good idea," Raquel agreed. "Smart. You'll get my sisters?"

"I'll get your sisters," Megan promised. "You get some rest, Ms. Williams."

Raquel whispered, "Raquel," and fell asleep. Megan pulled the covers up, murmured, "Raquel," and went down to the front desk to ask them to keep an eye out for Raquel, although she thought it probably wasn't necessary any longer. Still, they agreed, and Megan left the hotel with a sigh, only realizing as she went out into the night that she had completely failed to keep her promise to Bourke. From the car, she sent Cillian a text saying all was well, Bourke a text saying she was once again employed by Leprechaun Limos and also driving the Williamses despite his request, Jelena a text saying she wouldn't make it to the gym tomorrow after all, and finally, a text to Brian saying she'd be home soon and he didn't have to stay with the puppies all night. "Remember when you'd have had to have made four actual phone calls to tell people all this?" she asked herself. It seemed like a long time ago.

Brian and Cillian texted back. Bourke, Megan hoped, was at home asleep like a sensible person, although the Irish were generally as notorious about staying up late as they were about not getting up early. She was about to drive home when she got a text from Raf saying **good time to call?** and shook her head like he could see her.

Gimme half an hour, she wrote back. **Good news, I got un-fired.**

Aw man, he said. **I was looking forward to you living on our couch**.

Half an hour later, the car back in the garage and Megan flopped out on her own couch with puppies on her belly, he called through the video phone app, took one look at her, and said, "Ten-minute call tops. You look exhausted."

"Boy, and you're the one who just got off an all-night shift." He didn't look like it, though, his brown eyes bright and his dark gold skin a lot healthier in tone than Megan's own, in the tiny picture of herself at the app's lower corner. The shadows made her eyes look deeply sunken, and it didn't help no matter how she held the phone above herself. "Thanks for calling, Raf. I think I'm okay now."

"Sarah filled me in, *pero que pasa, hermana*? You're un-fired?"

"Oh, god." Megan rolled her eyes and caught him up on the past few hours, his eyebrows growing increasingly crinkly as she did so.

"You ever hear the term *toxic workplace*, Megs?"

"Yeah, of course. Mostly it's not like this. She's just a pill, usually."

Raf said, "Mmm-*hmm,*" in a much more emphatic way than Brian had earlier, and managed to sound so much like his mother in doing so that Megan began to laugh. Raf looked pained, and for a minute or two they caught up on how his parents were doing. "You talked to your folks lately?"

"I think you talk to them more than I do. No, I'm going to call them this week, though. Just to say hi."

"Good. I know you're not close, but I hate to think of you not talking to them."

"We're not *un*-close. Or not unfriendly, anyway. Just . . . they have their lives and I have mine. Still, I don't know, this thing with Raquel tonight made me think about them. I should talk to them more."

"I talk to Mama twice a week and I'm still a neglectful son," Raf assured her. "It's never enough."

"Still, I could do better. Okay, look, it's past eleven and I have to be at the airport before seven to pick up two more people whose mother just died, so I'm going to . . ." Megan changed her focus from the phone to the ceiling. "Drink heavily all night?"

"Probably not a great idea."

Megan smiled back at the phone. "No, probably not. Okay, fine. I'll just get some sleep, and deal with tomorrow when it comes."

"Aight. G'night, Megs."

"Night, Raf. Or g'morning, or g'afternoon, whatever it is there." They hung up and Megan dragged herself off to bed, pausing only long enough to do her nightly ablutions and get her uniform onto a hanger where it belonged. The puppies climbed onto the bed with her and she set her alarm for fifteen minutes earlier than usual so she'd be able to brush dog hair off and iron her uniform. Just after she got comfortable, her phone, still in the living room, buzzed with the urgency of an incoming message. Teeth gritted, she ignored it and went to sleep.

CHAPTER 7

The alarm went off much, much too early. Megan lurched out of bed, followed by two bouncing puppies, and only got dressed to take them for a walk because it was too cold out to do it in pyjamas. Still, *dressed* was an optimistic term: She put sweatpants and a huge jumper on over her PJs without bothering to put a bra on, and shoved her feet into cloppy shoes she'd bought just for the purpose of early-morning walks. The cold air did less to wake her up than she'd hoped—five hours of sleep just wasn't enough at this point in her life—and she put coffee on to brew when they got back to the flat. "I could use a place with a garden," she told the empty apartment, as if it would take dictation on her personal needs. The puppies, content with their empty bladders, flopped down and went back to sleep. Megan mumbled, "Traitors," and went to shower.

The hot water, followed by the scent of brewing coffee when she emerged, went miles toward awakening her. Increasingly chipper, she ironed her uniform, stole eight minutes to do the most basic yoga stretches possible, and headed out the door with her insulated coffee mug in hand. The previous evening's text message was from Brian, sending her information about the people she was supposed to meet later that morning. A second one, sent while she was sleeping, was from Jelena, saying she'd miss Megan at the gym, and to call when she got the chance. Megan muttered, "See, not every text is mission critical and has to be checked immediately," to a world that was neither listening to nor interested in her heretical opinions.

Leprechaun Limos employed about thirty full- and part-time people, with a dozen or fifteen drivers and roughly the same number of maintenance and support staff. Usually, not more than six or ten of them were in the shop at any given time, and there were usually far fewer this early in the day. Today an astonishing bustle filled the garage, well over a dozen people there despite it being just after six on a Wednesday morning. Furthermore, it all basically came to a stop when Megan walked in, everyone's gaze swiveling toward her. Megan blinked in confusion, opened her mouth to speak, and released a wicked little cackle instead. "What is this, my twenty-one-gun salute?"

Tymon, the Irish-born child of Polish immigrants, glanced nervously at their coworkers, and, at their encouraging nod, stepped forward. He'd clearly been appointed their spokesperson, despite being barely into his twenties, but he spoke two of the three languages used in the shop fluently, and a third—Irish—that almost nobody else did. His communication skills outstripped most of theirs, including Megan's. "First we wanted to make sure you're okay?"

"Yeah, I'm grand. I'm okay. I'm fine." The lady, Megan thought, doth protest too much, but Tymon's shoulders relaxed a little and he nodded.

"Good. Good. Grand. The second thing is we're unionizing." Colour flushed Tymon's cheeks as he made the bold statement, like he was afraid of Megan's opinion. His nervousness drained away, though, as Megan's astonished smile bloomed.

"Seriously? You are? *We* are? That's brilliant!"

Relief swept not just Tymon's face, but everyone else's too. Suddenly they were crowding around, offering hugs and sympathy for the madness Megan had been through with Orla over the past day. Someone was saying how they'd been afraid Megan wouldn't be on board with unionizing because so many Americans didn't seem to like them, while someone else lifted their voice to say no one should be treated the way Megan had been, and Tymon talked over them all, saying, "Our power is in working together. Orla can't replace us all at once, even with drivers in Dublin looking for work, especially if we sit in. We won't let her fire you, Megan. This isn't right."

"You're amazing. You're all amazing." Megan waded into the group, hugging and trying not to spill her coffee on anyone. "Don't do anything dumb on my behalf, though, okay? Don't get fired over me. If you're going to engage in industrial action, wait until you've got all the union paperwork, or whatever it takes, in place. I don't want anybody else in tro—"

"The whole world is in trouble," Tymon said fiercely. "We'll stand together so we don't fall apart."

Megan smiled. "A modern-day Benjamin Franklin." At Tymon's quizzical eyebrows, she said, "When they were signing the American Declaration of Independence he said 'We must all hang together, or we will certainly all hang separately.' Same idea."

"Smart man."

Megan's smile turned to a laugh. "He's generally considered to be, yeah. Look, lads . . ." She smiled around at the group of them, aware that in this particular case they were all, in fact, lads. The first time she'd heard a teen girl address her all-girl cohort as "lads," she'd laughed so hard she'd nearly wept, although she knew it wasn't actually any more peculiar than the generic American use of "guys." It was one of a hundred cases of being separated by a common language, and there were aspects of it Megan figured she'd never really get over. "Thank you," she said. "Thank you all. I don't know what I've done to deserve this, but thank you."

"Learned Yoruba," Dayo said dryly. Tymon said, "Stayed late to help clean the cars when you didn't have to," and Cillian, who had just come in from dropping his vehicle in the back, added, "Taken late shifts so we could go see our new nieces," over several other peoples' responses. Megan had to wipe her eyes, and sniffled as she tried to stop the rush of answers.

"Well, okay, thank you. Thank you. I have to go or I'll be late, but thank you." She was mobbed with hugs again before they let her leave, but got on the road with just enough time to drive the forty minutes up to the airport. Traffic through O'Connell Street and Drumcondra, the two bottlenecks, was still light enough that she reached the M1 motorway in good time, and made it into the reserved parking area at the airport with two minutes to spare before the official landing time.

Of course, it turned out the flight from Dallas had already landed, but the Williams sisters would have customs to get through, and possibly luggage to collect. Megan still made a face as she scurried through the airport, nodding greetings to porters and security she recognized from her regular visits there, and scooted up to the arrivals gate with *Williams* in bold text across her phone screen.

Then she had to wait for forty minutes for them to clear customs and collect luggage, but she vastly preferred having to wait over the perpetual worry that she would somehow arrive late and have upset clients waiting on *her*. She rang Jelena, updating her on the entire ridiculous saga with Orla, who had thoroughly earned the pretty Polish woman's pique. Tempting as it was, Megan turned down Jelena's offer to go have a word with Orla, although the idea of watching her buff not-officially-a-girlfriend loom over her boss was pretty appealing. "Maybe next time," she promised, and Jelena said, "I'll hold you to that," before hanging up.

Personal business taken care of, Megan meandered up to the waiting area in front of the arrivals doors and stood around with other drivers holding their clients' names on phones and printouts. Chats that sprang up about new grandchildren, enraging family members, the latest sports, and politics kept the drivers occupied while they waited, and Megan's American opinion—or more accurately, her ability to explain often incomprehensible-to-Europeans American decisions—was highly sought after. "Explain it again," one of the older drivers, a white guy named

Liam, said to her that morning. "The part about being embarrassing millionaires."

Megan laughed. "No, 'temporarily embarrassed millionaires.' America's got this national mythology about how we can all pull ourselves up by our bootstraps, and that we'll all be millionaires if we only try hard enough. So the 'temporarily embarrassed' there means 'we have somehow accidentally found ourselves without the millions we deserve, but as soon as we have them, we definitely won't want to pay taxes on it.' The thing is that while they're feeding us the bootstraps mythology with mother's milk, they don't explain graduated taxes or how few people are actually millionaires or how much money a million—or a billion—dollars really is."

"I just read that a million seconds is eleven and a half days and a billion seconds is thirty-two *years*," another driver said incredulously. Like Tymon, Alannah was young and Irish-born to immigrant parents, her Kenyan heritage clear in dark brown skin and tightly curled black hair. She was, also like Tymon, very cute. Megan kept wanting to introduce them to each other. "If I had a billion euros and spent one a second I would be *fifty-three* before I'd spent them all."

Liam proclaimed, "That's mental," and went to collect his clients. That signaled the breakup of their morning chat. Megan would repeat something like it later in the week with another group, or maybe just admire baby pictures and—maybe—laugh over the story of Ms. Kettles and the dinner disaster of the evening before. Those loose-knit friendships and the glimpses into other people's lives were among the reasons she really did love her job.

A text filled with exasperated emojis, their faces frowning and their hands thrown in the air, came through from Detective Bourke, and she wrote back a **sorry not sorry? I mean, I'm glad I'm not 100% fired** . . . before putting her phone back in her pocket. A mix of contentment and sorrow settled in her chest as the Dallas flight passengers began to flood through the arrivals doors into the cordoned triangle, and then out to the airport proper.

Like Raquel, Jessie and Sondra were obviously their mother's daughters, though one of them had the hip-length hair and soft-looking clothes of a hippie, and if Megan hadn't been looking for facial resemblances, she wouldn't have pegged her as a Williams. The other looked buttoned-down and strained, wearing four-inch heels and carrying her shoulders so high that Megan thought she spent most of her life stressed, and that she was now near to breaking. They were both pale with grief and lack of sleep, the strained one marked with hot spots of colour on her cheeks.

The hippie saw Megan's sign first and pointed, guiding her sister toward Megan. The strained sister, whose hair was pulled into a braid so tight Megan got a sympathetic headache, nearly crumpled when she saw Megan, and it was the hippie who said, "I'm Jessie. This is Sondra. Thank you for coming," as they approached the cordoned barrier.

"Megan Malone. Leprechaun Limos, and I, would like to extend our sympathies. I'm so sorry for your loss," Megan said gently. "Let me help you to the car." She gestured down the length of the cord, indicating they could come that way, and they both followed obediently. They only had one suitcase and one carry-on between them, plus a couple of personal bags, and Megan offered to take the former with another small gesture. Sondra immediately handed the suitcase over but Jessie shook her head, whispering, "I can handle it."

"Of course. Don't be shy about changing your mind, though, please." She guided them out of the airport to the car service private parking lot, held the Lincoln's door for them, and wasn't surprised, when she got in the car herself after putting the luggage in the trunk—the boot—to see the buttoned-down sister staring glassily out the windows. Jessie cast first Megan, then Sondra, an agonized glance, but apparently didn't feel she could reach out to her sister with someone watching.

Or maybe, Megan thought, Sondra's rigid frame just never allowed anyone to comfort her. Megan herself liked to maintain a certain degree of professional attire when she flew, but she also chose those clothes carefully for comfort: knit skirts over leggings, flat shoes, layered shirts that could be taken off or put back on depending on the varying temperatures in the plane. Sondra Williams wore a structured skirt suit half a size too small, with an unforgiving waistband and a blouse too thin to keep an airplane's chill out beneath a lined, shoulder-padded jacket that would be too warm to keep on. Her one concession to the eight-hour flight appeared to be having undone the three buttons that snugged the jacket around her waist. It looked like hell to travel in.

"How long is it to the city?" Jessie whispered. "Is Raq all right?"

Megan, pulling out of the parking lot, glanced at the clock. "The drive in will be slow this morning, ma'am. We'll be hitting the eight am traffic head-on. I'm sorry about that. I saw Raquel late last night and I think she was as well as she could be under the circumstances."

"Oh, please don't call me ma'am. I'm Jessie. And you're American?"

"I am. From Austin, actually." Megan offered Jessie a little smile in the rearview mirror, and noticed that Sondra glanced her way too, at that confession. "I've been here in Ireland about three years now."

"Do you miss it?"

"Sometimes. I did twenty years in the military and stationed overseas and on tour a couple of times, so in some ways I've been gone a long time. I miss the instant family the military brings, but it's not quite the same as missing the States. I suppose in the end I felt separate enough from the idea of America to be comfortable living outside of it, at least."

"What'd you do in the military?"

Megan smiled. "Drove cars, mostly. Field medic too, because it seemed like it went well with driving people in and out of combat zones, but mostly I drove."

"And you're still driving."

"And I'm still driving," Megan agreed. "I love meeting people, and this is a great way to do that."

"Ever met anybody famous?"

Megan's smile grew. She knew the young woman— Jessie Williams couldn't be more than twenty-five—was distracting herself with questions, but crawling through morning traffic toward Dublin would be boring even if there weren't emotional trauma weighing the drive down. "You know Niamh O'Sullivan?"

"The actress?" Jessie straightened. "You've met her? Really?"

"She was actually one of the first people I drove for Leprechaun Limos when I got to Ireland. I ended up helping her out of a jam and we got to be friends."

"Oh my god," Jessie said breathlessly. "What's she like?"

"What's it matter?" Sondra broke in with a snarl. "Mama's dead. Who cares about some stupid actress?"

Jessie's face went even paler as tears rose in her eyes. "You think I don't know it doesn't matter? It's just a conversation, Sonny. Jesus. You won't talk to me so why shouldn't I at least hear about Niamh O'Sullivan?"

"What do you want me to say?" Sondra shouted. "All this bullshit about earls and Ireland got Mama killed and now you're sitting here gossiping about an actress like this is some kind of *vacation* and—"

"Shut up shut up shut *up!*" Jessie's face went red, tears spilling down her cheeks. "Oh my god, shut *up*, you awful bitch! It's not my fault you and Mama weren't speaking! It's not my fault Trevor left you because you're such an uptight bitch! It's not my fault your stupid business is failing and your kids hate you and that Raquel took the time off to come with Mama instead of you doing it like the oldest sister should! This was Mama's dream and all you could do was shit on it, and now she's dead and you don't get to say how I deal with that and if I want to hear about some stupid actress then I goddamn well *will* and you can just *shut up!*" She subsided into heaving breaths while Sondra, whose cheeks now glowed so red she looked burned, clenched her jaw and turned a hard, furious gaze out the window.

Megan had long since developed the apparent inability to hear personal details about clients' lives, and said, "Niamh's amazing," into the heavy silence, like nothing had happened. She went on, talking easily about her friend, not mentioning anything a magazine interview wouldn't reveal, but below the light flow of chatter, she thought maybe Detective Bourke wouldn't be so sorry she was hanging out with the Williamses, after all.

The Williams sisters, it turned out, were all supposed to be sharing a room. Megan privately gave it until noon before one of them—probably Sondra, but she wasn't sure—rented a second to get some privacy. She'd developed an idea of sororal affection between the sisters from what little Raquel had said about them, but that idea was obviously miles off the mark. Maybe Raquel was the peacemaking middle child, although Megan had also thought she was oldest. All of her preconceptions were going out the window, and she desperately wanted to be a fly on the wall during their reunion in the Gresham. There was, however, no way for her to invite herself beyond bringing their luggage up to the room, where she stood behind them an uncomfortably long time while they waited for Raquel to open the door.

She looked as though she'd been on a three-day bender when she did, with her hair unnaturally flat on one side and a tangled knot on the other. Her makeup was smeared into raccoon eyes, and she honestly looked as though she didn't know who her sisters were, for a few seconds. Then she burst into tears and fell into Sondra's arms, although the older Williams woman did little to actually catch her. Jessie stepped forward and put her arms around both of them—mostly around Raquel—and held on while two of them sobbed and the third maintained her stony silence. Finally, wet-eyed and snuffling, Raquel lifted a miserable gaze to Megan. "Thank you so much for getting them. I knew you wouldn't let us down."

"I'm glad I can help."

"You're being paid to help." Sondra extracted herself from the unwelcome embrace and took the suitcase. "I understand Mama engaged your services for the week but I can't imagine we'll nee—"

"Of course we will! We're going to Lyetrum—"

Raquel said, "*Lee*trim," for which Megan was grateful, and Jessie picked it up without hesitation. "Leitrim to see our great-great-granddaddy's lands—"

Sondra said, "Great-great-*great*," in tones more scathing than Megan had known could be applied to a generational listing.

Jessie made an obvious decision to ignore her and continued. "—and we'll need a driver for that, I don't want to try driving on the wrong side of the road when I'm tired and sad and—" Whatever else she had to say disappeared into quiet tears. Raquel began drawing her into the room and Megan made a small apologetic motion to get Raquel's attention.

"I'll wait with the car. If there's anything you need, please call."

"Of course," Raquel said hoarsely. "I had the most awful dream, Megan. I dreamed we weren't friends anymore and you weren't going to drive us."

Megan said, "Um," and smiled. "Good thing it wasn't real."

Raquel's visible relief lasted until Sondra, frigidly, said, "Tell us what happened, Raquel," and herded her sisters into the hotel room with her tone of voice alone. Megan, caught between relief and disappointment, watched the door close to exclude her. The temptation to press her ear against the door teased her. Amused at herself, she found the nearest staircase and trotted downstairs, dictating a text into her phone. "So the sisters arrived and it turns out they really don't get along. Oldest wasn't talking to Mom, youngest thinks everybody hates oldest, and Raquel is in bits."

The phone's voice recognition did it pretty well, except *Raquel is in bits* turned into *Brooke Allison Betts*. Megan, correcting that, couldn't help grin and wonder who Brooke Allison Betts was, and how the poor woman tied in to the Williamses' sisters' drama. She sent the text to Bourke and had barely settled into the Lincoln when her phone rang. Raquel Williams quavering voice came over the line. "Megan? We were wondering if you would drive us—"

"Of course she will," Sondra snapped in the background, so clearly that Megan thought Raquel must have her on speakerphone. "She's being paid to do what she's told."

"Jesus, Sonny, have you ever heard of a little basic politeness?" Jessie asked, and Raquel tried to strengthen her voice to be heard over her sisters' bickering.

"We were hoping you could drive us to St. Michan's," Raquel said. "I tried looking it up on the map and I think it's not very far, but—"

"If we're paying for the service we might as well use it," Sondra said acidly. "And I'm certainly not equipped to walk more than a block or two."

"You've got two functioning legs, don't you?" Jessie sniped back. "Oh, yeah, but you only buy shoes with four-inch heels so you can dominate everybody around you with an extra bit of height. I can't believe you wouldn't even walk to the hospital to see her bo—"

"Please!" Raquel's voice broke in a wail. "Mama hasn't even been dead for a whole day and you two can't just get along for her sake? For mine? Never mind, Megan, this is—"

"Don't be silly," Megan said gently. "I'll bring the car around to the front doors in five minutes, and we'll go to St. Michan's."

CHAPTER 8

The sisters came out of the hotel three abreast, though Raquel dragged behind a little. Jessie had her arm linked through Raquel's, though, as if she wouldn't let her walk in Sondra's wake for love or money. Seeing the three of them like that, Megan realized Sondra was the shortest, but made up for it with her heels, just as Jessie had suggested. Her own arches ached at the thought. They looked formidable together, though, even if they were as stylistically different from one another as was possible. She hadn't thought of Raquel as a soccer mom, but now, between Jessie's hippie vibe and Sondra's corporate shark look, Raquel slotted into that stereotypical image.

"Christ, are we going to all have to sit together like four-year-olds?" Sondra's nostrils flared and she refused to enter the car first. Raquel, looking too cowed to roll her eyes, walked around to the Lincoln's far side and opened the door herself, while Megan, holding the kerb-side door for them all, shot her an apologetic glance over the vehicle's roof. Raquel gave her a barely-perceptible shrug and got in, while Jessie, obviously not caring, gave Megan a nod of thanks and got in her side to sit in the middle. Sondra got in like she was doing everyone a favor and Megan closed the door gently behind her, then made sure she was expressionless as she went around the car herself to get in the driver's side.

"I'll drive one of our larger cars tomorrow, if you pre-fer, Ms. Williams."

"I'm sure that will cost us more," Sondra replied acidly.

"For God's sake, I can ride in front with the driver," Jessie said in exasperation, and Raquel said, "Megan," as if standing up for the use of Megan's name was easier than standing up for herself. Megan smiled briefly at her in the mirror and tried not to compare the bright, ener-gized dynamic of the woman she'd met yesterday to the daunted middle sister Raquel presented as today.

She drove them around via Parnell, avoiding traffic on the quays and coming up to St. Michan's from—effec-tively—the back. It wouldn't quite have been faster to walk, but it was a near thing as she pulled into the church's little parking lot and got out to open the Lincoln's door for the sisters on Sondra's side. Jessie, climbing out sec-ond, gave Megan a look that said she knew why Megan had done that and regarded it as pandering, but also couldn't blame her. Raquel opened her own door and got out the other side of the vehicle. Megan sent her a guilty grimace and Raquel made an expression exactly like the one Jessie had just given her. Megan bit the inside of her cheek to keep from laughing, and, at Raquel's tiny head-tip, followed the sisters into the church.

Peter the tour guide was in a pew, reading a paperback novel thick enough to use as a weapon. He hopped to his feet, putting the book aside, a welcoming smile crinkling into confusion as he recognized Megan but not the people she was with. "You remember Mrs. Williams, the woman I was here with yesterday," Megan said when it was clear none of the Williams women knew how to begin. "I'm afraid she died suddenly yesterday afternoon. These are her daughters."

Peter paled, blurting, "I'm so sorry, your mother was a lovely woman," to the Williams daughters. "What a terrible loss. What ha—" He got hold of himself, realizing that asking for details was probably inappropriate, and floundered a moment. "What can I do for you?"

"My sisters want to pursue this ridiculous link with the Earl of Lyetrum."

Jessie and Raquel both hissed, "*Lee*trim," at their sister, who gave them a withering look, but corrected herself. "Leitrim. We know Mama came here to exhume the mummies."

For the second time in two days, Peter cast a mildly panicked glance Megan's way, but she was rescued from having to come up with a response by the arrival of the priest, who gave her the same questioning look Peter had, upon recognizing her. The tour guide, though, took over her attempts at explanation, saying, "That charming Mrs. Williams from yesterday passed on unexpectedly, Father Nicholas. These are her daughters. I'm sorry," he said, turning to the trio of women. "I didn't get your names."

"I'm Sondra Williams," she said, drowning out the

other two. "Our mother's obsession with a ridiculous attempt at linking herself with some old noble Irish family is an embarrassment, but it's a—"

Raquel's shoulders dropped in resignation, but Jessie, visibly furious, shouldered her oldest sister out of the way, said, "She's Sondra, and I'm Jessie, and this is Raquel," while offering her hand to first Peter, then Father Nicholas. "Obviously we're not here to exhume anything, but we're trying to—"

"*Jesus*, Jessie, could you be any more rude?" Sondra shouldered in front of Jessie, whose jaw set with anger as her voice dropped low.

"Could *you*? You didn't even introduce us, and nobody needs your monologuing about how you don't approve of Mom's genealogical research, because what the hell does it matter if you approved or not? She's dead and the least you can do is be a little frigging decent about it."

"She wouldn't be dead if she hadn't come haring off to the other side of the world to find some stupid link to some stupid piece of land that we won't have any rights to even if we are its heirs! Who cares?"

"You don't actually know that," Raquel protested, although not strongly. "If someone really did m—m—m—" She took a deep breath and surged through the word: "*Murder*. If someone really did murder Mama, maybe they would have come after her in El Paso, too. Maybe there's something they wanted from her that didn't have anything to do with this at all." Tears collected in her eyelashes, threatening her mascara. "I just think it's right that we see this through for her."

Jessie lifted her chin and glared at Sondra. "What she said."

"We're here, aren't we?" Sondra demanded. "What more do you want?"

Peter clearly wanted to be anywhere but where he was. Megan doubted his pay grade covered bereaved, bickering sisters. Father Nicholas, on the other hand, obviously had experience with exactly this kind of thing. He turned a sympathetic gaze on the two younger Williams daughters while taking Sondra's hand and somehow making it seem as though he was offering her solidarity and support in the face of their unreasonable behaviour. Megan watched in awe as, with that simple touch, Sondra visibly thawed. Father Nicholas's voice dropped into a rather more low and sonorous tone than he'd used the day before.

"If it were at all possible, I'd get you that bit of bone my own self, so you could have the answers you're looking for in these dark hours. No one should have to face any more questions than necessary in a time of grief. I can see your mother in you," he said gently to all the women, but again it seemed to especially resonate toward Sondra. "I can see her pride and her determination and her passion, and I can only imagine how maddening and beautiful that must be for you. Families can be hard, and there's nothing harder than facing the moment when we've lost the chance to say everything we might have wanted to say. I take comfort in prayer, in times like this. I think—" and Megan noticed he laid the Irish on there, saying *tink* instead of *think*, as he offered a sweet smile to the sisters. "I think you're not of my own church, but I wonder if you would allow me to share your grief and perhaps ease your own burdens a little with prayer. Perhaps together we could find a way to say things that have gone unsaid, and with it, a measure of peace."

Sondra's glacial gaze melted into hard-won tears before he'd finished. She nodded and he, with a favoring glance at Raquel and Jessie, led her several steps away. They exchanged looks and followed at a discreet distance, close enough to seem part of the conversation but far enough away that their raging older sister could feel like she was being tended to alone. Megan, impressed, murmured, "Does he do exorcisms?" and earned yet another horrified look from Peter.

"Who needs one?"

"Me, kind of. It's complicated." Megan, after a pause, asked, "Does he?"

Peter spread his hands in ignorance. "Not that I know, but I'm just a tour guide. I don't even go to this church."

"Neither do they, but he seems to be working some kind of magic on them. Mrs. Williams was probably murdered," she said to the sudden anticipatory gleam in the young man's eyes. "That's all I know, and if you could not spread it around, the gardaí would be happier with me."

He mimed zipping his lips, though his eyes were round with unasked questions. "Honestly," Megan repeated. "It's all I know." The church's door opened and Peter glanced toward it, his face arranging itself into welcoming lines as he left Megan's side to approach the young man entering the nave. The hiking shorts and boots, backpack and tank top over a tanned torso could have been German, but something about him said *American*. He wore dark blond hair pulled back in a short ponytail, and a friendly smile broke the gold scruff coating sunburned cheeks beneath light eyes as Peter approached him.

"Welcome to St. Michan's," Peter said genially. "Are you here to see the mummies?"

"I guess, but not really." He was, in fact, American.

Megan chalked one up in an imaginary scoreboard as Jessie spun around, colour suddenly flushing her cheeks.

"*Reed?*"

"Jessie!" The lanky American ran across the church, catching Jessie Williams in his arms as she leaped toward him. Megan could hear him mumbling into her shoulder, promises and assurances that make the young woman hiccup with sobs. She said something and Reed put her on her feet, wiping her tears away with the ball of his thumb. "Of course I came, babe. It's your mom. What was I gonna do, stay in Austin?"

Jessie whispered, "It's so far to come overnight," and Reed wiped her tears away again.

"You did it. I told you I'd be there for you. I tried to get on the same flight. Sorry I couldn't."

"It doesn't matter. It doesn't matter. You're here now. Oh my god, Reed." Jessie threw herself into his arms again. He looked over her head at her sisters hopefully.

Whatever warming up Sondra had done had disappeared, leaving her face tight with disapproving anger. To Megan's surprise, Raquel, whom she would have pegged as a romantic, looked wearily unhappy too. Some of Reed's apology fell away into resignation and he hugged Jessie more tightly while Father Nicholas, behind them all, gave a small shrug, the body language of a man who had tried his best but couldn't compete with newly arrived family drama.

"What are you doing here, Reed?" Sondra's voice bounced off the church's old stone walls as sharply as any preacher could ever have hoped for. "This is family business."

"Reed is my family!" Jessie tore away from the young man, voice breaking with fury. "God, when are you going

to accept it? Mama liked him, I love him, and we're trying to build a life together! What is *wrong* with that?"

"He's a freeloader, J—"

"Oh, you think that about every guy ever since Trevor
left you for somebody with more money. Screw that,
Sondra, we all know he left because you're a goddamn
control freak who doesn't know how to have fun so nobody around you better either. The fact that his new
wife—oh, didn't you know they got married? I got an in-
vitation to the wedding," Jessie spat. "The fact that she
has more money than you do is just good luck for Trev.
And I don't have any stupid money anyway, so how
could Reed even be a freeloader?"

"Men like that always find a way."

"Whoa, whoa, whoa, babe." Reed caught Jessie as she
lunged toward her sister, hands clawing toward fists, like
she couldn't decide whether she wanted to scratch Sondra
or punch her. Megan sympathized with either impulse.
"Forget it, Jess. Hey." He tipped Jessie's face up as she
stopped fighting him, a tender smile on his lips. "Look, I
knew she wouldn't be happy to see me, okay? I didn't
come for her. I came for you. What I'm gonna do is get
out of everybody's hair, but I've got my cell phone and
I'm staying at a hostel in Temple Bar. Barnacles. You just
come on over if you need some time to process, okay?"

Jessie nodded and Reed dropped his head, not to kiss
her, but to bump his nose against hers. She smiled, suddenly teary, and hugged him hard before letting him go.
He nodded toward her sisters like he knew even the gesture was unwelcome, but he was darn well going to be
polite. He also gave Megan, Peter, and Father Nicholas a
warmer smile as he headed for the door. A few steps away

from it he hesitated, looked back, and shrugged. "I guess I could see the mummies, since I'm here. If that's okay?"

Peter sent a brief, longing glance at Father Nicholas, as if he hoped he could stay and watch whatever drama was left to unfold, but then put on a professional smile, said, "This way, please!" to Reed, and escorted him from the church.

The instant the doors closed behind them, Sondra rounded on Jessie. "What were you thinking, telling him any of our business? That we were here at the church? When did you even have time?"

"He's my boyfriend," Jessie said incredulously. "Why wouldn't I tell him? I've just been texting him to keep him up to date."

"He hasn't been all that reliable, Jess. You haven't even seen him since before Christmas, have you?" Raquel sounded like she didn't want to rock the boat, but felt she couldn't leave it alone, either. "And that whole window last year where he just took off?"

Jessie said, "We were on a break," with the emphasis of someone who had repeated the phrase dozens, if not hundreds, of times. "I knew he was going to travel, and I didn't want to go with. He didn't 'take off.'"

"You were devastated," Sondra snapped. "You said he was off chasing some girl. Dora or something."

Jessie rolled her eyes so hard it looked painful. "That's not what I said at all, but if you can't even get that detail right I'm not even going to talk to you about it. I'm glad he's here and I'd think you'd be glad for me. Isn't he being reliable now? Isn't that what you want?"

"Well, what about the thing with the band, though, Jessie?" Raquel said carefully. "That went on for quite a while."

"It's not easy to build a fan base, Raq. I couldn't expect him to just hang out in El Paso while I finished college. Oh my god. Why are we even talking about this? Mom's *dead*. I thought we were gonna pray or something."

Father Nicholas seized on that, stepping forward. "Let us," he suggested. "It would do my soul good." A few minutes earlier he'd been commanding and dignified. Now he sounded like a querulous old man afraid he'd lose his chance at a nice dinner. All three of the Williams sisters responded with remarkable sympathy, suddenly tutting and fussing over him. Father Nicholas tottered toward the pews in their company, evidently having turned frail and ancient inside of a few minutes. Megan's jaw dropped and she swore she saw the old priest slide a wink her way as the Williamses helped him to sit down. Judging herself temporarily released from duty, Megan slipped toward the doors, but took her phone from her uniform's inner jacket pocket to send a text to her friend Niamh.

Next time you need a convincing old man in a movie role, you should audition this old priest I just met. I think the guy's a consummate actor. She didn't expect an answer—Nee was in California, where it was about 2 am—and put the phone in her pocket as she went around the church to enter the crypt.

Peter was midway through his lecture, explaining how some of the coffins had rotted away over the years, leaving the mummies exposed. When he caught sight of Megan she saw him bite back referring to them as "free-range," and she grinned so broadly that he nearly started laughing himself. Reed turned to see what the fuss was and frowned—or smiled, Megan couldn't decide which—

with puzzlement. "I called them free-range yesterday," she explained, and he laughed.

"Right. Gross."

"But funny." Megan came down the low-roofed stone hall to offer her hand. "I expect we might see a little more of each other over the next few days, so I might as well introduce myself. Megan Malone. I'm driving the Williamses while they're in Ireland."

"Yeah, well, two of the three will be trying to make sure you don't see me."

"I noticed there was some tension." Megan grimaced apologetically.

"People in—I don't know, where's somewhere far away? Tipperary?"

Megan, solemnly, said, "It's a long way to Tipperary," and Peter said, "*Jaysus,*" as both the Americans started laughing. Megan said, "I didn't know if that would get any traction, the song is so old," and Peter walked away, throwing his hands into the air and sending Reed and Megan into more gales of laughter.

"Tension breaker," Reed finally wheezed. "Had to be done. Anyway, yeah, the Sisters Williams don't like me much. I was a jerk," he admitted. "Screwed around on Jess a lot. She's forgiven me, but they haven't."

"Should they?"

Reed rolled back on his heels. "Damn, woman, we just met."

Hackles rose on Megan's nape. "There's nothing about that sentence that makes me think the answer is *yes*."

Frustration flittered across the young man's face. "Look, I'm here, aren't I? I'm trying to be here for her. What else am I supposed to do?"

"For one, I would *strongly* recommend not referring to women as 'woman' unless you've got some kind of prior in-joke arrangement about it."

Reed bared his teeth and glanced away. "Yeah, all right. Sorry about that. I know better. I was trying to be funny and wasn't."

Megan hesitated a moment, then nodded. "Okay. Apology accepted."

Surprise creased the kid's face. "Really?"

"I've heard much worse apologies from people who should know better, so yeah, I'll take it. I hope things work out for you and Jessie."

Reed sighed and nodded. "Yeah, me too. I don't know, though. What do you think about all of this? Are they just crazy?" He gestured at the crypt, encompassing the whole idea of lost ancestors and mummies.

Megan shrugged. "I don't know. Their grandma's diaries and stuff, if they're for real, seem to provide a pretty good link." She blinked at the crypt's ceiling for a moment. "I mean, the diaries are real. Cherise had one with her yesterday. I just don't know if they're real in the sense of relating a true story, you know? It'd be kind of cool if it's all true, although I don't think it would mean you're bagging yourself an heiress."

"Hey, a guy can dream, right? But no, Jessie and me go back a long time before all this started, though. I met her at a concert and she w—"

"Driver!" Sondra's voice thundered down the crypt. "Come out of there at once. We're going to Leitrim."

CHAPTER 9

Megan exchanged a startled glance with both the young men in the crypt. Reed whispered, "I think I'll just stay here," and Peter returned to make an effort at continuing the tour, which Reed waved off. Megan left them behind and climbed into the darkening afternoon light. The sun wouldn't set for hours, but in the short while she'd been in the crypt, the clouds had thickened considerably. Megan gave them a wary look before turning her full attention to Sondra Williams.

For a moment, despite the woman's caustic nature, Megan's heart went out to her. On the surface, she was the most put-together of the sisters. She dressed both professionally and flatteringly, wore her hair and makeup well, and had a figure she obviously worked hard to keep, even if the fit of her skirt right now said she didn't always succeed in that. She was still considerably fitter than Raquel, even if she didn't have Jessie's advantage of absolute youth.

But at the same time, it was just as obvious that the entire ensemble was a kind of armor, and that the shell could crack at any moment. She already looked windswept and cold in the Irish winter, and her rigid jawline made veins pulse in her temples. Megan hated to think of the woman's dental bill if she kept her teeth clenched like that all the time. Whatever Sondra's contentious relationship with her mother had been, Megan wouldn't have wished an end like this to it on almost anybody. She hesitated, then let curiosity win out. "Ms. Williams?" At Sondra's tight glance of permission, she said, "I get the impression you weren't happy about any of this old Irish-connection story even before Mrs. Williams came here to investigate it. May I ask why?"

For an instant, Sondra's facade cracked, a lifetime of frustration glimmering through as her voice dropped into a hiss. "My mother liked nothing more than a good story all her life. She was the type who believed in every princess movie, every miracle diet, every pyramid scheme. My sisters don't know how many times I bailed her out. They think my marriage ended because I can't let anything go. Well, they're wrong. Trevor left me because I said I couldn't let the bank repossess Mama's house and he said I could, that she was a grown woman and could make her own decisions and live with the consequences. But I knew the consequences were that she would come live with *me*, because I'm the oldest and most responsible and Jessie's a fucking flake and Ray just wants everybody to get along and she'd let Mama run roughshod over her and destroy her life too. So I helped Mama and my husband left me and my sisters think I'm a bitch and I have to be back at work by Tuesday and act like nothing's wrong because there's a shareholders meeting next week and if I don't get the numbers in shape I'm going to be out of a job." Sondra wiped away furious tears and wrapped her arms around her ribs tightly, warding off the cold wind. "So even if every bit of this stupid story is true, it's still just a fairy tale that killed our mother, and will pull my sisters down into it if it gets a chance."

"I am so sorry." That, Megan bet, was the confession Father Nicholas had been hoping to get out of Sondra through prayer. She also bet the Texan businesswoman had been too guarded, too afraid of letting anything slip that would conflict with the idea Raquel and Jessie had of their mother, to have fallen for the priest's ploy. Out in the parking lot, under the threatening sky, it had been safe enough to admit to, especially to the help. Books and television were always showing how freely the wealthy talked when their personal servants were around, and Megan's experience as a limo driver backed that stereotype up. Even when employers realized they'd admitted everything to an employee, as the slow horror building on Sondra's face indicated she had, they still counted on—

"That must have been burdening you terribly, Ms. Williams. I promise anything you've said to me will remain in confidence." There were clients for whom Megan might have smiled at that point, and murmured something like *I don't remember you saying anything at all, ma'am,* but Sondra Williams didn't seem to have the trace of self-deprecating humor that would make that line work.

The beans having been spilled anyway, Sondra let her shoulders sag for just an instant, weariness aging her a decade beyond her years. "I can't tell the girls. They won't even believe me, not without the financial paper-work to prove it, and maybe not even then. Besides, I don't want to disillusion them about who Mama was."

"You're a really good big sister," Megan said gently.

Sondra gave her a look filled with bitterness. "Tell *them* that."

"I hope they're able to see it themselves soon." Megan took a deep breath. "If you'd like, Ms. Williams, we could drive back to the Leprechaun Limousines offices and I could upgrade the Lincoln to a four-seater, for your comfort on the drive to Leitrim."

"And how much more would that cost us? How much would it delay us?"

"I'll speak with my manager. It shouldn't be much more." It shouldn't be anything more, given how much Orla had overcharged Cherise Williams to begin with, but Megan didn't want to say that aloud. "If we leave soon it shouldn't delay us more than the time it takes to go over and switch cars. The traffic isn't too bad, so we should be able to head out of town in less than an hour, either way. We'd get to Leitrim before one."

Indecision wavered in Sondra's face for a moment be-fore she nodded sharply in agreement. "All right. I'll get the girls and we'll go. What?" she asked as Megan visibly hesitated again.

"I know you haven't had time to go to the Mater," Megan said carefully. "Is that something you want to do?"

"You mean to see Mother's body? No, thank you, Ms.

Malone. All that's holding me together is the fact that the last image I've got of her in my mind isn't as a dead woman. Jessica might want to visit later, but I will not be joining her."

Megan, surprised Sondra knew her last name, nodded and went to the car as Sondra went back into the church. After a moment's wait in the increasing drizzle, it occurred to Megan to call the garage, and caught Tymon on the first ring. "Hey, Ty. Could you get the Bentley ready for me? I'm switching cars for a long drive."

"Ooh. Does Orla know?"

"I'm banking on it being easier to get forgiveness than permission."

The kid laughed. "Orla never forgave anything in her life. It'll be ready when you get here."

"Twenty minutes," Megan promised, and hung up as the Williamses emerged from the church, arguing over whether Jessie's boyfriend should join them. Jessie was obviously in the minority, but she got in the front seat of the Lincoln and sent a text while Megan held the door for the two older sisters. The argument stopped once they were all in the car, either because etiquette demanded not fighting in front of the help or—more likely, Megan thought—because the vehicle's heater, running on low, warmed Sondra and Jessie up enough to send them almost straight to sleep.

Driving back to the garage took about twenty minutes and Tymon, as promised, had a Bentley Mulsanne already idling for them. Megan loved the big vehicle, which had the poshest interior of any of the Leprechaun cars, and which cost enough to rent that teenage debs and hen parties never dared hire it. Megan's day shift usually meant she didn't get to drive it, but just this once she planned to get away with it.

"Get out of here before Orla catches you," he said, waving off her apology for not helping detail the Lincoln. "You don't need her nonsense on top of it all."

"Her nonsense *is* it all." Megan checked the time as she got into the Bentley, the Williamses already settled comfortably in the back. "Would you ladies mind if I stopped by my apartment really quickly? It's two minutes away and I have puppies who need walking if I'm going on a long drive. I can call a friend if you'd prefer I didn't," she concluded, "but I thought it wouldn't hurt to ask."

To her astonishment, Sondra turned toward her eagerly. "Puppies? What kind?"

"Jack Russells. I accidentally adopted them about seven months ago."

Sondra Williams actually laughed aloud. "You accidentally adopted two dogs? One I could understand, but two? Bring them with us," she said with an impulsiveness Megan would never have expected from her. "We could probably all use some puppy love."

"Are you sure?"

"Absolutely." Sondra didn't seem to care what her sisters thought, but Jessie nodded enthusiastically and even Raquel smiled. "How did you accidentally adopt them?"

"Their mama snuck into a friend's restaurant and had her babies in the kitchen," Megan said as she drove down the block to her apartment. "Obviously they couldn't stay, so I took them home, and they sort of . . . stuck. If you don't mind, I'll walk them real quick and then tuck them into the carrier on the floor? But the carrier might get in the way of your feet, it might not be a good idea. . . ."

All three sisters got out of the car to walk the dogs with Megan when she came down from the apartment with them, and Sondra solved the problem of feet by taking the forward-facing back seat to herself when she got back in the car, and putting the kennel on the seat beside her. Megan saw the younger sisters exchange glances, but neither of them complained as they got into the backward-facing seats and settled down for the drive. Raquel reached across to rub Dip's nose through the wire door and said, "*What* did you say their names were?"

"That's Dip, because his face looks like it's been dipped in chocolate. His sister is Thong because I thought Dip Thong was funny."

Raquel smiled like she didn't understand, which Megan got a lot when she told people the dogs' names, and Sondra stared at her in faintly disbelieving horror, which she also got a lot, and which made her laugh every time. Sondra, in rather accusing tones, asked, "Were you an English major?"

Megan laughed. "No, but maybe I should have been. I did twenty years in the military straight out of high school and got combat medic training, but nothing more formal than that. It doesn't seem to stop me from making stupid linguistic puns with dog names."

"It's a terrible thing to do to defenseless animals," Sondra told her, then ducked her head toward the dogs and murmured, "Poor puppies. What a bad lady your owner is," as they stuck their noses out and licked her fingers.

"So bad she adopted homeless puppies," Jessie said, and for a minute Megan was afraid they would snipe at each other the entire drive up to Leitrim. Fortunately, though, within a few minutes Jessie put her head against the window and fell asleep, while Raquel's head bobbed and snapped up in the rearview mirror as she fought sleep herself. Only Sondra stayed fully awake, watching the scenery and putting her fingers through the kennel's wire door to play silently with the dogs.

Even in the bursts of heavy rain, the drive up to Leitrim struck Megan as lovely. Dark clouds with weak winter sun behind them lay close to the earth, Ireland's endless hills coloured a deep, lush emerald in their shadow. Every once in a while, in the distance, the clouds broke with a burst of what Megan called "godslight," sunshine falling toward the earth in thick, individual rays. Sometimes those patches of brilliance grew to expose the pale blue sky, and other times, simply disappeared like a wish. It made the world feel small, all nestled in close together, as if the horizons had never been all that far away anyway, and that they weren't particularly worth exploring. From inside the car it had a kind of serenity, as if, despite the rain, the countryside was warm and cozy and safe. Of course, the sideways spatter of rain, and the lashing nods of leafless trees made a lie of that, but it still had a comforting feel to it. Megan liked this kind of day, at least from through a window and with a hot cup of coffee to keep her company. Walking around in it up at Lough Rynn wouldn't be as much fun, but she'd worry about that when they got there.

Like a welcoming committee spilling out, though, the skies cleared unexpectedly just as they reached the Leitrim border, and Jessie lifted her head to mumble, "We're home." Raquel reached across to squeeze her sister's hand, and Sondra gave them both an impatient, uncomprehending look.

"Texas is home. This is a fairy tale."

"Mama loved fairy tales," Raquel said, and for a heartbeat Sondra met Megan's eyes in the mirror. Megan moved her gaze back to the road, all too aware that she shouldn't contribute to the conversation.

"Fairy tales," Sondra said, voice straining with emphasis, "aren't real. Do you even know what's on the land, Ray? Nothing. They have hundreds of acres going to seed, and an old house nobody lives in. Even when people did live there, it wasn't a fairy tale. Our ancestors owned tens of thousands of acres. Land they had taken from native Irish and claimed as their own, then made the Irish farmers pay taxes and tithes on just to farm what had been theirs, and starved them in the Famine. Didn't you do any research on this?"

The younger sisters both said, "No," with varying degrees of surprise and belligerence. "I'm sure Mama would have mentioned all that," Raquel added.

"Mama liked fairy tales," Sondra repeated through her teeth. "What's left isn't the family's, and it's not a fairy tale. It's blood money, and I think you should know that. The earl whose DNA we're trying to get? He was murdered for being Ireland's most notoriously awful landlord after the Famine, and even though they know who did it, nobody ever got convicted for it because he was so terrible."

Raquel, bewildered, said, "What famine?" and it took everything Megan had not to stare at her in the rearview mirror.

"A million people starved here in the 1840s," Sondra said incredulously. "Another million left the country, because English landlords—the ones we're descended from, if this nonsense is right—took their food and sent it away. Leitrim County—"

Megan mouthed, *County Leitrim*, but didn't say it aloud, not wanting to interrupt Sondra's history lesson. "—had a hundred and fifteen thousand people before the Famine," Sondra went on. "Know how many it's got now, nearly two hundred years later? Just over thirty thousand. And the people you want so badly to be our ancestors were part of that. The reports said the third earl's funeral was a riot, that his tenants wanted his body thrown into the streets so they could kick it. *That's* the legacy Mama was so excited about, Raq. That's what our so-called family did."

The prospect of ransacking St. Michan's to steal a noble bone or two was starting to sound like a decent idea. Apparently the third Earl deserved to have his bones disturbed, although Megan doubted the Williams sisters could handle the logistics of tomb raiding. She bit the inside of her cheek, keeping herself from offering suggestions on the topic.

"Is that why Mama was murdered?" It seemed Raquel had, melodramatically, decided to accept the worst possible scenario as fait accompli. "Because our ancestors were so awful?"

"That wouldn't be fair," Jessie whispered. "The man who did all that already got murdered. Who would punish Mama for it?"

"I don't know," Sondra said bitterly. "Irish who hate the British, maybe. There are people who still do."

A horrified little silence filled the back half of the car

before Raquel, chirpily, said, "But at least the title isn't extinct!"

"Which we can't prove without a DNA sample that no one is inclined to give us," Sondra said. "I don't know why it matters to any of you."

Raquel's attempt at cheerfulness failed and she snapped, "Well, maybe if you were more involved with the family it would matter more to you."

"I am more involved than you will ever know."

"Right, because you and Mama weren't even *speaking*—"

Megan, in the tone of a driver who couldn't hear family spats, said, "Would you like to stop for lunch? We're just outside of Mohill now."

"Oh my God, Mohill! I know somebody there!" Jessie's enthusiasm startled the dogs, who woke up from their naps with whuffs and whines. "I've got an Ancestry dot com friend who lives there. Oooh, I have to text him!"

She whipped her phone out while her sisters stared at her in brittle silence. Sondra finally broke it by saying, "Lunch seems like it might be a good idea. I'm sure the dogs could use a chance to stretch their legs too."

Megan gave her a genuinely grateful smile in the rearview mirror. "Probably. I'll take them for a walk while you ladies eat, and we'll drive the last few miles after lunch."

"Flynn says to meet him at the Soup Bowl Restaurant," Jessie said a moment later. "He says it's brilliant."

"We'll all walk the dogs," Raquel offered. "Then you can eat with us, Megan. It wouldn't be nice to leave you out of everything."

"Oh, it's all right," Megan promised. "I wouldn't want to intrude."

"Apparently Jessie's got an internet boyfriend who'll be intruding already, so one more person won't hurt. And I'd like to help walk them."

"He's not an internet boyfriend," Jessie spat, but much to Megan's relief, they were in Mohill and finding a place to park before the argument could really take off.

CHAPTER 10

Sondra lifted the carrier into Megan's hands when Megan opened the car doors, and crouched to meet the dogs as they came out of the carrier, shaking themselves and stretching. Megan had taken them on road trips before (in rented cars, not the Leprechaun vehicles), and knew they traveled well, but reaching their destination with no car sickness or accidents still came as a relief. Thong stretched long and leaned heavily into Sondra's hand when she offered it to her, and Dip ran in circles yipping and jumping for attention. Megan clipped leads on them and they tried going in opposite directions with her in the middle, until Jessie, smiling, took Thong's leash. "It looks like sort of a one-horse town."

"Pretty, though," Raquel said. Mohill, County Leitrim *was* a pretty town, built straight along a main road with some afterthoughts spidering out to the sides, as many

Irish villages were. Hardly a building to be seen stood over two stories in height, and often the upper stories were painted in another colour to the lower, or covered in brick and stone that gave each establishment a personality of its own. By the time they'd finished walking the dogs, Megan thought they'd seen most of the village, including a visit to a statue of the last Irish bard, O'Carolan, who sat forever playing his harp to the Mohill streets. Everybody, even Sondra, had paused at the brown-framed tourist information signs that cropped up in most Irish towns, highlighting local history and sights of interest, and Megan knew more about Lough Rynn when they got back to the car than she had when they'd started out.

"Someone here in Mohill must know something about the Edgeworth family," Jessie said eagerly. "We can tell them we're related to the old earls and see what they know about the Lough Rynn House and who lived there."

"No, we can't," Sondra said. "We have no proof and it's idiotic to go prancing around saying Cleopatra was your ancestor."

"I thought people always claimed to be Cleopatra reincarnated, not her descendants," Raquel objected, and Sondra's mouth tightened.

"Whatever. You get the idea. I don't want to be spreading absurd stories around."

"It's not absurd! We've got all of Gigi's diaries—"

"They're only anecdotal, Raquel, and we don't even have them with us."

Megan said, "You—" and swallowed it, not actually wanting to get involved in the argument.

Sondra didn't hear her at all, and continued on just as sharply as before. "Without genetic testing we don't know for sure, and people in Ireland are forever hearing about how some tourist's great-great-grandfather was Irish-born and they feel such a connection and all of it and I won't have it. Especially with Mom's death. What if it *is* related to this earldom nonsense? I don't want my baby sisters going around making themselves targets."

"I'm not a baby!"

"You're still my baby sister!"

Megan turned her attention down the street toward the café they were meant to lunch at, trying not to show any expression as the women fell into another argument. There were a few walkers along the road, mothers with buggies stopping to chat to each other, and older people making their way along, alone or in pairs, to whatever business they had that day. Maybe, she thought hopefully, maybe she could just suddenly dash down the street and join them, leaving the sisters to fight among themselves.

Jessie was saying, "I don't know what the big deal is, if they've all heard 'omg I'm Irish' before," and Raquel, whose larger-than-life personality of the first hour Megan had known her was apparently permanently buried, kept murmuring, "Let's not fight, let's not fight," until both Jessie and Sondra turned on her, instead. Tears welled up and Raquel's jaw trembled stoically as she knelt to pay attention to Thong, who had come to press against her ankles. Megan wondered if the three of them had fought so bitterly when their mother was alive, or if grief exacerbated latent tendencies.

"We don't have to mention the Edgeworth connection," Raquel said, mostly to Thong. "Sonny's right about not having proof. We don't even have any of Gigi Elsie's diaries with us, and I don't think we're going to get the DNA sample we were hoping for. But even if it is just a fairy tale, it's nice to believe in, so maybe we should just be happy with that. Why don't we have a look around the grounds so we can get an idea of what it might have been like when the earls lived here, and maybe that's enough."

Megan, for the second time, started, "You have—" but Jessie overran her, demanding, "What happened to doing this for Mama? Have we come this far to stop now?" and Megan went quiet. There was no good time to say *anything*; she was the hired help, not part of their conversation, even if having someone there to interrupt might be what they needed.

Raquel looked up, her face full of tears and her voice sharp. "I don't know, Jessie! Maybe!"

"Jessie . . . ?" A young man in a raincoat, one of the locals Megan had noticed earlier, approached, a tentative smile on a face pink with anxiety. "Jessie Williams? Hey, hi, it's . . . it's Flynn."

"Flynn!" Jessie shrieked in delighted recognition and threw herself at the young man. "Oh my god, *hi*! I can't believe I'm really meeting you! Raq, Sonny, this is my friend Flynn from Ancestry. He's really nice and I can't believe you're actually here!"

"We hooked up on Ancestry because she was looking into local genealogy," Flynn said to Sondra. "Nobody really looks for information around Mohill, so we got to talking, and—it's mental *you're* here," he said to Jessie. "Why didn't you say you were coming? You disappeared off social media and then all of a sudden you're here?"

"You *hooked up*?" Sondra asked incredulously. "What is this, taking advantage of Mom's death for an international booty call? And now I have to wonder if Reed was the cheater or if you were cheating on him!"

Jessie bellowed, "Oh my *God*, will you *lay off*!" at the

same time Flynn's pleasant features went white with horror.

"Your mom *died*? Oh my god, I didn't know. I should get out of here—I have to get out of here! I'm so sorry! I didn't mean that kind of hookup! We're just friends! Oh my god, Jess, I'm so sorry! I'll leave you all alone!" Flynn backed up several steps, looking around as if the one-street town would offer somewhere to flee without anyone being able to watch. *Everyone* was watching, though: people had come out of shops and paused on the street to watch the commotion.

Jessie, if she even noticed, didn't care. "You can stay right here, Flynn!" He froze like a rabbit in headlights, waiting to be squished. Jessie swung toward Sondra, still yelling. "First off, you hate Reed so much I figure you'd be happy if I *was* hooking up with somebody else, and second, Flynn and I have been friends online for like three years now and it's *really incredibly super-nice* that he's willing to meet me on no notice. And you know what, maybe it *would* be a hookup if Mom hadn't just died and maybe it would be anyway if you weren't so frigging judgmental—"

Flynn's expression flew through emotion, from excited hope to moral horror at his own hope and through to embarrassment about the whole thing. It was like watching Charlie Chaplin in a silent movie, his every aspect furthering the story. Jessie, oblivious, kept shouting. "Because—oh my god, I could use something nice right now—" Flynn lit up at this—"and all I want is to just live my life without people scolding me for it—"

Sondra thundered, "*Enough!*" so loudly that Dip, who had been sniffing along the sidewalk's edge, rolled over

on his back and peed in the air. Everyone fell silent,
Megan crushing a relieved giggle that no one else felt the
need to show quite as much submissiveness as the dog
did. A muscle twitched in Sondra's jaw, like part of her
saw Dip's display and wanted to apologize to Megan,
who would be cleaning pee off the puppy before they
could go anywhere, but also didn't dare break the spell
she'd cast with her roar. "We are going to lunch now,"
Sondra said through her teeth. "Just the three of us, with
our driver. Flynn, go home."

Jessie hissed, "Flynn, don't go home!" and Megan saw
barely contained fury flash through Sondra's face. Flynn,
who was about twenty-seven and should have been able
to read a room well enough to make a decision on his
own, froze, rolling his eyes from one woman to another
and finally alighting on Megan, at whom he looked as if
she were a source of reason in the midst of chaos. She
lifted her hands about a quarter of an inch, abstaining
from the whole mess, and panic settled in his gaze.

Raquel, the peacemaker, said, "Maybe Jessie can see
you later, Flynn, but this isn't a good time." The young
man took it as gospel and fled, leaving other locals to
duck their heads together and chuckle about the whole
scene. Raquel whispered, "Why didn't you tell us you
had an internet boyfriend?" to Jessie, who bugged her
eyes as a refusal to respond.

"Well," Sondra said acidly, "all we need now is your
actual loser boyfriend to show up, and everything will be
perfect."

A car honked down the road, and Jessie's actual loser
boyfriend drove up and parked beside them.

* * *

Megan put a hand over her face, knocked the tip of her nose, and remembered, with eye-watering clarity, that Dip had caught his tooth inside her nostril a day earlier. She'd obviously not needed to blow or rub her nose since then, because it hadn't bothered her at all, but it hurt so badly she missed Reed exiting his car. All she heard was the door closing and his hopeful voice. "Jess? I tried to catch you guys when you texted that you were coming up here, but I missed you, so I rented a car and drove like hell to get up here. Are you okay, babe?"

Jessie wailed, "No!" and Megan's vision cleared enough to see the young woman throw herself, theatrically, into Reed's arms. He looked as unwashed and travel-worn as he had earlier, which, given the time constraints he'd been under, wasn't surprising, but Megan thought if he'd made an effort, even Sondra might have thawed toward him a little. Bobbing into an emotionally-fraught family tragedy while looking like a beach bum didn't win him any points, even with Megan, who had no particular horse in the race.

She wiped her eyes and went to get a rag to clean Dip up with so he could be put back into the kennel, then quietly collected all the dogs and snuggled them into the kennel before putting the whole thing back into the car. Dip gave her the guiltiest look ever and she ducked her head over him, whispering, "It's okay, baby, you didn't do anything wrong, that was scary," and rubbed his head. Thong squirmed forward for some of that love too, and Megan stayed where she was, crouched by the side of the kennel and reassuring her puppies, while everyone else shouted at each other.

"—two hours to get up here, you couldn't have rented a car and driven up here and arrived a few minutes before

we did without endangering everyone on the road—"
Even without looking, Megan knew that was Sondra.

"—trying to support Jessie, I thought you'd appreciate
that—" Reed protested.

"—can't we just stop *arguing?*"

"*God*, Raquel, will you stop trying to make peace. You
can't make peace with a war hawk, and so what if he sped
a little, Sondra, he's here for me—" Jessie's irritation at
Raquel made her sound almost like their oldest sister.

"Like your little Irish boyfriend is?" Sondra snapped.

"Wait, what Irish boyfriend?"

"I don't *have* an Irish boyfriend, Reed, obviously I
don't, I just have a friend who was concerned when I
dropped off social media—"

"Wait, I came all this way and you were hooking up?
On your mom's deathbed?"

For an instant all three sisters were united in disgust.
Megan, watching from the corner of her eye, thought the
only reason Sondra didn't slap Reed hard enough to send
him spinning was that Jessie stood between them. Reed
inhaled and exhaled like a pretentious yogi, even bringing his arms up and around as if pressing away negative
energy. Sondra's lips hardly parted, but she still managed
to bare her teeth, her contempt of his affectations palpa-
ble.

"Jessie," Reed said, evenly, "I'm sorry. That was un-
called for, and gross. I shouldn't have said it and I hope
you can forgive me."

The youngest Williams girl wiped her eyes surrepti-
tiously and grunted, "Yeah. I'm not hooking up with anybody, Reed."

He sighed. "Of course you're not. It was ugly of me to

be suspicious. Look, I don't know how we always end up on the wrong foot—"

Sondra made a sound that indicated she had a few ideas, but Raquel elbowed her hard enough to be considered assault in some states, and she shut up. Reed continued as if oblivious to their byplay, which Megan thought he could very easily actually be. "—but I'm willing to let bygones be bygones—"

Neither Raquel Williams nor, Megan suspected, any other force on Earth could have stopped Sondra's derisive snarl that time, but she didn't engage with Jessie's boyfriend, just went to the car and stood by the door as if expecting Megan to hold it for her. Raquel wailed, "But we need to eat, Sonny," and the oldest sister looked suddenly tired, like she'd forgotten that in her pique.

Reed, on the other hand, looked genuinely surprised by Sondra's anger. Apparently he felt he was the aggrieved party, and couldn't imagine anyone thinking otherwise. "I just want to support Jessie. It's got to be weird, trying to face family you've never known, never mind having to do it when someone you love has just passed away."

"Well, we're not really facing anybody." Jessie's fire seemed to have dulled. "The original family doesn't even live on the land anymore and we don't have any proof anyway."

"What about the diaries?"

"Nobody thought to bring any of them with us."

Reed cast a startled glance at Megan. "But your driver said Mrs. Williams had one with her."

All three of the sisters looked toward Megan in astonishment. She rose, the dogs closed into the kennel. "She had a little blue diary with her on Wednesday at St. Michan's. Wasn't it in the hotel room?"

"No." Raquel's voice rose to an edge. Hairs rose on Megan's arms, her heart suddenly beating too fast as Raquel spoke faster and faster. "No. I know exactly which one you mean, and it's not with Mama's things, not at the hotel or at the hospital. Where is it? Where is it?"

"I don't know, but we'll find out," Megan promised.

"How?" Sondra sounded sharper, angrier, than Raquel. "How can we find one little diary in all of Dublin?"

"We can find it because we know when it disappeared," Megan said steadily. "She had it when she went into the CVS office at just before two pm on Wednesday, and didn't have it three hours later. Detective Inspector Bourke is already reviewing hotel security tapes and tracking your mother's movements between me dropping her off and five pm. I'll let him know he should be looking for that diary too. Had any of you read it? Do you know anything about what it said?"

"I read them all when I was a little girl," Raquel whispered. "The blue one with the gold heart on it, it was the most romantic of them and I read it like it was a novel, like Laura Ingalls Wilder. But I haven't read it since I was about fourteen."

The sky above darkened, spatters of rain slapping down, and Jessie suddenly took over the role of oldest sister, her jaw setting grimly. "We're not going to remember anything standing out here in a downpour. Let's go into that café and get something to eat, and then we can . . ." Her confidence faltered and Sondra took over, as if offended that her position as bossy sister had been usurped.

"And we can see what nonsense Raquel remembers. I don't see what possible use it could be." Her own jaw set and for a moment, she and Jessie looked very alike. "But if someone killed Mother and took it, there must be something useful in there. Reed . . ." Her nostrils pinched as she sighed. "You may join us for lunch."

Megan, in Reed's place, would have been hard-pressed to keep a civil tongue in her head at Sondra's holier-than-thou tone, but Reed only smiled in relief and murmured, "Thanks," to the oldest Williams sister. Megan tucked the dogs' kennel into the car, rolled the window down a few inches to let fresh air in, and followed the other Americans down the street to the restaurant.

CHAPTER 11

Jessie's friend Flynn had, it turned out, gone there after all, and sat huddled in a corner with the expression of a lost puppy. Jessie froze when she came in, gaze skittering around the cozy little space like she was trying to find somewhere safe to sit, while the locals all looked up from their coffee and soup and chips and made no pretense of not watching. Flynn shrank even farther into his corner, and Jessie, with an act of deliberate defiance, tossed her hair, marched over to him, and said, "Sorry about all that out there. Want to join us?"

He turned so pink his blond hair looked like the flame on top of a match. "That'd be grand, if you really don't mind." He got his coffee cup and shuffled to the table Raquel had claimed, shoulders hunched and eyes wide, as if he expected to be kicked. The whole café—Megan thought everybody in town who wasn't otherwise occupied with work or family might have come down for lunch today, in hopes of getting in on the drama unfolding in their midst—watched him eagerly.

Jessie, a little too loudly, said, "Of course we don't mind. This is my boyfriend, Reed. Reed, this is my friend Flynn, the one I was just telling you about."

The young men shook hands, neither appearing to try to crush the other's, which surprised Megan a little. Raquel, trying to act like everything was normal, gave Flynn a determined smile and gestured to the chairs. "Take any one you like. You can hold the table for us while we get our lunch."

"Thanks." Flynn sat down with his back to as much of the café as he could, which Megan felt was a good call. He had to know everyone was watching. At least he didn't have to meet any of their gazes, that way, or have to see the suspicious scowls Reed kept throwing at him. Hiding her own smile, Megan went up to the counter with the others, looking over the buffet-style offerings. Loads of Irish cafés worked on that principle, and after almost three years in the country, Megan still found it strange enough to be uncomfortable.

"I keep thinking I've adapted," she admitted to the Williamses, who stared at the café counter with a wariness not unlike Megan's own her first year or so in Ireland. "But then it turns out I'm still awfully American. Try the soup. It'll be pureed, but it'll be good."

All three sisters looked skeptical, but the soup—carrot, chickpea, and coconut milk—was, as Megan had warned, both delicious and pureed to a consistent smooth texture. Megan, at the end of the line, got a chunk of brown soda bread and extra butter to go with it, and by the time she joined the others at the table, an impassioned discussion had burst to life. Sondra, sounding exasperated, was saying, "I remember you poring over them when we were kids, like you'd found the door to Narnia or something. You talked about them incessantly," as Megan sat.

"And if you'd ever listened to anything I said you might remember something useful," Raquel said with a tired bitterness that obviously went back decades. "It was the story of why Great-Geepaw Patrick left Ireland, and how he and Great-Geemaw met and fell in love. I loved it because it was like a fairy tale. Our very own fairy tale, with an evil king and everything." She went silent a moment, staring at her soup. "I guess that's what you were talking about, Sonny. The landlords taking the farmers' lands and letting them starve. I never really imagined it was real. It was a fairy tale," she said again, unhappily. "Gigi Elsie wrote about how Patrick had wanted away from his family because of the evil king who had died before he was born. He was afraid the king's legacy would poison them all. But I guess it was probably an earl, not a king, and I just didn't know the difference."

Megan, gently, said, "I read a little about the family in the twentieth century. The next earls did better by the people. One of those was Patrick's father, and the other was his brother. So the old earl didn't poison them all, after all."

"So he left Ireland for nothing, and we didn't get to grow up as nobility."

"We wouldn't have anyway," Sondra said impatiently. "We wouldn't be us if we'd grown up rich Irish kids. Patrick would have married someone else and had different children and we'd be four generations of cumulative changes. We'd have been other people entirely."

Reed, who'd sat through it all, ignoring his food and

glaring at Flynn, took Jessie's hand and focused a contrived gaze of loyalty on her. "I'd love you anyway, Jess, no matter who you were."

"I bet, because I'd be rich."

Reed looked wounded, and Flynn, who had kept his eyes on his plate until that point, looked up. "You wouldn't even know her. I'd have grown up with her in school like, and we might be best mates, but you wouldn't even know her."

To Megan's surprise, Jessie gave Flynn a rather soppy smile that almost literally raised Reed's hackles. He huffed, aggrieved, and Megan accidentally caught Sondra and Raquel's eyes with an ill-concealed smirk of *Oh my god, twenty-somethings*. All three of them lost the plot as one, smirks turning to giggles and then, as Jessie, offended, looked between them, into full-on belly laughs. Even Sondra ended up clutching the edge of the table and wheezing with laughter. Raquel pushed her soup bowl away so she could put her head on the table to muffle her laughter, and Megan, gradually getting hold of herself, wiped her eyes and didn't dare look at the older Williams sisters again for fear of setting herself off again. The three younger people hunched together in shared insult, aware they were being laughed at without quite understanding why.

Finally Raquel lifted her head again, her face strained with contained sobs. Sondra scooted her chair closer and put her arms around Raquel, sharing the tears that laughter had brought on. Jessie's eyes welled up with confused anger and sorrow. Megan's heart went out to her, and she was glad when Reed hugged the younger woman, even if it left Megan and Flynn awkwardly on the outside of their grief. Megan glanced around the café, finding most of

Mohill's denizens unabashedly watching the antics at the Williams table. A couple of young mothers had the decency to skitter their gazes away, faintly embarrassed, when Megan met their eyes, but they looked back again as soon as they thought it was safe, and most of the older people just kept right on watching.

Megan rose, stepping between the sisters and the biggest chunk of viewers that she could, and settled into a parade rest. She wasn't particularly tall or broad-shouldered for her size, but the black chauffeur's uniform lent her a bit of authority, and the expressionless gaze she met onlookers with lent her a lot more. Within a few seconds the café patrons had decided their lunches were more interesting than gawking, and from then on any time someone looked their way, their attention bounced off Megan and returned to their food. A surprising number of people finished their coffees and left in the next five minutes.

After a while, Sondra, somewhat recovered, said, "Thank you, Megan. I think you can sit back down with us now."

"You finish up." Megan glanced over her shoulder to see Flynn gaping at her with something akin to hero worship. "I'll eat on the walk back to the car."

"This isn't part of your job," Raquel objected.

Megan permitted herself the ghost of a smile. "Sometimes it is, ma'am."

Somehow the formality made all three sisters smile a little in return, and allowed them go to back to their lunches without feeling like they needed to insist on Megan joining them. She listened while they talked, and watched how, when others came into the café, she drew their attention and then, with her stoic presence, sent it elsewhere. Even the most curious didn't dare do more than steal a glance or two when Megan's gaze kept finding theirs as they peered toward the Williamses.

"There were drawings of the grounds," Raquel said as she finished her soup. "Not ones that Gigi Elsie did, but ones from Patrick that she'd tucked into the book. Even when I was a kid they were fragile, so I didn't open them very often. And I had a hard time reading his handwriting. It was old-fashioned and pencil on paper so it'd gone all yellow and faded and there were cracks and holes from it being folded. I never thought to copy them. I wish I had."

"I always liked maps," Reed said. "I used to think about being a surveyor, when I was a kid. My grandpa was one." The last was defensive, like he had to explain himself.

Sondra, sourly, said, "And you ended up an itinerant musician?" which explained to whom he'd felt he owed the explanation. Megan worked to keep her face straight, knowing a crack in her demeanor would make the other café patrons feel like they could return to spying on the strangers.

"I'm not itinerant!"

"Oh my god, can we not," Jessie said tiredly. "Do you remember anything about the maps, Raq?"

The middle sister shook her head. "Just the house and the lake."

"There's loads more up there," Flynn put in. Even Megan glanced at him, and he shrank in his seat. "We weren't supposed to go messing about, but everybody did after the family moved away. They've a groundskeeper who's there enough that the old house isn't much damaged even though it's been empty since my mam was a girl, and they keep the land from going all to seed, but there's hundreds of acres to mess about on like. We used to go and piss on the grav—" Megan looked again in time to see him go white, and allowed herself a one-sided grin as she settled back to parade rest while the kid tried to find a non-incriminating way to finish that sentence.

Jessie helped by skipping over the confessional aspect of it. "There's a graveyard? I thought they were all buried at that church in Dublin. Why don't we just go dig one of them up?"

"Well, that's horrible," said Raquel.

"And apparently urine-stained," Sondra said more sharply. "Who would do that?"

"Lads whose ancestors were starved by those land-holders and died or fled the country to find a new life," Flynn said almost as sharply, and to Megan's surprise, Sondra subsided. "I could take you around, anyway," Flynn said. "Show you all the old bits, if you wanted."

"Let's," Jessie said decisively. "Megan, you should eat before the soup is totally cold and then we'll go. The place has mostly cleared out anyway."

Megan assessed the café, then nodded, said, "Thanks," and sat to eat her lukewarm soup, which was still pretty good. She spread butter thickly onto the bread and ate that on the way back to the car, licking her fingers before she opened the car doors, because she'd forgotten a nap-kin. The dogs made sleepy sounds as the doors opened, but even they couldn't really be bothered to wake all the way up as Sondra climbed in beside them. Everyone hesitated momentarily, trying to figure out the logistics of Flynn joining them, and Reed offered, "He can ride with me."

Jessie paused at the Bentley door, eyeing her two would-be suitors uncertainly. "Uh."

"It's five miles and we'll be driving right behind them," Sondra said. "He's not going to run him off the road."

"I could cycle," Flynn said to Jessie. "It'd take longer, but . . ."

"For God's sake." Reed tossed his keys to Flynn. "There, you drive. Does that make everyone happy?"

Flynn threw the keys back. "It would if I drove, but I don't. And did you sign a waiver for a second driver on the rental? You'd be in for loads of trouble if I crashed."

Megan, who hadn't been asked, said, "I think they'll be fine," and, as if her word was gospel, everyone got into the appropriate cars to drive up to the old Williams property.

The old cast-iron gates to the Lough Rynn House property were, in the strictest sense of the word, open. There were no chains holding them closed, and the heavy bolt that would normally bar them was not actually settled in the bolt-holder. Consequently, the two sides of the gate stood perhaps two inches apart, not exactly an inviting distance.

Flynn, with a youthful disregard for consequences, got out of Reed's car, shoved the gates all the way open, indicated that the two vehicles should drive through, and then, with a peculiar nod toward niceties, returned the gates to almost closed before getting back into the car. Megan drove ahead of them, not wanting to speed but also very much wanting to get the gates out of her rearview mirror, as if not seeing them would absolve her of trespassing.

The driveway had an air of benign negligence, with

sharp yellow and white gravel clearly having been laid down deliberately at some point. Even now it stayed within the road's boundaries rather than melting into a mess at the shoulders, but tufts of grass grew up in sparse rows between the gravel too, and pothole incursions had developed over the years. All of the Williams women fell into a hush as they crept up the road toward the house itself, and Megan, amused, felt her own heart rate accelerating, as if a wonderful surprise awaited them.

A few minutes later a curve in the road revealed the old house, and Megan had to hold her breath to keep from having an opinion before the sisters could come to terms with what they saw. She pulled the car into a parking spot and got the doors for the sisters, who got out with unabashed awe brightening their faces. Even Sondra's tension faded as they gazed at the glorious old building.

Megan couldn't tell, at a glance of the building's front face, what had stood for two centuries and what had been built, or restored, more recently. Under the changing winter light and dripping rain, the bricks looked grey or gold or white, set on absolute acres of wilding lawn and framed by thick leafless trees that nestled the old building comfortably into its surrounds. Slate roofs with more chimneys than Megan could count in one go rose toward the clouds, peaking over windows with complex wooden frames. Megan wondered if any of them held the original glass, and if it wobbled and shaped the view of the endless gardens stretching around the house. It wasn't a castle the way Americans thought of one, with turrets and towers, but a magnificent, multistory manor house that looked as though it had slowly grown into its position, like the dark trees around it.

Sondra bleated something like a laugh. "I guess it would have been all right."

They were all suddenly in tears, regrets and loss and maybe a certain sense of the absurd overwhelming them. Megan stepped away, giving them the space they needed to mourn and recover, and when Reed and Flynn drove up, shooed them away with a protective ferocity. They both made as if to get out of Reed's vehicle and she gave them a warning look, since she didn't want their company right then herself. Especially since she needed to text Detective Bourke, although—inevitably—the signal out in the hinterlands of Ireland ranged between one bar and none. She typed up a text anyway, describing the diary and explaining its absence, and spent several minutes pressing *send again* until the message finally went through.

The sisters seemed to have almost collected themselves by then, and Reed and Flynn were sort of sulking inside the rental like they couldn't decide whether to get out or not. Megan wondered if they would keep being cowed by her gimlet glares, or if they'd overcome their own indecision to act. Maybe Jessie drew indecisive men to her, or maybe it was just that they were in their twenties and hadn't figured it all out yet.

Not that Megan herself, in her forties, had figured much out either, given that less than forty-eight hours earlier she'd been begging for a couch to crash on if her life went any more haywire. And honestly, between Brian, Jelena, and Niamh's often-empty apartment, she probably wouldn't have ever needed to flee all the way back to the States, but for a minute it had seemed a genuinely viable option.

Sondra, more or less composed, waved at Megan, beckoning her over. "We don't know what to do next. It seems so . . ."

"Rude," Jessie put in, when Sondra didn't finish her sentence. "To just go stomping all over the place. On the other hand, it's kind of what we came to do, right? And nobody is here to stop us."

Raquel murmured, "We should have worn different shoes," and Sondra, still in tall heels, gave her a look that fell somewhere between rueful agreement and total irritation.

Flynn and Reed finally got out of their car, joining the women at the edge of the house's formal grounds. Like the driveway, the acres of lawn suffered from benign—or perhaps something less benevolent than benign—neglect. Under the gray January sky, yellow hay that Megan suspected were summertime wildflowers met brambles and saplings at the lawn's farthest edges. Tremendous older trees sprang up suddenly at those edges, though, with no gradient between the knee-high little trees and their vastly taller brethren. The groundskeeper Flynn mentioned apparently worked at keeping the forest from eating the lawn, but if they didn't return soon, it would be a lost battle.

The house itself, set an easy couple hundred metres from where they'd parked, had the same kind of feeling to it. The doors were sealed tightly and it somehow gave the impression of resting until life returned to it, but a few windows were broken, and Megan imagined the whole place could fall in on itself with just a little more neglect.

"C'mon," Flynn said. "Nobody's around to give out to us, so we might as well have a look around." He cast Jessie a quick look to see if he'd impressed her, then struck off for the house as if he hadn't a care in the world. Reed, not to be outdone, followed hard on his heels while the women exchanged glances.

"Jessie's right," Sondra said with a shrug. "Megan, you might as well get the dogs and let them stretch their legs, too."

"Oh. Yeah, good idea. Thanks." Megan hurried back to the car and released the hounds, or at least the terriers, and clipped their leads on them before they could go surging off after the Williams women. "No way. There's too much land for you to get lost on out here and I'll need to drive everybody home in a couple hours, not chase puppies all over kingdom come." All three dogs strained at their leashes, wanting to catch up with the others.

It only took a moment to do so. Megan's shoes were comfortable and flat and easy to both drive and walk in. Sondra, on the other hand, had to keep to the gravel-paved walkway that led toward the house's front doors, her weight tipped forward a little to keep her heels from sinking in. Raquel had hurried to offer Sondra her arm, and Jessie ran to catch up. They looked momentarily happy, like a family just out to do something silly together. They slowed a little as they reached the house, nerves overtaking them, but Jessie gave a firm nod and they split up, everybody beginning to peer through windows and try doors.

Reed shouted that he was going around to the back to do the same. He disappeared around the side, which looked like enough of a hike to get his ten thousand steps in for the day. Flynn followed soft of half-heartedly, like he felt he needed to be a bold explorer in order to impress Jessie. Megan made a cup of her hands and peered in one of the windows, trying to see through the gloom and grime that had built up on them.

Even through the muck, it was clear the interior had been magnificent in its day. Although it had been abandoned decades ago, it retained its stateliness, and the detailing—heavy-weighted cornices, window frames swollen with age and water, broken-tiled floors—cried out with their former glory. Jessie walked along the windows, peeking in as silently as a ghost, while Raquel kept her fingers pressed against her mouth, eyes large above them. Even Sondra looked pained, as if seeing what the old building had become was more than she could bear. Megan heard her murmur, "We couldn't restore it," and knew she was trying to convince herself.

Megan couldn't imagine how much it would cost *to* restore it. The property had been largely empty since the last of the family had moved away from it in the 1970s, and decades of neglect had to take an impossibly pricey toll. But even overgrown and forgotten, its bones were still good. Megan didn't know how much longer they'd stay that way, if the estate continued on without residents, but letting the old manor fall into total disrepair seemed like an actual crime.

In fact, she thought it might literally be, given the laws about restoring and maintaining listed buildings. There were ruined castles held up by scaffolding all over the country, preventing them from becoming any more ruined than they already were, but without the cost and effort of restoring them. A manor like the Lough Rynn House, still just on this side of dereliction, had to be a site of interest for the heritage groups.

"We couldn't restore it," Sondra murmured again, and Raquel sighed.

"Do you think . . . if we proved we were the heirs . . . they wouldn't give it to us, would they. It doesn't work that way." She hesitated. "Does it?"

"It still belongs to somebody," Jessie said unhappily. "They must not want it anymore, but it still belongs to them. And honestly, what would we do with it?"

"Turn it into a hotel," Sondra said, suddenly brisk and businesslike. "It would cost a fortune and we could never do it, but that's what you'd do."

"Shut your mouth," Raquel said primly. "Can you imagine what Mama would say if she heard you talking about turning her ancestral home into a hotel?"

"If it meant her ancestral home didn't crumble into dust, I think she'd have been all for it. She didn't have any sense when it came to money anyway."

Raquel, genuinely shocked, gasped, "Sondra!" and her older sister exhaled noisily.

"Ray, it's God's own truth, whether you like it or not. If somebody came along and said, 'Here, Cherise, I want you to pour every penny you've got into restoring a building that will never love you back, and might bank-rupt you before you finish,' she'd have been signing her name on the dotted line before they were even finished talking."

"*Sondra!* She's our mama! And she's dead! You can't speak ill of the dead!"

"Believe me, if I was speaking ill, you'd know it."

Before it devolved any more toward an argument, the manor's broad front door suddenly banged open. Reed, dusty and cobwebbed, stood in its frame. "Come in," he said hoarsely. "I think you'd better see."

CHAPTER 12

Not even Sondra put up more than a pro forma protest, a combination of curiosity and inborn conviction that they had some slight birthright to be poking around the crumbling manor, allowing them the mental latitude necessary to do a little more invasive trespassing. Even Megan and the dogs, on their leashes, went in. "In the name of reporting back to Paul," she murmured to Thong, who took the trouble to sit down, tilt her head, and cock an ear dubiously at Megan.

"Yeah," Megan whispered, "yeah, okay, it's total bull, but we're running with it anyway, okay?"

Thong, evidently satisfied that Megan had thought this through, gave a soft whine of agreement, rose, and trotted up to her brother, who had been obliged to stop at the ends of his leash while Megan had a conversation with his sister. They hurried to catch up with Reed and the Williams sisters—they could be a band, phrased like that—who had all gone upstairs, walking in each others' footprints so the dust was hardly disturbed. The dogs were less concerned about that, and small paw prints appeared in a wide swath, wiping out another set of Reed's footprints, presumably from his first exploration.

The old house had over a dozen bedrooms, and even after decades of disuse, some of them retained their grandiosity. Megan saw four equally deep impressions in the wood floor of one of the rooms, as if a heavy bed had once sat there. A flowery ceiling above the empty bed space must have once held a candle-laden chandelier. Hairs rose on Megan's arms as she thought of the age and glamour of that era. Then, more pragmatically, she also imagined being the housemaid who had to climb up and scrub that intricate cornicing free of wax and smoke, and some of the romance faded.

"Careful of the floor here," Reed said. "I found a weak spot the hard way." Boards softened with age had clearly taken too much weight, splinters jabbing up from a divot just shy of being a hole.

"I always wondered what would happen if somebody stepped all the way through floorboards," Raquel said with a kind of macabre interest. "I used to be afraid that would happen to me and I'd fall all the way into the basement."

"Does this place even have a basement?" Jessie asked.

"Probably cellars," Sondra replied. "Not basements like at home."

Raquel, irritably, said, "I didn't mean falling through *this* house, anyway," and Reed said, "Shh," as he pushed open a door that had clearly been broken through at some point in its history.

The room beyond it didn't even have windows, light coming only from the torch on the phone Reed held as they entered. The walls were awkward; some short, some long, all of them angled, as if the room had been built as an afterthought, taking space out of the rest of the house for this space. It made it the innermost room, as protected from the elements as could be possible, and as her eyes adjusted, Megan understood why it had been built that way.

Whatever history the family had, whatever memories and heirlooms had been worth keeping, but not keeping close to hand, had been packed into the odd little space. One by one the other torches came on, illuminating the room. Hope chests were crammed together, curving cedar tops holding the weight of portraits above them. Other boxes, much more modern in make, were stacked in tall piles, someone's neat handwriting labeling the fronts and sides with information about what they contained: photographs, papers, books, letters. One, near the top, simply had *Patrick* written on it. Raquel went to that one, shifting boxes away to take it from the pile, and knelt to open it. Everyone gathered around, even the dogs. Thong put her nose over the edge of the box and blew into it, then backed up and sneezed violently.

It released a string of tension that had entered the room, allowing everybody to laugh. Raquel took a few pieces of newspaper out, gingerly, and turned them over, searching through the pages. "They're the last earl's search for Geepaw Patrick." She put them aside, lifting envelopes and letters out. Jessie lost interest and began looking around, lifting sheets off portraits and peeking beneath them. Reed paced after her to the degree it was possible in the little room: They came close to bumping into one another as they each looked through different boxes. Megan backed up, tugging the dogs with her, and watched Sondra never quite touch anything, her hands drifting above boxes and chests and portraits as if encountering a force field that kept her from making contact. Aside from the box Raquel had opened, no one else intruded on the material that much. Megan thought the permission they'd granted themselves to enter the house had a hard limit, one that they probably weren't fully aware of hitting.

"Jess." Raquel's voice broke in little more than a whisper, but they were all so quiet the shock of it sent chills up Megan's spine. Jessie went back to Raquel as she lifted a 120-year-old photograph from near the bottom of the box.

Jessie said, "Oh, shit," and stepped back.

Her own face, or near enough as to make no difference, gazed up at them from Raquel's hands. Their great-to-the-third grandfather's eyes were narrower, perhaps, and his mouth less full than Jessie's. The faded sepia tones of the photograph washed away comparisons of hair or eye colour, but the jaw structure, the shape of the nose, and the set of the eyes were direct echoes of the young woman standing at Raquel's shoulder. "He's even got your eyebrows, Jess."

Jessie, offended, said, "My eyebrows are nowhere near that thick," and even Sondra chuckled quietly.

"No, but the shape is the same. Look at his hairline." She reached over to smooth Jessie's hair back, showing the same strongly triangular hairline on her sister as their grandfather had. She let Jessie's hair fall and spread her hands as if admitting defeat. "I believe it now, at least."

"People can look like people they're not related to," Raquel murmured, "but yeah. This is . . ."

"Freaking *weird*." Jessie stepped forward again, staring at the photo. "Gigi Elsie had some pictures of him, but they were all older. I never thought I looked like him or anything. He must have been . . . he must have been about my age, when this was taken?"

Raquel turned the picture over, looking for a date. "Nineteen-oh-four. He was a little younger than you are now." She put the photograph down, faceup, and took a picture of it over Sondra's sound of wordless objection.

Jessie proclaimed, "Fuh-*reaky*," and shivered. "Look, I think we should put this all away. It's not . . . it's not really ours, is it."

"Aww. I thought you'd want to . . ." Reed gestured. "Root through it all. There's got to be some good dirt in here. Family secrets. Ghosts. Buried treasure. Something."

"Something that might explain why Mother was murdered?" Sondra squatted and took the papers from Raquel, beginning to put them away. "Maybe, but Jessie's right. We don't have any real right to be going through these things. Not without permission. And I don't think anybody imagined there was buried treasure on the land anyway."

"Geepaw Patrick used to bury treasures," Raquel said, sounding surprised. "Gigi's diaries talked about it. He'd take things from the house and bury them for his brother to hunt for and dig up. He drew maps, like I said." She put her hand on Sondra's arm, stopping her from packing

anything else up, and went through the papers again, finally shaking her head. "None of them are here, though.
That's too bad. There might have been some that weren't
folded up, that I wouldn't be as afraid to touch. I know
they wouldn't have led to anything except maybe some
old crockery, but they'd be wonderful to look at. We
could see how the land had changed since he was a child.
There—" Raquel's breath caught. "Oh. Oh, Sonny. Flynn
said there was a graveyard."

Sondra, lit by the hard white light of the phones'
torches, looked especially unforgiving and uncomprehending. "So?"

"What if . . . do you think Mama would like to be
buried here?"

Strains of conflict shot through Sondra's expression,
her initial impulse to reject the notion clear, and then the
idea of her mother's romantic notions obviously displac-
ing that impulse. "I don't know, Raq," she finally said,
wearily. "I think she might love it, but would we want it?
And we still can't prove we're related, even if we had the
diary. Even with that picture. Which we're not supposed
to have seen. You can't show anybody that picture,
Raquel."

Raquel looked inclined to be stubborn, then, as
quickly, let it go. "I'll keep it, though. For us."

"Fine." Sondra finished putting things away and put
the box back where they'd taken it from. "Let's go look
for the graveyard. It's probably in too much disrepair to
be used anyway. And weren't they all actually buried in
that church in Dublin anyway?"

"Just the earls themselves," Flynn volunteered from
the doorway. Everybody startled, looking toward him,
and he set his jaw defensively. "I was looking around and

you all disappeared. I just caught up. It's only the earls who were buried at the church. The rest of their family was buried at the chapel on the family land."

"That's too bad. Mama would love being a mummy," Jessie muttered.

Raquel hissed, "Jess!" although Megan thought Jessie might be right. "Anyway," Raquel went on as if the mummy idea hadn't been floated, "I bet she *would* like being buried in the ancestral graveyard."

"Don't get your heart set on it," Sondra warned. "Do you know where it is, though, Flynn?"

"I do so." He cast a look at Sondra's shoes. "The path out to it might just be solid enough yet for you to walk, Ms. Williams. I wouldn't want to go anywhere else, wearing those shoes."

"Is there anything around that we *can* look at, even with Sonny's shoes?" Jessie asked.

"Not much," Flynn said dubiously. "You'd want hiking boots for loads of it."

Sondra gave an enormous sigh. "Is there really anything out here we'd need to see? Aside from curiosity?"

Flynn cast an uncertain look at Reed, then Megan, as if they might somehow have the answers. "I'd say no? The house is the grand bit, and the rest is just land going to wrack and ruin. You might fancy the druid's altar, but it's not . . ." He waved his hand. "It could be a thousand years old like, but it's probably just a lump of old stone somebody dropped there a couple hundred years ago for gas."

"For gas?" Raquel blinked. "Were they drilling for natural gas?"

"It means for fun," Megan murmured. Raquel's expression cleared, while Flynn's went through a visible struggle not to laugh. "Tell you what," Megan offered. "It's going to be dark soon and we're not going to want to be tromping around out here in the dark, especially if it starts to rain. How about I take the dogs for a walk to this druid circle, and see if it looks like something cool enough for you to come back and see, and you go see if there's anything left of the chapel and graveyard?"

Gratitude flashed across Sondra and Raquel's faces while Jessie looked a little disappointed. She looked at her own feet, though—Birkenstock sandals, with bare feet already bluish with cold—and reluctantly went to stand with her sisters. Megan, satisfied, said, "Okay, which way is the druid's circle?" and looked skeptically at Flynn when he pointed southeast and said, "It's a ten-minute walk."

"An Irish ten minutes or a real ten minutes?"

He looked mildly bewildered. "Ten minutes."

"Right. I'll be back within an hour," Megan said dryly to the sisters, who frowned at her in confusion. "I never met an Irish ten minutes that wasn't at least twenty," she explained, and set off with Reed sort of edging after her.

Flynn, cheerfully, said, "Go on, mate, I'll bring the ladies to the chapel my own self," and when Megan looked back, Reed, scowling deeply, was stomping after the Williamses. Megan grinned, and as soon as they were out of earshot, said, "All they need is a quirky best friend to be a rom-com, huh, pups? Who do you think she'll choose? Who would you choose, hm? Yeah? Not me. I'd take a year or two off from dating and reconsider the kinds of boys I wanted to hang out with, but that's proba- bly because I'm old and sensible, right? Right. Right. That's probably it," to the dogs as they walked along.

There had probably been a path to the druid's circle,

once upon a time. Now there was a track of slightly-less-overgrown grass through fields and trees, and Megan's calves were wet with rain clinging to the grass before the shape of another lake appeared, reflecting grey clouds and lined by winter-black trees. "What was that," she murmured to the dogs. "Fifteen minutes? Yeah? Yeah, I thought so too. Not ten at all. It's never ten." Megan looked back, but the Lough Rynn house had disappeared, leaving her alone with the dogs in a very tame sort of wilderness. "Okay, five more minutes, and then we're heading back, because otherwise we'll be leaving the Williamses standing in the cold for an hour."

In less than five minutes, though, a crowd of trees opened over what had to be the druid's altar, with three or four lichen-stained stones piled on top of one another, and another leaning at a dramatic angle away from them. They were all at least six inches thick and curved like gravestones, obviously shaped rather than natural, but their positions made them look more like a lounge chair than an altar, to Megan. There were trails of mashed-down grass around it, as if other people had been that way fairly recently. She supposed if someone needed a bit of privacy and a little magic, the Lough Rynn grounds were a fine place to find it.

The puppies pulled at their leashes, wanting to climb and sniff the stones, but Megan shook her head. "It's not nice to pee on druid altars."

A dry-voiced old woman said, "Worse has been done to it," and Megan stifled a shriek by turning it into a high-pitched laugh. The woman emerged from behind one of the massive old trees overhanging the altar, leaving Megan to imagine, for an instant, that she was a dryad or some other tree spirit herself. She'd never imagined dryads as wearing wool jumpers, thick plaid skirts, wellies, and a cloche hat jammed over their ears, though, much less carrying what appeared to be a metal detector. "I should know," the old woman went on. "My parents would've been shocked to hear what I got up to on those rocks. You're American?"

"I am," Megan admitted, still smiling with surprise. "You snuck up on me."

"It's the dogs," the old lady said. "I've had a fear of them since I was a girl, so I hid and then I said to meself, Maire Cahill, I said, you're seventy-eight years of age and not one of those creatures is higher than your knee, so what is it you're afeared of? And the woman's got them on their leads like a decent sort, so screw your courage to the sticking point and go on out there, I said, and so I did."

"Oh! I'm sorry! They're friendly," Megan promised. "And I don't let them off their leads, but I didn't mean to scare you. I didn't know there was anyone out here to scare. And you've got a weapon," she said with a nod at the bulky metal detector.

Maire hefted it thoughtfully. "I hadn't thought of that so. And there's not usually anyone here to be scared by," she allowed. "What's your story, young woman?"

"My employers wanted to see the old house, and the gates weren't *locked* . . ." At the old lady's grin, Megan smiled back. "What's your story, if you don't mind me asking? Treasure hunting?"

"Even an old lady needs hobbies," Maire replied haughtily.

Megan laughed, and the puppies, interested in the sound, came to wind around her ankles. Staying unentangled kept her feet busy while she talked to the old lady. "Any luck?" She forbore to mention that she was pretty certain using metal detectors for treasure hunting was illegal in Ireland, on the basis that Maire probably already knew, didn't care, and wasn't finding much anyway.

"Eh. A bit of iron ore here and there, but all those Vikings and Normans don't seem to have left a damn thing worth digging up. What good is a history of invasion if it doesn't provide a treasure or two?"

"Well, they had a lot of Ireland to bury things in," Megan said solemnly.

Maire cackled. "That's true enough so. I can see what you're thinking, though. What a way for an auld wan to spend her time, hm? Shouldn't I be knitting things for the grandbabbies and having my sisters around for tea?"

Megan, truthfully, said, "The thought never crossed my mind. Besides, think how happy the grandbabbies will be when their nan makes the whole family rich."

"The sisters will be bitter over it, though," Maire predicted and Megan laughed.

"Family can be tough, huh? But treasure hunting seems like fun."

"It gets me out walking and at my age, that's a good thing."

"At any age," Megan agreed. The dogs finally gave up on winding around her and sat down in the damp grass with sighs of melodramatic patience. Megan clicked at them, encouraging them back to their feet, and smiled at Maire. "I think they're telling me it's time to go."

Maire clicked her tongue. "Here and I was going to ask them to do the digging for me if I found a bit of gold. Ah, well. Be careful driving out of here. The gardaí like to lurk and see if they can catch trespassers if they know strangers are in town."

"And I reckon all of Mohill knows we're here." Megan rolled her eyes. "Thanks for the warning. Good luck with the treasure hunting."

"I'll give ye a gold coin if I find a trove," Maire promised, and Megan, smiling, took the dogs back toward the house.

CHAPTER 13

Her phone buzzed with a message as she reached the car, and she paused to towel the dogs off and get them into their carrier before checking it. Just a note from Paul saying he'd keep an eye out for the diary, and had she learned anything interesting herself. Megan, reluctantly eyeing the walk up to the graveyard, tried to think whether they'd learned anything interesting enough in the house to mention having done a little breaking and entering. She could hear the sisters and their incidental escorts coming back toward her, and decided to spare herself the walk to the graveyard.

"It's a mess," Jessie announced as soon as she was within Megan's earshot. "I don't know how you'd even know where was safe to dig. You might end up putting Mama in on top of somebody else."

"Jessie," Raquel said in despair, but Sondra, walking awkwardly across the gravel in her tall heels, shook her head.

"Jessie's right, Raq, and you know it. Even if we convinced them we're family, the work that would have to be done just to clean that space up enough to bury someone in it wouldn't be worth it. And we have a plot at home where everybody is buried together, even Geepaw Patrick. I think Mom would rather be there than in some half-rotten churchyard in Ireland."

"*You'd* rather be there," Raquel snapped. "Mama had a more romantic soul than you do."

Sondra's nostrils flared and Megan saw the young men exchange wary glances. Apparently forty minutes alone with the Williams sisters had made allies of them, which—honestly—Megan sympathized with. She wanted to imagine their strife came from shock and heartbreak, but she kind of doubted it.

Jessie said, "I am so tired," with a note that belayed Megan's instant suspicion that she was just trying to head off another spat between her sisters. "Was it actually only this morning that we got in? Has Mama really only been dead for a day? How is this even happening? I want—" Her voice wobbled. "I want to go home. I want this to not be happening."

Reed tried to step in and offer comfort, but Sondra got there first, enveloping Jessie in a weary hug. Raquel came to join them, and they all sort of crawled into the car without letting go of one another, like an amoeba of Williamses. Megan closed the door behind them, found the two young men looking to her for guidance, and shrugged. Even she felt it had been a terribly long day, and she didn't have the weight of grief and jet lag pulling her even farther down. She got in the Bentley herself, waved to Reed and Flynn, and left them to figure out their own ways home as she drove the Williamses back to Dublin.

Rain started falling at the Leitrim border, and once the tears had subsided, Megan's only companions in the drive back were the hiss of tires on the wet roads and the occasional soft snore from the back seat. She turned the heat up to keep the exhausted sisters warm, and watched Dublin's amber glow brighten on the horizon as the night grew darker and the drive took them nearer. It was absolutely lashing in city centre, and she got an enormous umbrella from inside the hotel before waking the sisters up to walk them to inside. None of them looked like they even knew where they were, although Raquel gave her a sudden, hard hug as she left them in the Gresham's lobby.

The streets glittered black with water that rushed past overfilled gutters as Megan drove across town to drop the dogs off at her flat, then brought the car back to the garage. The cleaning crew was swamped with vehicles all coming in wet at once, so she took half an hour to detail the Bentley herself. Tymon waved gratefully and she nodded, then went into the main office to get a glass of water, but stopped short just inside the door.

The outside curtains were drawn and the front door's *OPEN* sign had been turned to *CLOSED*, although normally Orla kept the shopfront open and blazing with light until 9 pm. Tonight, though, the reason for closing up early came in the slim, well-shouldered form of Detective Paul Bourke, whose sandy red hair had undergone a neat trim since Megan had last seen him. He'd gotten Orla out from behind the counter somehow, then put himself between her and the way back behind it, leaving her in the space near the door. Although the door provided an obvious escape route, Orla had the aura of being a trapped animal, with her shoulders high and her body language shrinking away from Bourke.

The detective lifted his gaze from the notepad he wrote on and acknowledged Megan with a short nod. She said, "Oh, hi, sorry, I didn't mean to interrupt," and scurried to the far wall, where a water cooler sat in a recess. She filled a cup, mumbled, "Sorry" again, and hurried back to the garage, where she all but seized Tymon and hissed, "What's going on in there?"

"We don't know, we were hoping you'd find out! He's your friend and all!"

"Yeah, but he's a cop first. It's not like he told me he was coming out to talk to Orla. Why's he talking to Orla?"

"Because Orla can't keep her gob shut." Cillian Walsh, who was tall, black-haired, strong-jawed, and, at twenty-eight, much too young for Megan to be interested in, got out of the vehicle he was pulling into the garage just in time to hear the end of their conversation. "She's after telling everyone that one of her clients is a countess of the old blood. You know some of her mates are IRA from the old days, and they don't care for the idea of an heir turning up. There's folks still alive who remember when the old earl died."

"They must have been kids," Megan protested. "He died in 1952. Well, okay, I guess some of them could have been adults, but there can't be many left."

"It's not how many they are, but how bitter. And some of those lads, it's not themselves doing the killing anymore, but their sons and grandsons who've been radicalized."

"Right, but—wait. Are you telling me Cherise Williams might be dead because Orla couldn't stop bragging to her old militant friends about the heiress to an Anglo-Irish earldom and they just couldn't stand the idea of somebody like that being around?"

Cillian gave a shrug that meant *basically, yeah*, and Megan's voice rose with urgency. "But doesn't that mean that her daughters are in danger too?"

"Shite. I guess it might?"

Megan's hands turned themselves into claws that she rattled toward the office. "I swear I could *kill* her, if that's what's happened!" Detective Bourke walked past the main garage doors and Megan shouted, "Paul!" after him. He paused, obviously not surprised, and waited for her to catch up.

"You know I can't comment on an ongoing investigation, Megan." He flipped the collar of his trench coat up, protecting himself against a northerly wind driving the rain hard.

"I'm not asking you to. I'm asking if the Williams girls are in danger and if anything is being done to protect them."

"That is, in fact, commenting on an ongoing investigation." Bourke sighed and lowered his voice. "I have people watching them, all right, Megan? Does that satisfy you?"

"On the one hand, no, because I'm desperate for details, but yes. Yeah." Megan put her hand on his arm. "Thank you, Paul."

"It's my job, Megan, and you might not end up thanking me if your boss goes down as an accessory to murder."

"Wouldn't that mean she helped move the body, or something? Gossip isn't accessorizing." The warmth drained from Megan's body. "Oh my god, she didn't help move the body, did she?"

Bemusement flickered over Bourke's face. "When did you get so familiar with the details of what different terms mean?"

"I've had a weird year, Paul."

"I suppose you have, at that. Just stay away from it, Megan. For my sake, if you can't keep your nose out of it for your own. My boss is spitting nails."

"All right, well, I'm probably driving the sisters around some more tomorrow, if that's any use to you and your protection detail."

"I wish you wouldn't."

"But I'm going to anyway, so there we are."

"There we are." Bourke sighed, turned the collar of his coat up again, and left Megan behind on the sidewalk. She watched him for a moment, all drama with his long stride and the trench laden with rain, then shivered hard and went back inside the garage as a fresh deluge of fat raindrops started to splash down.

The company staff descended on her like locusts and looked collectively skeptical that she'd learned nothing in her chat with the garda detective. Megan said, "Do you know how much trouble he could get in for telling me anything?"

"He's done it before." Cillian scowled after Bourke. "I thought he fancied you."

"Bourke? I don't know why he would. He's dating

Niamh O'Sullivan. Besides, even if he did, he can't go around telling me everything about his job."

Cillian's gaze went back to where Bourke had disappeared down the street. "Seriously? That . . . *guy* . . . is dating Niamh O'Sullivan? He's nowhere near her league."

"And yet you think he's appropriately into me, which means I must not be anywhere near Nee's league either, doesn't it?"

"What?" Colour rushed to Cillian's cheeks and he shook his head, flustered. "Uh, no. No, that's not what I meant at all."

Megan said, "Uh-huh," with all the admonition she could muster, and walked off. To be fair, she didn't consider herself in Niamh's league, either. There was a reason Niamh was a movie star and Megan wasn't. Granted, she liked to think that at least part of that reason was that it had never even crossed her mind, whereas Niamh had wanted to act since childhood. Still, she felt Cillian had deserved the nose-tweaking. She went into the office, mostly because it took her out of sight, and she thought after that withering conversation, a full-on exit was the only appropriate final commentary.

The shades were still drawn and the door still had the *CLOSED* sign turned outward. Orla sat on the couch, hands clasped tightly at her compressed knees. Her head was lowered, making her look hardly bigger than a child, although she lifted her gaze when Megan came in and rose, suddenly flushed with relief. "Megan. That detective there thinks I've something to do with the murder."

"Have you?" The chill in Megan's own voice surprised her and took Orla completely aback.

"I'd never! You know that!"

"What I know right now is that you kept mocking the 'countess' and mouthing off to everyone about her pretensions, and that you fired me for even being in proximity to her death. I could see how a person might get suspicious about that. Maybe I saw something that would tie her death to you."

"But you didn't! And you've got to prove it!"

Genuine anger rose in Megan's chest so hot and fast that she spread her hands on the welcome desk and leaned in on it, eyes closed while she breathed through the spurt of fury. When she trusted her voice again, she said, "Why on earth would I have to do anything for you?" in as mild a tone as she could manage.

Judging from Orla's flinch, it was mild enough to be frigid. "I've given you a job and a home—"

"You *hired* me to work for your company, and I rent my apartment from you as my landlord. 'Give' implies that I haven't offered anything equitable in exchange, like my skill as a driver or my rent money. It also tries to shift a burden of guilt and responsibility onto me, as if I owe you something. I don't owe you squat." Megan had seen so many low-ranking military kids try to pull something like this over on people beneath them in the pecking order, and it made her angry every time. Orla nominally had more power over her, in fact, than those young troops had over each other, but there was nothing Orla provided that Megan couldn't equip herself with if necessary. Even if she couldn't, being the target of a power play was enough to make her prepared to burn it all down.

Orla's cheeks paled as she recognized the genuine anger in Megan's voice. She lowered her gaze, pressing her thin lips together, and looked up again with an expression Megan had never seen before, at least not on her. She'd seen her boss do contrite (not very convincingly, but she'd tried), and she'd certainly seen her do manipulative. This time, though, vulnerability shone in Orla's blue gaze, and Megan actually believed it. "All right," Orla said stiffly. "I've treated you unfairly, and I'm sorry. I need your help."

Megan, thinking of the decent apology Reed had offered, said, "Would you be sorry if you didn't need my help?"

Irritation flashed in Orla's eyes, but to her credit, she said, "Probably not," with sufficient honesty that Megan huffed angry laughter.

"And what do I get for helping you?"

Orla's irritation turned to outright ire. "You're already getting paid contractor rates for this damn job. What more do you want?"

"My regular job back? The threat of eviction lifted? A fifteen-percent raise for the whole staff? For you to not fight back when we unionize?" Orla's face grew increasingly outraged as Megan went on, and the last prompted a burst of wordless indignation. Megan smiled. "I think if we can agree on all that I might be willing to try helping you."

"That's extortion!"

"Mmm, no. I'm pretty sure extortion involves threats. I'm not threatening anything. I'm bargaining. I have something you want, and I also have terms that need to be met for you to get it."

"But a union?"

Megan shrugged. "Up to you. I've got to get home. You can give me a call when you make up your mind."

She got her winter coat, which she rarely wore while actually on duty, off a rack behind the counter, and pulled it on as she brushed past Orla toward the exit.

She was nearly out the door when Orla's answer, half-shouted, came after her. "All right, *fine*! But you'd better clear my name, d'yis hear me? You'd better clear my name!"

CHAPTER 14

Megan, with a sigh, glanced at the time and closed the door again. "I have things I need to do, so you'd better just tell me who you've been talking to and what kinds of connections they have." At Orla's shifty look, she shrugged. "It's your neck, Orla. What is it—are you IRA yourself?"

"I'm a republican, so I am," Orla said stoutly, almost defiantly.

Megan's sigh turned to a groan. The word *republican* carried a completely different meaning in Ireland than it did in the States. It meant supporting a united Ireland, one in which the northern counties were no longer part of Great Britain, but instead part of the Irish Republic. That in itself wasn't especially controversial, but the violent splinters of the long-since disbanded Irish Republican

Army were considered terrorist groups by the British, and sometimes other, governments. "There's a world of difference between being a republican and being IRA, Orla, and you know it. Don't be fucking coy."

Orla took a shocked step backward. "You don't swear."

"No, I don't, so don't be fucking coy!" A surge of satisfaction rose in Megan as Orla, still gaping, tried to gather herself to answer. She'd realized early in her career that foregoing curse words could both defuse a situation—people tended to laugh at a well-timed *gosh darn it*—and that it made the occasional f-bomb considerably more effective. The Irish swore so much, though, that she hadn't known if Orla would even notice her dropping one. Apparently she would.

"We're none of us IRA, or Real IRA, or New IRA, or any of it, not my lot," Orla muttered in sullen cooperation. The rain suddenly blew sideways, sending thick drops slapping loudly against the windowpanes. Megan pushed the blinds open a few inches with her fingers and made a face, not looking forward to walking home in the storm. Orla hunched up as if the rain was spilling down her back as she continued. "We'd know them as are IRA, or who run with them as are. Or were. Most of it's all blown over now, even with the bloody stupid Brits and their Brexit and the troubles it's caused. What's left is talk." Her gaze rose to meet Megan's, an abrupt, worried discomfort in it. "That's all it is, is talk. No one gives a tinker's damn about some eejit American claiming to be a countess. There'd be no point in killing the likes of her. If they were looking to make a statement, they'd pick a bigger target."

"Would they, though? It's a lot easier to get to an eejit

American than the British prime minister, and they've never had any compunction against risking civilians with their tactics."

"Have *you* heard of any bombs going off in Dublin?" Orla demanded, and Megan had to give her that. Every group claiming to be the old IRA's heir tended toward using bombs and guns, not sneaking up on people and filling their veins full of air. Explosions made a statement in a way more subtle assassinations didn't. "I told your detective all of this," Orla muttered.

"Did you give him any names to talk to? People I should check up on to see if I can find a way to help clear you?"

Orla looked wary. "That could be dangerous for yis. Can't you just figure out who did it instead of bothering my own?"

"Just tell me who you talked to, Orla, and who they might have talked to as well."

"It's not only who I had a word with my own self," Orla replied cagily. "I might have had a thing or two to say down the pub about countesses and lost heirs and the like."

"Oh my god, Orla! Which pub?"

"Maybe Slattery's. Maybe Rody Boland's. Maybe Murphy's or even out the Hill if I was feeling like a wander."

Megan put her arms and head on the counter, slumped in despair. "What happened to a local where you go every night without thinking about it?" she asked, muffled.

"Then you've the same audience every night," Orla said with a performer's disdain. Megan thunked her head against her arms a few times, then straightened.

"If you had to guess, where would you say rumour would fly straightest to trouble from?"

"Either where the youngest lads or the oldest gather, but I wouldn't know which of the pubs that is, if any of them." Orla's jaw set, and Megan knew she wouldn't say more for fear of painting a friend's establishment with a black mark. Paul Bourke would know more about it than Megan did, by dint of being local, but Megan would have to make the rounds herself, with a plausible story to get her into the gossips' good books. She leveled a finger at Orla.

"Word might get back that I'm bad-mouthing you. If it does, be forewarned that it's how I'm trying to get people to trust me."

Orla sniffed. "I'm a pillar of the community, I am. Watch what you say or it's your own self who'll be in trouble."

"Uh-huh." Megan thought anyone given a chance to complain about Orla's sharp tongue and tight-fisted ways would leap at the opportunity, but there was no profit in saying so. Orla's eyes narrowed with irritation, suggesting she'd followed Megan's line of thought, and that she suspected Megan was right. "I'll do everything I can," Megan promised. "And you'll keep your word."

Orla's jaw set even harder, but after a moment, she nodded grudgingly. Megan sighed. "Fine. All right. I'll let you know what I've learned tomorrow evening. Good night, Orla."

Her stomach suddenly rumbling, Megan walked home in the lashing rain so she could eat.

* * *

Not even the puppies wanted to go out in the miserable weather. Megan herded them out the door to do their business and a while later ate chili and cornbread muffins with two small, dripping dogs staring reproachfully at her every move. Well, not dripping: she had, for her own sake as much as theirs, toweled them off when they got back in, but somehow they managed to emote drippiness. By the time she'd finished eating, though, Dip and Thong had forgiven her and equilibrium was restored. Megan crawled on to the couch with the puppies and lay there staring at the ceiling, trying to figure out how to both clear Orla and steer away from the rough sorts Orla obviously imagined her having to tangle with in order to clear her.

The answer was to find out who was actually responsible, which she wanted to do anyway. The trip up to Leitrim hadn't shed any light, not unless old Maire had actually found a treasure after she and Megan had parted ways. But really, unless there was a sword in a stone which, when drawn, would proclaim the heir to Leitrim as the rightful ruler of all Ireland, Megan didn't know what else she might have expected to find up there that could help Orla or the Williams daughters.

"Besides," she said to Thong, who crawled up to lie on Megan's stomach and lick her chin, "the Lia Fáil is the Irish version of the sword in the stone, and it's in County Meath, isn't it. Yes it is. Yes it is. Hello, baby. Eee, you're kissing me." She wrinkled her face and rubbed the puppy's head. "Good girl. Should I bring the Williamses to Meath, huh? Should I bring them out there and see if the stone screams when they lay their hands on it? Can you imagine Sondra's face if that happened? Huh? Can you? Yeah, me too. It'd be gas."

Lia Fáil meant "Stone of Destiny," and the waist-height pillar of pale stone at the Hill of Tara was meant to recognize the true kings of Ireland. No one believed it, of course, but despite that, everyone hoped a little when they put their hands on it. Thong licked her chin again and Megan crossed her eyes at the puppy on her chest. "Oh, you'd stay out of the family dramas, would you, huh? Yeah, that's good advice."

Thong blew air through her nose and settled down, apparently feeling that was answer enough. Megan rubbed her head, then looked at the time on her phone and considered a pre-bedtime nap there on the couch. The puppies didn't help her decide against that notion, either, as both of them had fallen asleep, Dip sprawled across her thighs and slowly sliding to the side, where she could squish between Megan's ribs and the couch. Megan scrolled through a few pub reviews, like one of them would helpfully mention that modern IRA sympathizers hung out there, and finally put her phone on her chest, willing to drift off with the dogs for a little while.

She was just about asleep when the buzzer from the street-side door intercom blared. Megan jolted upright, the puppies coming awake with a series of startled barks. Megan dislodged Dip and let Thong slide the few inches to the couch cushions by getting up and walking blearily to answer the buzzer. "Yeah?"

"Megan?"

"Paul?" Megan buzzed the detective in and opened her door to watch him come up the stairs, shaking water off his shoulders. Dip and Thong went barreling out to meet him and he picked them up at the top of the stairs, smiling as they wiggled in his hands. His hair, dark brown with water, was plastered to his head, rivulets streaming down his nose and cheekbones. Megan left the door open and went to get him a towel, which he took gratefully after coming in, closing the door, and putting the puppies down. He hung his coat up and dried off a bit, then sat on the front edge of an armchair, trying not to drip as the puppies wiggled around his ankles. Megan, smiling, said, "How's Mama Dog?"

"Grand. She's come all the way around so. I knew she would. It just took a little patience so, as I'm not whatever ginger bastard who did her wrong. She knows that now, and she's a good girl, *mo croí*."

Megan knew the Irish words meant variations on "my darling," and smiled at his affection for the aloof little dog. "What's the story?"

"How fast did Orla enlist your help?" Paul lifted his eyebrows under messy, damp hair, his blue gaze both amused and challenging.

A surprised, guilty flush rushed Megan's cheeks. "Fast enough and urgently enough, that I'm a hundred percent un-fired. Do you really think she's got any part in this?"

Bourke shook his head. "Probably not, but there's been a lot more New IRA movement since Brexit, and it's not impossible."

"Cherise Williams isn't much of a political target, though."

"But she was accessible and makes a good flashpoint, especially if she turns out to really be the heir to Leitrim."

"I don't see how we're ever going to know that, though. Can I get you some tea?"

Unfettered gratitude shone in Bourke's eyes. "Please. I'm frozen through. It's desperate out there."

"If it weren't so desperate, I'd have probably gone out

to try sizing up potential bad guys at local pubs," Megan admitted as she went to put the kettle on. Fortunately, the kitchen and living room were both open-plan and small, so it meant walking about ten feet away from where Paul sat with puppies leaning on his feet. "Have you eaten? I can reheat some chili and there's cornbread left over."

"What's cornbread?"

"Oh, you sweet summer child." Megan got him a couple of muffins to go with his tea and reheated the chili, putting the whole meal on the table. "There's no rice to go with it," she told him severely. "I'm not a barbarian."

He came to the table and sat, completely nonplussed. "What do you eat it with, then?"

"Cornbread!" Megan sat across from him, tucking her legs up into her chair. "It took me ages to figure out that you lot regard chili as a kind of curry and that's why you put it on rice. And let's not even talk about the disservice you're doing to Indian food by referring to it all as 'a curry,' anyway."

"We don't call it *all* a curry." As Megan raised skeptical eyebrows, Bourke shrugged in defeat. "All right, maybe we do so. Oh my god," he added around a mouthful of cornbread, and moved the muffin back to take a better look at it. "This is brilliant. What is it?"

"Mama Malone's sweet cornbread recipe. Not too sweet, though. It's corn flour, except not what you call corn flour. That did my head in too," she said irritably. "You call corn*starch* corn flour, and I bought like three things of it before I realized I was never going to get what I was looking for. Separated by a common language, dang it. You call this cornmeal, or polenta, although your polenta's more finely ground than what I use in the muffins or already mixed up in to actual polenta that you just put on things. Not that anybody actually puts it on anything."

Paul took all of that with the air of a man who expected it to end, or at least reach a point, eventually. Not even Megan imagined she'd made a point, but she did at least wrap up, upon which Bourke said, "Whatever it is, it's gorgeous. Mama Malone's recipe, huh? So it's secret?"

"No, I'll email it to you. I don't believe in secret recipes."

"I never heard of anyone who didn't believe in secret recipes."

"Well, now you have. Eat." Megan got the brewed tea and came back to the table as he spooned up a bite of chili. "I assume you're here to tell me to not go poking around the IRA."

"I would if I thought it would do any good. Wow. This is gorgeous too." Bourke looked into his bowl of chili like it contained a surprise.

Megan, vaguely offended, said, "What did you expect?"

"Tesco's Own?"

"Oh. No, I'm constitutionally incapable of buying chili spelled with two L's. This is homemade. I just put it in the slow cooker for a day, freeze it in meal-sized packages, and eat it whenever I want some."

"I didn't think you cooked."

"I got out of the habit when I got the puppies. They wrecked my life, yeah, didn't you, guys?" Megan's tone changed enough that the dogs, who had gone back to lie on the couch, stood up to look over its back, then hopped down and came over to see if anybody was going to give them a treat. "Okay, that was my bad," she said to them, and got up to get them snacks. "So if you're not here to tell me to stay away from the IRA, what is the story?"

"Apparently it's that I was hungry and needed home cooking. My mother wants me to marry a nice Irish girl, but she'd probably accept an American if she came with that cornbread recipe."

Megan snorted. "First, technically, I am a nice Irish girl. Second, I already said you could have the recipe. Third, that was a terrible proposal, but fourth, that's probably a good thing, since you're dating Niamh."

"I'm more seeing her for occasional weekends in the midst of her strange, larger-than-life life, but I can't quibble over the rest of that. I put in a request to get the earl's DNA."

"You did what? Why?"

Paul shook his head. "I don't see how they could claim anything, but the family association has to be why she was killed. Either someone wants to make a statement about how welcome British landlords are in modern Ireland, or they think there's something about the title worth having. I can't imagine the legal mess involved with actually claiming it, but either way, finding out if the link is legitimate may help to unearth something." He ate a few more bites of chili, sipped his tea, and finally added, "And it seems like they ought to at least know, after all of this."

"You're a good man, Detective Bourke."

"I try. What's in the diary?"

Megan blinked around like she might have one she didn't know about, then shook herself. "Oh. Cherise's diary. Or Gigi Elsie's, I guess. It's a family heirloom, and maybe their best bet at establishing a connection to the

Edgeworths. Well, not if the DNA thing goes through, but it's the best they've got otherwise. It didn't sound like there were any deep dark secrets hidden in it, but Raquel's the only one who'd even read it, and that was more than twenty years ago. Their family is a mess," she added. "Cherise was gullible. Sondra, the oldest, kept bailing her out financially, but her sisters don't know that. Raquel's apparently a lot like Cherise, and Jessie, the youngest, is angry at everything. Generally, I mean. I think it's how she goes through the world, not just right now in the wake of her mother's death. They all want different things and they're like cats and dogs with each other trying to get it."

"Would any of them have killed their own mother?"

"Jesus." Megan rolled back like she was taking a hit. "I don't think so, but more importantly I don't see how they could have. Raquel was flying into Dublin when Cherise died, and I don't see how either Jessie or Sondra could have flown in, murdered her, gotten back to Dallas, and gotten on another plane to fly back here fast enough to arrive at eight this morning."

"Hired killer, maybe? How deep was Sondra in, financially?"

"She lost her husband and her house over it, I guess. But . . . well, I don't know." Megan sighed. "I certainly don't want to think any of them hired somebody to kill their mother. Wouldn't you be able to follow the money on that, anyway?"

"Not if you hired somebody online and paid in cash that you'd been saving up. I could follow a browser history, maybe, if they were mad enough to do their searches from home." Bourke finished his chili, sighed in contentment, and got up to rinse his dishes. Megan followed him with her gaze, astonished.

"You can hire assassins on the *internet*?"

He made a face over his shoulder. "For surprisingly little dosh, although the cheap ones aren't, em . . ."

"Very professional?" At his nod, Megan put her face in her hands. "We live in a strange, strange world, Paul."

"We do so." Bourke sounded almost cheerful about that. "It's less likely, though, than Orla shooting her mouth off to somebody who thought he'd take a chance."

"I honestly don't know which is more awful." Megan rose to look out the window at the pouring rain. "It's miserable out there. Are you going home or back to work?"

"Home." Paul finished washing the dishes and came back to glance out the window. Thong ran over and leaned on his ankles, so he crouched to rub her ears. She sighed and rolled onto her back, feet flopping without dignity, so he could rub her belly instead. For a moment or two he was engaged in that serious activity, but he finally stood up with a sigh. "I'll be no use to anybody if I don't get some sleep. I'm calling a taxi, though. I don't think I can face another drenching. Look, Megan . . ."

"If you're going to tell me to stay out of trouble, I'm pretty sure it won't take."

"I would so, but I know you better than that by now. I'm serious about this, though, Megan. Stay away from the political side of things. Don't go digging into who Orla knows and who she doesn't. That's dangerous business, and it's not your job."

"I was planning on clearing her name by figuring out who really did it, not by interviewing people with dubious political connections."

A smile twisted Paul's mouth as he took out his phone and pulled up an app to hail a taxi with. "That's not your job either, but it's as good as I'm going to get from you, so I'll take it."

Megan flicked a sharp, if not official, salute. "Assistant Investigative Detective Adjunct at your service, sir."

Amusement crossed Bourke's face. "Someday I'm going to take you to the opera. In the meantime, keep me apprised of anything the Williamses let slip, since you're going to be nosing around anyway."

"You keep *me* apprised of whether that diary shows up again."

"It is definitely not my job to do that." His phone buzzed with the announcement his taxi had arrived and, with a wave, Bourke left Megan and the dogs to their night's sleep.

CHAPTER 15

A text from Jelena woke Megan at a quarter to six: **are you gymming today?**

Megan, sleepy and slightly guilty, responded with **I am now** and got a series of happy emojis in return. She got to the gym before the doors opened, mostly because it was literally across the street from her apartment, and Jelena, her curly hair beaded with rain, jogged in a few minutes later to join the warm-ups. A good-natured spotting session turned into a laughing, sweating attempt to out-lift each other—Jelena won—and both women were staggering with the effort by the time they'd finished their workout. Giggling at their wobbliness, they made their way to the door, and Megan tilted her head toward her apartment across the street. "Coffee?"

Jelena shook her head. "I can't today. Work starts in forty minutes and I need a shower. Are you all right, though, Megan?" During their workout, they hadn't talked much about the chaos the Williams family had brought to Megan's life, partly to keep focused on the exercise, but mostly mindful of others who might be listening in. "You know you can stay with me a while, if it comes to it."

Megan shook her head. "Orla's been forced to her senses for the moment. I'm never staying in that apartment with her as my landlord, so I'm not, but I don't have to find a new place immediately." She stepped forward to curl a hug around Jelena's waist, even if they were both sweaty from their workout. "Thanks, though," she mumbled. "It's nice to know I could, if I needed to."

"Thank goodness." Jelena returned the hug, sighing against Megan's hair. "You have too many adventures, Megan."

"I don't mean to!" Megan stepped back to smile up at the other woman, whose bright eyes sparkled with amusement.

"I know you don't, but they follow you. I want you to be careful, hm? And we can have coffee on . . ." She looked around like the rain-wet streets would tell her what day it was. "Maybe Sunday?"

"Sunday. Should I get cinnamon rolls or would that defeat the point of going to the gym?"

"It would. I'll bring some." Jelena stole a kiss and headed down the street. Megan watched her go before running back across the road to shower and get ready for work herself. By the time she got out of the shower, Orla had texted her schedule for the day, which was essentially *"get the Williamses and do what they want."*

Megan texted Raquel in return, went and got a car, and got to the Gresham just after Raquel's answering text came in. She sent a note up saying she'd arrived, and sev-

eral minutes later the sisters emerged from the hotel, hud-
dling under a huge umbrella even though it wasn't actually raining just then. Megan sprang out of the Bentley
and held both the door and the umbrella for them as they
got into the vehicle.

"Sorry it took so long," Raquel said. "We didn't expect
you to be here already."

"It's no bother," Megan promised. "Did you get any
rest?"

"Yeah." Jessie's voice was raw, heavy with grief and
exhaustion, but she twisted to give Megan a tired smile.
"Raquel shared some of those Ambiens and I think we
were all asleep before seven." Tired as she sounded, she
looked better than she had the day before. All the sisters
did, even Sondra, whose concession to the inclement
weather was two-inch-heeled boots instead of the four-
inch stilettos she'd worn the day before. She was no less
put-together, but seemed more comfortable, which could
have been the sleep as much as the footwear.

"We're supposed to go to the embassy to deal with the
legalities of an American citizen dying overseas," she
said grimly. "Do you know where that is?"

"Of course." Megan smiled gently at her in the rearview mirror. "Would you like quiet, or the ten-cent city tour
on our way over?"

Two of them said, "The tour," and one said, "Quiet,"
then closed her eyes and waved wearily, giving them all
permission to have the tour despite her wishes.

Megan smiled again and pulled out of the parking bay
onto O'Connell Street, saying, "About three hundred
years ago this was Drogheda Street, a proper narrow
cesspit of a road, until a banker bought this half we're on
now, the upper half, and razed it to make it into houses

for rich people. It took another fifty years to complete the whole street to this width and to build O'Connell Bridge. A lot of the Easter Rising was fought along this street. There are still bullet holes in the GPO's pillars." She nodded at the General Post Office as they drove by, and all three women moved toward that side of the car to see the gorgeous old Georgian facade more clearly. A minute later they were over the bridge and crawling down Dame Street, then turning up onto George's.

Jessie, still mostly mashed up against the window, said, "This is all really pretty," and Megan nodded.

"Georgian, mostly. Back in the day, the north side, where you're staying, was the fashionable side of the city, but right after they finished the bridge we just crossed, the Duke of Kildare built a huge fancy house on this side of the river. His architect and everyone thought he was out of his mind, but it became a kind of 'if you build it, they will come' thing. The south side became fashionable and there's all sorts of gorgeous early Georgian architecture over here because of it. And his house is the seat of government now, actually."

"Did you know all of this before you moved here?"

"Oh, god, no. I've picked it up living here, and sometimes by . . ." Megan dropped her voice into a furtive whisper. "*Researching* stuff."

"Oh no, not that," Jessie said in mock dismay, then, more seriously, added, "I'm glad you know it all. It's a distraction." She cast a worried look at her sisters, as if she might have said too much, but Raquel only nodded. Jessie's eyes still filled with tears, and Megan, trusting that distraction was as important as driving, said, "This stretch near Embassy Row is pretty posh, as you might guess from being near all the embassies," and all three sisters nodded along attentively, clinging to the diversion. Megan dropped them in front of the American embassy, a building she thought of as clunky and bunker-like, and was always surprised to see was actually three stories of windows laced in a kind of concrete honeycomb. The only part she'd been inside was cramped, filled with waiting-room chairs, and rather grim, so she supposed her knowledge of the interior somehow informed her feelings about the exterior.

"I don't know how long this will take," Sondra said as they got out of the car.

"Don't worry about it. There's street-side parking here, so I'll just wait around the corner with my book and unlimited Wi-Fi and it'll be grand. Just text or call when you're done and I'll pick you up."

Raquel said, "Thank you," and Megan left them to deal with the heartbreaking legalities of a death abroad. Once she'd parked, she left the car to take a walk. A little extra exercise after yesterday's long drive wouldn't do her any harm, and she reckoned she'd better do it sooner rather than later, just in case the meeting at the embassy took less time than she imagined it would.

When she'd moved to Dublin they'd been doing some kind of work beneath the River Dodder, just a few dozen steps up the road from the embassy, and it had been a riverbed empty of water but full of heavy equipment. That work was long since finished, but she had a strange fascination with seeing water in the river now, as if some part of her expected it to disappear again without warning. She turned down a little side street and walked down to the river's side, collecting small stones to throw in. Her phone buzzed and she took it from her pocket, creating a bad moment where she almost threw it instead of a rock.

Grimacing, she dropped all the pebbles and took a step back from the river, like the extra distance would keep her from doing anything stupid.

To her surprise, it was a text from Niamh, saying **I'll be home for three days from the Sunday for press junket stuff. 1. Can you drive me around town? 2. Wanna go out to eat? I'm dying for a coddle.**

Megan wrote **holy beans, absolutely!** back, then, after a moment, added **I don't suppose you're bringing my Favourite Chris along? Also isn't it like 1am there? Why are you even up?**

It took a minute before Niamh wrote back again, and Megan, glancing warily at the sky, decided to risk a walk down the river path. She'd just about given up on Niamh answering when another text buzzed through. **No, Fave Chris press junket won't be until next year, we only finished filming in Nov. This is for things going mental with the little Irish thing I did last year. And I'm in NY so it's only 4am. Wait, that's not better, is it . . .**

Ugh, no, it is 100% Not Better. Are you still up or just up?

Neither answer to that is very good, is it? I'm just up, but they're coming to take me away for press junket stuff. I'll ring you Monday morning when I know where they want me driven around to? Paul's picking me up at the airport & we're stealing a night together before the madness hits.

Megan said, "I'll book you in," aloud, sent a thumbs-up emoji in response, and tucked her phone back into her inside breast pocket. "The little Irish thing" was a home-grown film that had garnered unexpected awards attention, great for Niamh's career but harder, Megan thought, on her burgeoning relationship with Paul Bourke; Nee had been planning to be home for four months after her last film wrapped, and instead had found herself on the awards circuit, doing press and trotting the globe. Megan, one step removed from Niamh's increasingly fabulous lifestyle, loved watching it, but couldn't imagine living it herself. Driving her friend around Dublin and glimpsing the glamour from inside a limo was, by and large, close enough for her.

Well, unless Niamh brought Favourite Chris with her to the next Irish premiere. Megan might presume on their friendship *just* a little, in that case. Grinning, she hunched her shoulders against the January wind and broke into a much brisker walk, trying to warm up without turning back and resorting to a cup of coffee. She'd gotten just far enough to start sweating when genuinely enormous raindrops began pelting from the sky. Megan spun on her heel and scurried back to the car, climbing inside barely ten minutes after she'd left it. She sat in the driver's seat a minute, beating a tattoo on the steering wheel and staring thoughtfully at the ballerina skirts blooming in the gutters in front of her. Most of the morning traffic had cleared away, and it was only a few minutes' drive to the Central Statistics Office. The Williamses would probably be in the embassy for at least another half hour. Megan couldn't get very *much* snooping done at the CSO in ten or fifteen minutes, but faint heart never won fair lady, and they'd be closed for the weekend, so she decided she'd better get while the getting was good.

A few minutes later she was driving along the Grand Canal, one of the two canals connecting Dublin with the River Shannon in Ireland's west, not that freight had been moved along it for decades. One of her bucket list goals was to take a pleasure cruise across the island on the canal system, but she supposed she would have to take a vacation to make that happen, and her American sensibilities hadn't quite caught up with the idea that European law insisted on a minimum of four weeks of mandatory holiday for all full-time employees. She was terrible about taking it.

The receptionist at the CSO building remembered Cherise Williams, and, unsurprisingly, had already talked to Detective Bourke about the Texan woman. Megan, leaning on the counter, said, "Did he ask about Mrs. Williams's diary?" and the receptionist—a bulky bald man in his late forties who looked like he could also be the security guard—shook his head curiously.

"Little fabric blue book, about this big, with a pattern on the cover. She might have—"

"Ah sure," he said, "that was her proof so. I had a bit of a look through it. It's a lovely old book full of brilliant stories, but it's a bit of Bridey Murphy too, isn't it?"

Megan smiled reflexively. "Hardly anybody knows who she was, anymore, but you're right, it kind of is. Only Mrs. Williams's nan was just writing down her father-in-law's stories, not remembering them herself like a past life. Do you know who Mrs. Williams talked to here?"

"Sarah Brennan, up on the third floor," he said promptly. "But she's gone on holiday now, left right after seeing Mrs. Williams yesterday, in fact. Mrs. Williams came down in a right state, saying she couldn't see why anybody wouldn't help her when all she was after was—" His brows crinkled, sending wrinkles all the way back across his shining, shaved pate. "Was a DNA sample from the mummies at St. Michan's? That can't be right, can it?"

"I'm afraid it is." Megan looked toward the lifts, vaguely exasperated. Ms. Brennan rushing off on holiday after talking to Cherise certainly made a good exit strategy for a murderer, but unless she'd first followed Cherise to the hotel and stabbed her full of air, Megan didn't see how the timing could work. "Did Ms. Brennan take a taxi to the airport?"

"Acht, I wouldn't know. Yer wan, Mrs. Williams? Did when she left, though. I called it for her."

"Do you remember what company?"

The receptionist's eyes narrowed. "Are yis with the garda, then?"

"No," Megan said, vaguely guiltily. "Just a hopelessly nosy American."

"You're all of you bold so you are," he told her without any real severity. "I only used the app, but I can tell you the driver. Yer man will have talked to him already, though, that ginger guard."

"Probably. Do you know if she had the diary when she left?"

The bald man shrugged expressively. "I'd think so. Where else would it be, up in Sarah's office?"

Megan widened her eyes hopefully and the receptionist burst out laughing. "You're a fine wan, aren't you? I can't let you into Sarah's office, lass."

"I'd never ask you to, laddie," Megan said dryly, and snorted amusement at his surprise. "I'm maybe five years younger than you. Don't go 'lass'-ing me. Could *you* pop up to Sarah's office and have a look around?"

"And leave the desk unmanned? Hnf." He did pick up the phone, though, and, visibly amused, put a call through to somewhere upstairs. "Áine? Yeah, it's Declan down the desk. I've a lady here who thinks she forgot something in

Sarah's office yesterday. Could you look to see if there's an wee little blue book—" A guffaw burst from him. "No, not one of the car resale types. A diary, like. It's old, with a gold—?" He met Megan's eyes, his eyebrows lifting. At her nod, he went on: "A gold heart on its cover. Ah, you're grand so, I'll hold a minute, sure."

Megan whispered, "You're a scholar and a gentleman," as he tipped the phone's mouthpiece down.

"I'm neither," he said, clearly pleased. They waited in silence on Áine's return, and a couple minutes later she came back with what was clearly a negative response. Declan put the phone down, obviously disappointed. "Sorry, love."

"Hey, you even calling up to ask was going above and beyond. I really appreciate it." Megan meant it, too.

"Here's the taxi details." Declan wrote a name and number on a piece of paper and handed it to Megan. "Maybe your book was left in the taxi. It's gone missing, has it?"

"Mrs. Williams's daughters can't find it," Megan admitted. "I don't know if anybody's looked under the bed."

Declan guffawed again. "Good luck with it so."

"Thank you." Megan lifted the note and repeated, "Thank you. You're a star, Dec."

"Ah, we're mates now, are we? I'd best have your name then."

"Megan," she said with a smile. "Thanks again."

"Come back and tell me how it all turns out." Declan waved her off and Megan went back to the Bentley, unfolding the paper with the taxi driver's details on it. It was barely after ten, but she drove back to the embassy before calling the number so that she would be on hand if the Williams sisters needed her.

An African accent answered when she rang, and Megan said, "Hi, Mr. Omondi? I'm calling from Leprechaun Limos in Rathmines. A client of mine might have left a book in your car yesterday. Did you find anything like that?"

"The dead American woman, eh? No. She left nothing. Are you a guard?" The other driver sounded wary, and Megan couldn't really blame him. Immigrant taxi drivers caught more than their fair share of grief from not just the police, but other taxi drivers as well. It pissed Megan off, particularly because she largely saw herself as an immigrant, and was all too aware that being an English-speaking American immigrant put her into an entirely different class as far as most people were concerned.

"No, I just work for a car service, like you. Well. I bet you own your own car." She had no particular urge to drive for herself, but put a note of wry admiration into the words anyway, and the man on the other end audibly thawed.

"It is not always easy, but yes. The police did not ask me about a book."

Megan shook her head even though he couldn't see her. "No, we only realized it was missing late yesterday. It's a family heirloom, I guess."

Omondi was silent a moment, then said, "Let me look again." She heard him rustling, even opening and closing the car boot and a side door before he came back. "No, there is nothing. I'm sorry."

"That's okay. Thank you for looking, that was really nice of you. It's looking like somebody took it, then."

Megan held her breath a moment. "I know you talked to the guards already, but . . . is there anything you've remembered since then?"

A hesitation came over the line, before Omondi said, "You are not the police?" again, as if balancing between increased suspicion and the impulse to tell her something.

"I'm really not. My name is Megan Malone and I drive for Leprechaun Limos in Rathmines. You can look me up if you want."

Several moments of silence passed before he blurted, "You are the murder driver!"

"Oh my god." Mortified, Megan slid down in the driver's seat, one hand splayed over her face. "Yeah. Oh god. Yeah, that's me. I didn't know I . . . had a reputation?"

"We talk about you often," Omondi said eagerly. "How do you do it?"

"Sheer incredible bad luck."

He laughed, a big booming sound that made feedback in the phone. Then his voice lowered. "Now I know you are not police. I will tell you this, but you must tell no one you heard it from me. I do not wish attention."

"I promise."

"I believe you, murder driver. I left your client at the hotel, as I have told the police. But I waited, yes? In the taxi ranks in front of the hotel. And I watched the doors, to see who might come out needing a driver. A white man met your client as she went inside. He held the door for her, and caught her arm as if she slipped. I did not see her slip, though."

"Oh my God." Megan straightened again in her seat, eyes wide as she gazed, unseeing, at the street ahead of her. "What did he look like?"

"Tall, with light hair. He wore a young man's clothes, jeans belted around his hips and a large, long shirt, a sports jacket over it, do you understand? A baseball cap and expensive runners and winter gloves. Sunglasses, although it was—" He made a sound as if he was gesturing to grey, cloudy, rain-laden Irish skies, and Megan chuckled.

"Anything else? A beard or anything?"

"No, he was not . . . hipster. Gobshite, perhaps, but not hipster."

Megan laughed. "Right. I know exactly what you mean. Okay. Oh my god. Thank you so much. Anything else?"

"Only that she went into the hotel after that as if nothing was wrong. He walked with her a little way, then returned, but I did not see his face. You will not tell anyone I told you this?"

"I won't. I promise. But thank you so much. Thank you *so* much."

"She was a loud and rude American," Omondi said after a few seconds. "But she tipped well. I hope that her killer is found."

"He might just be, with this. Thank you *so* much," Megan said again, and Omondi chortled.

"Good luck, murder driver. You are our own personal superhero. I hope you vanquish your enemy once again."

CHAPTER 16

The line went dead and Megan took a minute to do a stomping, air-punching victory dance in the driver's seat before putting a video call through to Detective Bourke. He picked up immediately, his pale gaze wary. "Did you find another body?"

"No, but I got a description of a man seen with Cherise Williams on her way into the hotel right before she died."

"*What?* How did you do that?" Bourke sat back, visibly stunned, then pulled a notepad toward him and propped the phone against something on his desk so he could write and see her at the same time.

Megan, loftily, said, "I have my sources," and then, in a more normal tone, added, "Honestly, I can't tell you. I promised I wouldn't. But I was able to talk to somebody who trusted another civilian more than they trust the cops."

Bourke lifted his eyes to her for a moment, then sighed. "I'd like to say that's insulting and there's no reason anyone shouldn't trust the guards, but I'm not that naive. What's the description?"

"White male, light hair under a baseball cap, no beard, dressed young but wasn't, necessarily." Megan gave the details, including the fake stumble, and ended with, "My source described him as a gobshite but not a hipster."

Bourke laughed sharply. "Sure and I know just what that means."

"So did I," Megan said, amused. Hipsters, in her reckoning, could be gobshites, but gobshites weren't necessarily hipsters, only people with a look of troublemaking about them, or who were indulging in what Irish vernacular referred to as *antisocial behaviour*. There was, she'd found, a fine line between *obnoxious* and *gobshite*, but, like plenty of other things in life, people tended to know it when they saw it.

"Anything else?"

"My source said—"

"You're really enjoying saying 'my source,' aren't you?"

"I am so," Megan said with a smile. "Anyway, my source said the suspect wen—"

Paul gave another sharp laugh. "I think you mean the person of interest."

Megan's smile broadened. "Do I? Okay. I'm not entirely up on my police terminology. The person of interest went inside the hotel doors with Cherise, but came right back out, but my source didn't get any better of a look at his face."

"Do we know what time that was?"

Megan's face fell. "I didn't think to ask, but . . ." She

did a rapid calculation. "I dropped Cherise off at just before two, and Declan said she was at the CSO fo—"

"Declan? Declan Ahern at the Central Statistics Office? Megan, what were you doing talking to him?"

"Nosing around, obviously. Anyway, it would have
been between two-fifty and three-thirty at the latest, I'm
guessing, because Raquel and I got back to the hotel at
about five-thirty and Cherise's skin was already cooling,
so she couldn't have died less than an hour before that at
the most."

Bourke frowned, blond eyebrows pulled down in a
deep V. "I suppose if a civilian has got to keep getting involved in local crimes, one who keeps their head about
things is better than the squeamish sort, but it's a little
weird listening to you be so cool and collected. I know,"
he added before she said anything, "you're trained for it.
But I think of you as a limo driver, not a combat medic
and . . ." He shook his head. "Well, never mind. It's good
work you've done here, and I owe you for it. Get back to
me if you learn anything else." He hung up, and Megan,
immensely satisfied with herself, sat back to wait for the
Williams sisters to return.

She'd gotten most of the way through her book—a
fantasy novel about a shaman in Seattle—before the
Williamses emerged, all three of them hollow with grief
and exhaustion. Megan held the car doors for them, and
as soon as she'd gotten back in the car herself, Raquel
spoke in defeated tones. "It costs so much to send a body
back to America. They said we should consider cremation, but we've never been a cremation family."

"Could you bring us back up to Leitrim?" Jessie asked.

"We know the cemetery on the house grounds is a mess, but they said if we got permission we could bury her there, so we thought . . . we thought we'd go ask. And even Sonny agrees it'd be better if we asked in person."

"Who do you ask?" Megan asked, both morbidly curious and mystified. "The local parish? The current landowners?"

"Both." Even Sondra's voice was heavy. "And we have to try to get it done today. It's Friday and I—I'm told nothing happens in Ireland over a weekend."

In most cases, that was true enough that ordinarily Megan would laugh about it. She thought that death, what with it waiting on no man, probably fell under different auspices, but she also remembered that Sondra Williams had a board meeting early in the next week that she was desperate to get home to. Glancing at the other two, Megan suspected they didn't yet know that, and wondered who Sondra was protecting. "Do you know where the current landholders are living?"

"I looked them up. They still live in that little town we were in yesterday, just not at the big house." Jessie pressed the heels of her hands against her eyes. "If we'd known we could have just . . ."

"Gone and said we thought we were long-lost cousins, with no proof?" Sondra, for once, didn't speak with bitterness. "I'm sure they already know we were up on their land without permission."

"Still," Raquel whispered. "It's too strange a request to make if we weren't pretty sure, isn't it? So if we went up and asked, at least we'd know whether they were willing to consider it. I wish we had the diary. Maybe some of it would sound like old family stories they knew."

"Should we stop and get your dogs?" Sondra asked.

Megan blinked in surprise, then smiled. "That would be great, if you didn't mind."

"I think we could all use some puppy love. And maybe lunch, before we go. What time is it?"

"Just after eleven." They'd been in the embassy longer than Megan had expected, although on the other hand, she also wouldn't have been all that surprised if it had taken all day. "Do you want something familiar and comforting and carb-y, or local ambiance?"

They exchanged a wordless conference and Raquel said, "Comfort carbs."

"I'll take you over to Five Guys."

Sondra's sense of self reawakened and she said, icily, "Christ, no, I don't eat Five Guys," then curdled red from her collarbone up as her sisters froze in shock for a heartbeat before doubling with laughter. Jessie slumped in the leather seats like a child, one arm wrapped around her ribs as tears of laughter spilled down her face, and Raquel fell toward her, wheezing as she wiped her eyes. Sondra's mouth grew pinched, first with embarrassment, then with resignation, and eventually twisted into a dry acknowledgment of humor. Their laughter finally wound down, and Sondra, with tremendous injured dignity, said, "I suppose I'll have Five Guys just this once," and watched in nearly invisible satisfaction as it set her sisters off into whoops of laughter again. They were still giggling and blotting their faces as Megan put the car in drive and took them through the Dublin streets toward lunch.

Sondra snuck the puppies out of the kennel one at a time, snuggling them and handing them to her sisters to cuddle, too, on the drive up to Leitrim. Megan pretended not to notice and the dogs wriggled with utter joy. Eventually Dip went to sleep with his chin on Jessie's jeans-clad thigh. Megan was going to have to vacuum the whole car before she would even dare bring it back to the garage, and then do the detailing herself, but having the puppies licking and snuggling was clearly so good for the sisters that she didn't mind. They didn't talk much on the drive, distracted by the dogs or drowsing because of emotional strain and burger-filled bellies. They'd even brought a cheese dog, fries, and a milkshake back to the car for Megan, who would also have to apply a lot of air freshener. Still, she appreciated the gesture and enjoyed the meal (eaten one-handed on the drive), and managed not to drip any ketchup on the Bentley's seats.

Her phone buzzed a couple of times as they crossed into Leitrim, but she ignored it in favor of catching Sondra's eye in the mirror. "Do you know the family's address, or would you prefer to go to the church first?"

Sondra's "I don't know," seemed like a much more dramatic confession than it would have from either of the other two sisters. "The dogs need a walk, though."

"Flynn will know where they live," Jessie offered rather tentatively. "I mean, I'm sure he will. I could call him."

"That's actually a really good idea," Raquel said into the little silence that followed. "Why don't we stop and walk the dogs and you can call him and we'll . . ."

They reached the little town of Mohill before Raquel found a way to finish that sentence. Megan pulled into a street-side parking lot not far from the café they'd eaten at the day before, and Sondra herself took the dogs' leashes to clip them to their collars before opening the doors and leaving the vehicle.

It hadn't been warm in Dublin, but the Leitrim air had a fresh, cold edge to it, like more than rain might fall from the gloomy skies. Sondra shivered, but the puppies leaped about in delight, wiggling their whole bodies into the air and snapping at invisible motes around them. They hadn't been out of the vehicle thirty seconds before locals were gathering hither and thither, making a production of not noticing them. Jessie, unencumbered by a dog leash, walked several steps away, putting her phone to one ear and her hand over the other, as if it would keep interested strangers from overhearing her conversation.

"Flynn? Hi, this is Jessie." She took a few more steps, moving out of Megan's easy earshot. Megan clicked at the dogs, encouraging them on their walk. To her amusement, the older two Williams sisters trotted along obediently, even though the puppies were more interested in stopping, sniffing, and exploring.

By the time they got back to Jessie, she was leaning on the Bentley's hood, arms folded around herself to ward off the cold. She was better-dressed for the weather than she'd been the day before, with a multitude of long, decorative scarves and a longish, if lightweight, coat. In fact, they were all dressed more appropriately, but even Megan, in a long coat over her uniform, thought it was bitter, and she hadn't just come from Austin, where the winter temperatures ran eight or twelve degrees Celsius warmer.

"Flynn says—" Jessie smiled briefly. "He says Anne Edgeworth lives 'down the country,' whatever that means, but he gave me her address. It's a big, lonely old house, he said, but nothing like the estate house. I checked my maps app. It's about a fifteen-minute walk, or just a couple of minutes' drive. I don't know which we should do. Flynn said he'd come bring us there if we wanted."

"We can read a map," Sondra replied. "I think we should drive, though."

"For a fast getaway?" Jessie asked, but didn't argue as she got back in the car. Megan held the door for the older sisters, then paused to towel dirt off the dogs before herding them into their kennel. It really was just a couple of minutes' drive, down around a bend in the road and up a slim driveway that led to a two-story, eight-room manor on a hill.

Flynn was right: It was a lonely old house, with dark windows and tall grass growing up to brush its lower window frames. It didn't quite have an air of neglect, but it felt forgotten in a way that even the estate house didn't, with paint aging on the door and ivy spilling over walls. A thin stream of smoke rose from one of four chimneys in the middle of the roof, and the car in the driveway had been new when Megan was a baby.

"God," Raquel said nervously. "Do you think anybody actually lives here?"

"They must." Jessie got out of the car and marched for the door with enough purpose that her sisters scrambled after her, with Megan tagging along, curiously, in their wake.

A door knocker the size of Jessie's face took the place of any more modern method of announcing their presence. She lifted it and rapped several times, then stepped back, suddenly pale with nerves.

Enough time passed that even Megan was beginning to have her doubts, but the door finally creaked open, first a few inches, then wide enough for a small woman to frame herself in it and stare up at them.

Anne Edgeworth probably hadn't cleared five feet of height even in her youth, and age had long since taken inches from her. She wore white hair in a fluffy bun above a network of wrinkles, and a hand-knit cardigan over a high-collared blouse and calf-length wool plaid skirt. Ankles gone thick with age protruded over the collar of black leather shoes that were both exceptionally sturdy and exceptionally ugly. She looked at each of them in turn, dismissing Megan with a flick of her sharp brown gaze, and lingering longest on Jessie.

"Jaysus," she finally said, mostly to Jessie, "you're the very image of my sister. I suppose you'd better come in, then."

CHAPTER 17

The interior of Anne Edgeworth's house had the thick, damp stillness Megan had come to recognize in old stone buildings. The exterior walls were a solid two feet deep, cut of enormous stone, with windows set shallowly in them, and the central hall had, as Megan had suspected, four original doors, two on each side, and a stairway leading up. A fifth door at the back of the hall led into what she bet was a modern—or modern-ish—kitchen, and maybe into other additions to the original building. A low-watt yellow bulb flickered in its setting, barely illuminating the hall. Megan thought she probably would have believed this house belonged to a witch, when she was little. Or maybe not just when she was little.

Anne Edgeworth pushed open the first door on the right, its weight shushing over a rug threadbare from decades of such activity. The room beyond had a formal, mid–twentieth-century air to it, with walls that had been painted when lime was popular for home decorating. If the car outside hadn't also been forty years old, Megan might have thought the whole room had been done up in a deliberately high-quality retro fashion, but she had no doubt every piece in the parlour was lightly used vintage. All four of them sat gingerly on the front edges of the furniture, even Jessie's posture suddenly flawless.

"I suppose you'll be wanting tea," Anne announced with the air of one prepared to be inconvenienced. She hadn't yet taken a seat, adding to the impression of having been disturbed, but looked somewhat thrown for a loop when the visiting sisters all said, "Oh, no, thank you," as one.

Megan, who had been in Ireland long enough to understand this game, said, "Please, if it wouldn't be a bother. Maybe I could help you? Or even get it for you, if you like? I'm only the driver."

The three Williams women looked at her in abject horror, clearly thinking her rude beyond belief for taking their reluctant host up on the offer, but a sort of peaceful relief came over Anne herself. "I wouldn't mind, at that. The kitchen's only down the hall, and the kettle is beside the cooker. There's a box with the tea in."

Megan smiled, both genuinely glad to help and amused, as always, at how the ritual offering of tea set the stage for Irish conversations. "I'll find everything," she promised, and rose to go explore a stranger's kitchen, an opportunity she relished. Conventional politeness meant closing the parlour door behind her, because an Irish peculiarity was often to only have heat on in the room they were occupying, so she couldn't really eavesdrop, but she had some confidence the Williamses would tell her what she'd missed, later.

The manor's kitchen was modern in the sense that it had electricity, a cooker and oven, and both a refrigerator and a washing machine installed under the counter, but if any of them had been upgraded in the past thirty years, Megan would eat her chauffeur's hat. Even the electric kettle was vintage. A small cardboard box of commercial limescale remover sat on the counter beside a larger, teak box with the word *tea* inlaid in intricate lettering on its top. Megan filled the kettle, setting it to boil, and opened cupboards until she found one with an heirloom china tea set, complete with a pot, cups, trays, a platter, sugar bowl, and milk jug. "Oh, wow."

She opened even more cupboards, looking to see if there was anything less delicate to use, but even the solitary teacup in the sink was one of the blue and white china. Feeling vaguely like a child getting away with something, she took them down and opened the teak tea box, which fastened with a bit of ivory and a woven thread loop.

The tea was loose-leaf, which, in retrospect, she felt she should have expected. She opened drawers until she found a tea strainer, whispered, "This is amazing," like someone might overhear her, and peered around the kitchen while the water boiled.

A single-pane window with cracks in the caulking let cold air blow in over the sink, despite heavy, attractive curtains hanging around it. Knickknacks lay on the window frame, including a handful of old Irish punt coins from before the country started using euros, that were tarnished black with age. One of them, thicker than the others, was bent almost in half, with the light barely able to catch the lumpy shape of what was presumably some long-forgotten Irish politician's face. Next to it stood a slender, deep orange bottle vase that looked, both in colour and style, like it had been on the sill since 1973, held a few delicate stalks of yellowed straw with burrs and ears poking upward. Beside it, incongruous on an orangey-red pillow, sat a little china doll. Or a little Japanese doll, more accurately, because her faded flowers were the print of a kimono, and her hair was upswept in a geisha's hairstyle. Nothing on the sill was dusty, and Megan supposed their presence there meant they were, in some way, objects of affection in the otherwise lonely house.

The kettle clicked off and Megan filled the teapot, then checked the fridge for milk. A half-full pint sat in the door, so she poured the meanest measure she could into the tea set's milk jug, not wanting to use up all of Anne's milk on uninvited guests. Armed with the whole kit and kaboodle, she left the kitchen, pushing the door closed behind her, and invaded the living room with offerings of tea.

"Oh! Megan!" Raquel sounded like she'd forgotten Megan even existed. "Ms. Williams was just telling us . . . well, everything. Her father inherited the estate after the last earl died—"

"He never stopped hoping Patrick would turn up again," Anne said rather sourly. Megan, having only heard the woman speak two or three sentences, was beginning to think she had no other way of saying things, and that less separated her from Sondra than Sondra might want to imagine. "My sister and I were almost grown by the time

Father inherited, but we lived there a few years. But then Patty got married and I was left to take care of him and the whole old wreck of a place. When he died I walked out that front door and never looked back. I've had a hundred fortune hunters come after me in the past fifty years, but not one of them looked like Patty, not until that wan there." She poked a finger in Jessie's direction, and Megan, pouring tea for everyone, bet she'd already said all this already to the sisters, but relished the chance to growl at another captive audience.

All three sisters took their teacups politely, but only Jessie actually took a sip, then looked at the cup in surprise. "This is amazing. What kind of tea is it?"

Anne looked viciously pleased. "It's a Ceylon tea. My one vice. You," she said imperiously to Megan, who had almost gotten as far as sitting down. "Go across the hall and get the photograph on the mantle. You'll know which one."

Raquel's eyes widened in horror at the old woman's peremptory tone, but Megan, genuinely amused, did as she was asked, privately delighted to get to see another room in the house. As she was clearly expected to come right back, this time she didn't close the door behind her, and only took a few seconds to glance around the other front room, which was as vintage, but more lived-in, than the parlour they'd been invited in to. A hand-woven shawl lay dramatically over the back of a very comfortable-looking chair by the fire, which was banked low and made the living room considerably warmer than the parlour.

The mantle was crowded with framed photographs, but the old lady was right: Megan knew which one as soon as she saw it. She gathered it up, glanced again at the others, and returned to the parlour to offer Anne the picture.

The old lady batted it away irritably. "I've seen it, gell. Show it to *them*."

Jessie put her tea down as Megan handed her the photograph. "Oh my god."

"My sister Patricia," Anne said in triumph. "I said you're the spit of her, didn't I so."

Patricia Edgeworth—or whatever her surname had become, because it was clearly a wedding picture—must have been very close to Jessie's age when the picture was taken. Aside from the beehive height and dramatic upward flip at the bottom of her hair, it could easily have been a picture of Jessie herself, the resemblance even more striking than the portrait of Patrick Edgeworth had been. "Oh my god," Jessie murmured again. "I could be her twin."

"Or her ghost," Anne said. "She died not two years later, thanks to that bastard she married."

All three of the Williams sisters and Megan turned to her with a gasp. "Ah, he thought he was fancy, with that fast car and not a care in the world." Anne's anger, nursed for six decades, had clearly lost none of its edge. "The wheels couldn't catch on the gravel roads, though, and it was too narrow to correct, the way he took corners. They smashed into a wall, all three of them."

Raquel whispered, "All three. Oh no," and put her hands over her mouth, tears filling her eyes. "Oh, Anne, I'm so sorry."

"That was the end of the wretched Edgeworth line, except for me, until you lot showed up." Anne glared from one sister to another. "I never wanted it to continue.

We're cursed, we are. But maybe Patrick cast that all away when he left, along with everything else. I suppose you want the house. The grounds. The whole damn estate."

A series of startled noises, part protest and part astonishment, burbled from the sisters before Sondra cut through them, speaking firmly. "It's not what we came here for. Our mother had a dream of reconnecting with her Irish history, and we're just trying to . . . to give her what she wanted. We came to ask permission to bury her on the land, in the old graveyard. We thought she would like that."

"Well, you can as far as I'm concerned. You can have the whole lot, as far as I care. There's probably a cousin somewhere on my mother's side who thinks it's for them, or maybe I'd only be the mysterious rich aunt who died and left them a fortune, except there's no fortune, only a mouldering old house that will take every bit of money and every last drop of love you ever had in you, and drain it all away. The state would only take it anyway. It might as well be yours. Get up, gell," she said again to Megan. "Go on and get me my will from the other room; it'll be in the desk. I'll amend it right now."

Spluttering disbelief and genuine objections rose from the sisters while Megan, not about to argue with eighty-plus years of angry, got up to do what she was told. The desk in the other room was an absolutely magnificent rolltop that she guessed was twice as old as Anne herself, and lined with carefully dusted knickknacks in the same way the kitchen windowsill was: coins, an antique Parisian paperweight snow globe, fountain pens, and—less fussily—a stack of gorgeously heavyweight paper for writing on.

The will, unsurprisingly, wasn't in immediate sight, and busybody or not, Megan felt a little uncomfortable opening the desk's drawers, though it appeared Anne Edgeworth was prepared to reveal all to her visitors. Once she'd opened the first one, though, Megan had to quell the impulse to check for false bottoms, just in case there were really excellent secrets hidden away in the antique desk. There were, however, only old letters, neatly bundled, more knickknacks and pens, and, eventually, an aging manila envelope with *the Last Will & Testament of Anne Edgeworth* inscribed in elegant penmanship across the front. Megan collected it, and a pen, and went back to the parlour, where Sondra and Anne were about ten seconds from a knock-down, drag-out over the topic of inheritance.

"You don't even *know* we're related!" Sondra roared, but Anne gestured theatrically at Jessie.

"That girl could be my own dead sister the very last day I saw her alive, and even if you're not, what's to stop an old woman doing what she likes with her estate? I've no use for it *now*, never mind when I'm in the ground, and if it's the dream of another dead woman, who am I to stand in its way? Give me that," she ordered Megan, and took the will out to amend it with a flourish.

Sondra sputtered, but Raquel, the peacemaker, interrupted with a smooth, "You have a lawyer, don't you, Ms. Edgeworth? Someone to look over the will and to protect your interests?" At Anne's nod, she smiled. "Wonderful. We'll understand if you ultimately decide against this, of course, but we're honoured that you'd even consider it. Our mother would be beside herself." Her smile went watery, but she held on to its edges, if only just. "And . . . if you're really okay with us burying her in the Lough Rynn graveyard . . ."

Anne Edgeworth rolled her eyes. "I'll ring Father Anthony and have him meet you up there to discuss the details. It's no matter to me, save that it'll give me a bit of fresh company when my own time comes."

Megan bit the inside of her cheek hard to keep from laughing with shock while Cherise's daughters struggled, unsuccessfully, to contain their expressions of dismayed horror. "Let me clear the tea away," Megan said a little too loudly, and stood. "Will I wash up, Ms. Edgeworth?"

"Miss." Anne gave Megan a disdainful glare down her nose, which required a certain admirable amount of talent, since she was sitting and Megan wasn't. "*Miss* Edgeworth. And I might as well wash up my own self, it's something to do."

"Then I'll just clear it away, and then we'd best drive up to the chapel to speak with Father Anthony. We do have to get back to Dublin this afternoon," she explained apologetically.

"It's no matter to me." The old woman sniffed while the Americans began gathering themselves to leave, all of them still with slightly shell-shocked expressions. Megan brought the tea tray into the kitchen and poured the older sisters' untouched cups into the sink and rinsed all of them before returning to follow the Williamses out the door to the sound of their polite goodbyes.

As soon as they were out the door, a shrill giggle burst from Jessie's throat and slid directly into tears. Raquel put an arm around her shoulders and guided her to the car, holding her younger sister as she sobbed once they were both inside. Sondra squeezed in awkwardly beside them, fitting herself around the dog kennel so she could put her arms around both of them. "That was the most awful thing," she murmured, sounding almost impressed. "Fresh company."

Just as suddenly as Jessie's tears had come on, all three sisters were howling with laughter and hiccuping with sobs, repeating the awful phrase to each other and heightening their collective mania. Megan, wryly sympathetic, drove quietly up to the estate while the puppies, concerned about the high emotion, whined and poked their faces through their kennel gate, making the sisters laugh more gently. "Yeah, this is crazy, isn't it?" Jessie asked one of them, and Megan glimpsed Sondra sneaking them out of the kennel's top again. By the time they got to the Lough Rynn house, though, the women had calmed with the help of puppy kisses, and everyone, including the dogs, piled out of the car in relative equanimity.

"You didn't see the cemetery yesterday," Jessie said to Megan. "Come on up so we can show it to you. It needs work, but . . ."

"Mama would like it," Raquel said firmly. Megan, after clipping roll-out long leads onto the dogs' leashes so they could explore at a distance without actually escaping, got them all moving the same direction and followed the sisters. Jessie took Dip's leash, and Sondra took Thong's, leaving Megan with no leads to trip over, for which she was grateful. The two dog-walking Williamses went ahead at a pace the puppies preferred, and Raquel hung back to keep Megan company. "Do you think she meant it?"

"I think her lawyer will talk her out of it, unless there's actual proof that you're family." Megan once again remembered that Bourke was looking into just that, and bit back the impulse to mention it, still not wanting to raise false hopes. "I mean, more than paintings and photographs that look exactly like Jessie."

"And we always thought I was the one who looked like Mama." Raquel smiled weakly, then shook her head. "Well, I guess I am, but Jessie looks like the Edgeworth family, it seems. Funny how the look can hang on through generations, isn't it? That's the graveyard gate, up there." She gestured, as if Megan couldn't figure out that the aging, angled cast-iron gate that the other two women had just gone through—the one with gravestones beyond it—was the cemetery. A small chapel, its stone walls green and orange with lichen, lay not more than twenty feet past the gate, a solitary stained-glass window and a tired-looking cross above it the only real hints that it was a chapel and not just an ordinary outbuilding.

"Is the whole thing fenced in?"

"Yeah. The fence isn't very good, but there's a lot of grass grown up against it and tangled through it, so it's kind of thick. We're going to have to clear a section out to—" Raquel's breath caught. "To bury Mama."

"I'm sure we'll be able to find someone who can take care of that kind of thing," Megan promised, then called "How about we let the puppies run around free for a few minutes?" to the other women. She pulled the gate closed behind herself as Sondra and Jessie let the puppies off their leads, and for a moment all four of them just stood there smiling at the rambunctious little dogs gamboling around the greenery. Then Raquel sighed and nodded toward the chapel.

"It looks less overgrown over there. We were thinking maybe in that area. There doesn't seem to be any real rhyme or reason to how it's laid out."

"If there is, Father Anthony will probably know. I suppose you'll have to make sure there's room for Miss Edgeworth, too. For her fresh company." Megan darted a nervous look at Raquel, not sure the timing was right for a joke.

Dip began barking as if offended, but Raquel blurted a little laugh. "I can't believe she said that. But yes." She laughed again, another liquid sound that could obviously turn to tears. "We might as well. Mama would want somebody to talk to, too. What *are* they barking at?" The puppies were dancing frenetically, their high, sharp yips cutting through the damp January air.

Megan made a face. "I don't know, but that'll teach me to let them off their leads. C'mon! C'mon, puppies! C'mere!" She was already on her way toward them before she'd finished calling, all too aware that she'd been a bit lax in their training and coming when called was a thing they did on whim, rather than command. She made her way around a couple of gravestones, glancing at the letters wearing off on them, and called, "This could be a really beautiful little site again, couldn't it?" to the sisters.

"It'll have to be." Somehow, Jessie managed to mutter that loudly enough for Megan to hear, despite the dogs barking. "Mama wouldn't want to be left in a mess."

"She's left *us* in enough of one," Sondra replied, and Megan, like the other women, looked toward her in surprise. She had a hand over her mouth and distress in her eyes, and the quiet graveyard suddenly had the aura of a volcano about to blow as Raquel turned on her. Sondra shook her head rapidly, though, clearly horrified. "I'm sorry. I shouldn't have said that. This isn't her fault. Of course it's not. I just—I'm sorry. I didn't mean that."

Raquel, partially defused by the apology, struggled for something to say over Sondra's apologies. Megan, feeling like she shouldn't watch even if she wanted to, glanced away, and blurted, "Oh, Christ, no!"

Dip was still barking and bouncing around a trench in the grass, but Thong had lain down inside it, beside the prone body of treasure hunter Maire Cahill, and was licking her ear as if it might wake the old lady up.

CHAPTER 18

"Oh, holy—Sondra! Jessie! *Raquel*!" Megan dropped to her knees and Thong hopped up and moved back, like she'd only been waiting to get Megan's attention. Dip, worried, tried to wrap around Megan's ankles, but Thong herded him aside with absolute authority, and Megan was only distantly aware of their whining concern as she felt for Maire's pulse.

To her shock and relief, she found one, fluttering but strong. "Call 112," she shouted at the other Americans. "Tell them we've found a woman in her seventies uncon-scious in a ditch."

"Oh Jesus, we have?" That was Raquel, coming closer, but Sondra was on the phone already, putting the call through in the crisp, calm tones of a woman accustomed to dealing with other peoples' panic.

"I know her," Megan said grimly. "Maire Cahill. I met her yesterday."

"Cahill?" Now Jessie's voice rose in alarm. "But that's Flynn's last name!"

Megan muttered, "Great googly moogly," with no particular idea of why she'd landed on that phrase. "There are a lot of Cahills in Ireland, Jessie."

"But how many of them live in Mohill? I should call—"

Megan snapped, "You really shouldn't," although she shared the younger woman's sentiment. Blood leaked through the white hair at the back of Maire Cahill's head, but there were no tree branches lying nearby, nothing that Megan could see might have fallen and knocked her out. A glance at the grass around her suggested nobody had dragged her unconscious form there, either, but she didn't have a clue what the old lady might have been doing in the Williams graveyard. Her metal detector wasn't even nearby, so she probably hadn't been looking for treasure amongst the graves.

A thought struck Megan, and she gently moved Maire's hair, looking at the shape of the wound in her scalp. It could have been caused by the round end of a metal detector, although Megan didn't know if those were sturdy enough to stand up to slamming into someone's head. She checked Maire's breathing—shallow but steady—and the alignment of her neck. Nothing seemed out of place and Megan lifted her voice. "How long will it take for paramedics to get here?"

Sondra said, "Five minutes," briskly, and Megan exhaled in relief. Odds were she could safely turn Maire over—she'd had enough practice in her career—but if there were paramedics close to hand, they would have the right equipment to stabilize the old lady, and a stretcher to lift her on to. For the moment she shrugged her coat off and laid it over Maire to help her retain some warmth, even if *under* her would really be a lot better.

"What's she doing in our graveyard?" Jessie wailed. "Is she okay?"

"For God's sake, it's not *our* graveyard, Jessica!"

"Well, Mama's going to be buried here, isn't she? It's close enough to ours. Oh my god, I've got to call Flynn. What if it's his grandma?"

"Then he should hear through the proper authorities!" Sondra barked. "Don't make this worse than it is!"

"I don't see how she could," Raquel said faintly. She came to stand beside Megan, looking helpless, and smiled with relief when Megan handed the dogs' leashes over to her as something to do. She clipped them onto their collars, then crouched to pet the puppies, who leaned hard on her and looked soulfully at Maire's gently breathing form. By then Megan could hear fire engine sirens in the distance, and jutted her chin toward Jessie.

"Why don't you go out and meet them, show them where they need to come?"

Jessie, sniffling, fled to do as she'd been told. Sondra watched her go, then exhaled a sigh that came from the bottom of her soul. "Five minutes," she said to no one in particular, then looked at Megan. "We could use five minutes of calm. Who is this woman?"

"Just a nice old lady I met yesterday when I took the dogs for a walk over to the druid's circle. She was treasure hunting, or at least she had a metal detector."

"There can't possibly be any treasure on this land." Sondra glanced toward the house, obviously remembering the room of keepsakes, and what Raquel had said about Patrick Williams's maps. "Can there?"

"I might be able to figure it out if we had the diary," Raquel said miserably. "Probably not, but . . . it feels like a mystery, doesn't it? There's something strange going on here."

Sondra gave her a direct look. "You think? Mother's been murdered, this poor old woman has been assaulted, someone stole the diary . . ." Her eyebrows drew down and her tone changed. "I hadn't said it all out loud before. You're right. It does feel like a classic mystery. I'm sorry for being sharp."

Raquel accepted the apology with an astonished nod. Maire Cahill groaned, her eyelashes fluttering open before she sank back into unconsciousness. Megan felt her pulse again, then rose, looking for the paramedics. They were just driving up, taking the fire engine as far down the soft earth lane as they could without it miring. Two of them swung out before the vehicle had fully stopped, getting a stretcher and following Jessie, who led the whole little procession, at a trot. Megan stepped out of their way, saying, "I have some medical training. Her pulse is faint but steady and she just opened her eyes for a moment. She's cool from lying on the wet ground, but I don't think she's hypothermic yet. There's a wound on the back of her head, but I didn't want to try moving her, knowing you were on the way."

One of them, a stocky man in his fifties, gave her a quick nod. "Thanks. Any idea what happened?"

"None, except the last time I saw her she had a metal detector and she doesn't right now."

"Ah, hell, Maire." The other man, slim but broad-shouldered, knelt beside the unconscious woman. "What're you doing out here, lass, ye great eejit. That treasure hunting was always going to get you in trouble." The two of them slid a neck brace into place, then carefully but effortlessly moved the little old lady onto the stretcher. A blotch of blood stuck to her hair and the grass, some of the greenery pulling away as she was moved. The stain on the grassy earth was larger than Megan liked to see, and the fact that the wound was clotting meant Maire had been there a while. The younger paramedic crouched, lifting the old woman's head just a fraction of an inch to examine the wound before sighing and meeting Megan's eyes. "Looks like something curved, heavy, and blunt hit her."

"Something like a metal detector," Megan suggested, and he nodded.

"Not that I'd be saying so in any official capacity, but aye."

"Yeah. I'd kind of thought so myself. Okay. We'll see if we can find it, maybe." As soon as she said it, Megan rejected the idea. The gardaí would need to see the scene, and them tromping all over looking for the metal detector might ruin some key bit of evidence. "Or not."

"Probably not," he agreed. The two men hefted Maire's stretcher and carried it back to the fire truck. Megan and her clients all stood there watching them, as if at any moment an opportunity to be useful would arise. Unsurprisingly, one didn't, and in the echoing silence after the truck had driven away, its noisy engines fading in the distance, all four women looked at each other, a little at a loss.

"Somebody thinks there's treasure out here," Megan finally said.

"Maybe we should go look in that room again," Raquel said at almost the same time.

"We don't have *permission*." Sondra's rules-following inclinations returned to their usual snappish tones, but Jessie gave such a large, disbelieving snort that she started coughing.

"Anne said we could have it, as far as she was concerned. That's good enough for me."

"Jess, just because you happen to look like her dead sister—"

"*And* Geepaw Patrick," Jessie interrupted with such a perfect mix of defense and "so-there" that Megan thought she might finish up with *neener-neener*.

Sondra went on as if she hadn't been interrupted. "—doesn't mean we have the right to go crawling around that old house, digging through her family's old papers—"

Raquel bellowed, "Well, I don't care! I don't *care*! Ms. Williams said we could have it all and if there's some answer to why Mama's dead in that house I'm going to go find it! I don't *care* if we're really the heirs to the title or not, I just want to know why our mother is dead! You can stay out here in the graveyard, for all I care," she shouted at Sondra. "I'm going to go find out everything I can!" Tears of rage and grief streaming down her face, she handed Megan the dogs' leashes, stalked past her sisters to the lane, and only wiped her eyes when she had fully passed them. Jessie threw a challenging look at Sondra and chased after Raquel, the two of them going through the damaged graveyard gate together.

"Shit." Sondra, obviously stunned at having her power usurped, walked after them with the air of one *choosing* to do so rather than being forced into it. She made Megan think of a cat who had accidentally fallen off a sofa arm. The dogs, who had sat down to watch the theatrics, swiveled their gazes to Megan as if waiting to see what the leader of the pack thought they should do.

"Well, it'd be stupid to miss out on it all at this point, wouldn't it?" she asked them, and they all trundled along after the Williamses.

By the time they got to the house, less than two minutes behind Jessie and Raquel, Flynn Cahill had arrived in a flurry of flushed freckles and wide, panicked eyes. His bicycle lay, wheels spinning, a few metres behind him, and his chest heaved as he ran toward Jessie. Sondra was already shouting about how Jessie shouldn't have contacted him, but the Irish lad caught Jessie by the shoulders and, almost weeping, said, "Where's my auntie? What's happened to her?"

"You should have gone to the hospital, not come here," Sondra said icily. "Didn't Jessie tell you we'd called the paramedics?"

"They're here and gone already?" he asked frantically. "Jesus, that was quick. Is she all right? What happened? Jesus, I've got to call me ma." He released Jessie and fumbled for his phone. "Why are you up here? You've saved my auntie's life." He stopped trying to get the phone out and burst into tears on Jessie's shoulder again. She patted his back awkwardly and pulled a grimace at her sisters, both of whom watched as if they had never seen someone break down with worry and relief before.

"She had a head wound," Megan said when it appeared the sisters didn't know what to say. "Her pulse was steady, though, and they took her away to hospital

and will take good care of her. We were up here to look at
the graveyard again. Old Ms. Edgeworth said she didn't
mind if Mrs. Williams was buried here. I'm glad we were
here," she offered, and Flynn gave her a weepy, grateful
smile.

"Me too. Me poor auld auntie. She was after looking
for treasure again, wasn't she? She and herself found a
couple of coins when they were just girls and Auntie
Maire has always been sure there must be more. It didn't
help that herself had a few coins from when her grand-
uncle was a lad, either, so it seemed all the more real.
Jesus, I never thought it would get her half killed,
though."

Megan, baffled, said, "Who's 'herself?'" and Flynn
looked at her like she was daft.

"Anne Edgeworth, of course. She and Auntie Maire
were thick as thieves when they were girls, but they fell
out when Patricia Edgeworth married the man Auntie
Maire fancied. Auntie was furious glad when herself finally left the grounds after her da died."

Megan exchanged a glance with the sisters. "Furious
glad?"

"She hated the idea of the house going to ruin, but she
wanted to be able to poke around looking for treasure. I'd
say she's walked every inch of the grounds in the past
forty years."

"So there's not any treasure." Raquel's shoulders
slumped. "So why did someone murder Mama?"

"There have to be answers in there," Jessie said with
determination. "Flynn, you should go see your aunt. I'm
sorry I didn't think to tell you they'd gotten here and
brought her somewhere safe already."

"I wouldn't have seen it anyway, biking hell-bent for

leather like I was." Flynn looked back at his bicycle, which had gone still except for what motion the wind could tease out of its wheels. "What an eejit I am, thinking I could get here fast enough to make a difference. Or that I'd be any help at the hospital, either."

"She'll be happy if you're there when she wakes up," Jessie whispered. "We didn't get that chance. You should go and see her."

"Oh." Flynn paled. "Shite. I'm sorry. I didn't think—"

"Just go," Sondra said wearily. "Let Jessie know how she's doing, when you find out. We hope she'll be all right."

Emotional colour flooded the young man's face again. "Thanks, that's very good of you." He righted his bike and rode off much more slowly, Megan suspected, than he'd arrived.

Raquel, watching him, said, "I really hoped there would be a treasure," and began, quietly, to cry again. Jessie crowded close to hug her, and Sondra joined them, although with a somewhat impatient sigh. Megan squatted to pet the dogs, keeping her head bowed so she wasn't intrusively watching the sisters, but keeping an eye on them through her eyelashes.

"Come on." Jessie sounded utterly wrecked. "There's got to be some kind of explanation. If it's not here, maybe we'll find it somewhere else, but that room seems like our best shot."

Everyone looked toward the house, with its dark windows reflecting clouds and scattered patches of blue. At least it hadn't rained in the past few hours. Megan shuddered to think of what would have happened to Maire Cahill if it had.

"We didn't even try turning any lights on yesterday," Sondra said. "There's probably no electricity anyway. We should have brought real flashlights."

"Oh! I've got some in the boot! For emergencies," Megan clarified as the sisters turned surprised gazes toward her. She hurried back to the car, dogs tangling around her ankles, and got two torches from the Bentley's trunk. Both of them shone with intense LED brilliance when she tested them, casting blue shadows across the yellowed lawn. Satisfied, Megan brought them to her clients. Jessie and Sondra each took one, leaving Raquel faintly put out, but not enough to argue. She and Megan trailed behind the other two, both of them pulling their phones out to add to the light once they'd entered the house.

A message notification from an hour or so earlier scrolled across Megan's screen as she turned the phone on. She flicked it open and stumbled, reading it. Raquel caught her. "Megan? Are you okay?"

"I—I—yes. I just—you . . . here. This is . . . this is for you. All of you." Heart hammering, she handed the phone with its open message to Raquel, and the other two sisters turned back to see what was going on.

The text had come from Detective Bourke, and said, in its entirety, **The DNA results came back. They're the titular heirs.**

CHAPTER 19

The Williams sisters weren't, in Megan's experience, usually harmonious, but their chorus of half-shouted, "*What?*" sounded as if it had been rehearsed to be pitch-perfect. The next several seconds were considerably less melodious, with all three sisters repeating variations on *what* in higher and more incredulous tones, with Megan trying to explain without shouting. Finally Sondra dropped her voice and blared, "Who had the DNA test run?"

"Detective Bourke." Megan took a deep breath and waited for more shouting to subside before going any further. The dogs, agitated at all the noise, ran in circles and whined, which helped to quiet the Williams sisters more, Megan thought, than much of anything else would. "Detective Bourke thinks, like you do, that your mother's death must have something to do with the title. He didn't think proving it would necessarily lead anywhere, but . . ."

She sighed and shrugged. "But he's a nice man, really, and he thought you'd like to at least know for sure, so he put a priority request through to get a DNA test run."

"You knew this?" Sondra asked incredulously. "You knew and you didn't tell us?"

"I didn't want to raise your hopes."

Complex expressions flashed over Sondra's face, ending in resigned acceptance. "I suppose it would have been just one more thing to get wound up over." Abruptly, like she had only just realized what Bourke's message *said*, she took a step back, looking faint. "We really are the heirs?"

Raquel whispered, "I knew it. Mama knew it. Oh, I wish she was here now . . ." Tears welled up and Jessie reached over to wipe her eyes like she was a child, then wiped at her own eyes.

"She'd be so happy. And—I guess we can tell Miss Edgeworth that we really are family. That priest she mentioned will let Mama be buried here in that case, right?"

"Father Anthony." Sondra looked toward the front door, like she could see through the heavy oak to the driveway. "She said he'd come up here. I wonder where he is."

"It could be hours," Megan said wryly. "There's no point in hanging around waiting for him. We might as well go upstairs and do our sleuthing."

"At least we know we've got a right to the materials," Raquel said. "That makes me feel better."

Jessie gave her a thin smile. "Not that it was going to stop us."

"Right." Raquel returned the smile, took her little sister's hand, and went up the stairs with her. Sondra, Megan, and the dogs followed a few steps behind, dust blurring under their feet. They'd left a lot of prints the day before, with Sondra's pointy-toed high heels the most distinctive of them. They'd also taken more care to walk in each other's footprints on the way up than down: Sondra's points were only visible occasionally at the tops of the upward prints, but clear and distinct coming down again. The dogs' prints were all over everything, and Megan thought if they'd been trying to sneak, it hadn't worked very well.

"Holy crap," Jessie breathed as they got to the top of the stairs. "Holy crap, this whole place—it's not, but it *could* be ours. Like, it's our . . . legacy. Holy crap. That's . . . holy crap!"

Even Sondra blurted a giggle at that. "Yeah. You're . . . yeah. Can you even imagine?"

Her sisters said, "No!" and "Yes!" simultaneously, sending them all into another giggle. "Not that we want it," Sondra added more grimly, but like she was trying to convince herself. "The upkeep on the place would be impossible."

"Only if there's no treasure," Raquel said with a sigh. The door to the odd little storage room stood ajar, and she pushed it open as Jessie lifted her torch up to light the space. They both stopped so suddenly that Megan and Sondra nearly ran into them, and the puppies did squirm between their ankles to sniff around. Raquel whispered, "Oh no," and Jessie lowered the light as Megan and Sondra peeked around them.

The tidy piles and stacks they'd left the day before had been upended, papers and chaos everywhere. The box of Patrick's things lay on its side, entirely empty, and his portrait had been thrown to one side, its glass broken. Raquel whispered, "Oh no," again, and backed out of the doorway as Sondra, her jaw set, shouldered her way in and growled, "I'm gonna kill somebody."

Megan thought she might well do it, if the perpetrator were to present themselves in that moment. Enraged colour stained Sondra's jawline and cheekbones, and she held her hands in claws like she would tear something apart if she could. "These are *ours*," she snarled. "This is *our* family's history. How dare they, how—" The next sound she made was of inarticulate anger. It turned to equally furious tears in a heartbeat and, trembling with fury, she righted Patrick's box and picked up a handful of papers to tap them together into tidiness. She put them away neatly and selected another pile to make neat again, faster this time. By the third handful, her sisters had joined her, all of them acting with the swift, strangely precise motions of rage cleaning. Megan pulled the dogs, who both wanted to "help," back a few steps. First Sondra, then Jessie, found somewhere to put her torch, and all three of them ended up kneeling in the mess, not just tidying papers, but sometimes gently looking through them, then putting them away as if they'd become suddenly precious. Megan backed further away, whispered, "Let's just look around," to the dogs, and crept down the hallway, leaving the sisters to their grief and anger and cleaning.

There were more bedrooms beyond the storage room, and a narrow servants' stairway that led both up and down. Megan looked at the dogs, one of whom wanted to go up, and one of whom preferred down. "We'll go down next," Megan promised Thong, and climbed the stairs, testing their strength before putting her weight on each one. Someone else had come up them relatively recently, and more than once: even her single torchlight from her phone showed a man's footprints, or what she assumed was a man's, from the size.

The wee small upper bedrooms managed to be damp, cold, *and* stuffy, as if the last summer's heat had made the air stale in a way it couldn't recover from. The first couple had rusting metal bed frames in them, and the next few were empty, but one at the farthest corner, where as much of the driveway as was possible could be seen, had a futon mattress in it and modern, unmade bedclothes. Megan stopped short in the doorway, staring incredulously at a pile of clothes peeking out from under a satin baseball jacket. Her heart accelerated along with her breathing and she edged forward, casting nervous glances in every direction at once. No one approached on the drive, no one came up the stairs behind her, no one leaped out from behind the door. She whispered, "That's a little anticlimactic," at the dogs, who were busy sniffing around and didn't care.

Megan *ought*, she felt, to be able to recognize something that would tell her instantly whose room it was. The clothes fit the description that Omondi, the taxi driver, had given her, but there were no identifying features to them, and she probably shouldn't just dig through them to find things, much as she wanted to. She did take pictures of the whole room with her phone and texted them to Paul, saying **I found the bad guy's lair in the Lough Rynn house**, then tiptoed a little farther into the room, still looking for identifying objects. The unmade sheets rumpled over something square. Feeling somewhere between guilty and thrilled, Megan pushed them back a few inches.

Cherise Williams's little blue diary lay there, proof positive that Megan was in a murderer's room. She clapped a hand over her mouth and did a nervous dance back, then forward again, trying to decide if she should pick the book up.

The correct answer was obviously *no*: this was, if not exactly the scene of a crime, certainly the discovery of evidence. On the other hand, somebody had taken that diary for a reason, and there might be a *clue*. On the third hand, she wasn't supposed to be investigating clues, what with being a limousine driver rather than a detective. On the fourth hand—

By that time she'd picked the diary up, curiosity being far greater than sense. She could put it back, if Detective Bourke needed it to be in situ for his purposes. Diary clutched against her chest, she scurried downstairs in a flurry of dogs. They nearly pulled her down the second set of steps, but she tugged them toward the storage room instead, and they course-corrected in little kicked-up tufts of dust. "I found it! I found the diary!"

The sisters met her at the storage room's door, all three of them trying to crowd out while Megan and the puppies tried to crowd in. For a few seconds the air filled with excited, disbelieving cacophony. Megan fell back, giving the Williams women room, and they burst forth like chickens escaping a coop. Raquel snatched the diary from Megan's hands and hugged it, tears streaming down her face. Sondra visibly tried not to take it from her, while Jessie all but hopped up and down, crying, "Where was it? How did you find it? What's going on?"

"I found it upstairs," Megan said over the noise. "We'll have to put it back because I think it's evidence, but I wanted you to at least see it. Someone's living in the house."

All three women went shockingly silent, leaving the

puppies' exciting whining the only—and very loud—sound. Raquel whispered, "Who?" while Sondra braced herself like she expected to have to defend her younger sisters from an unknown adversary.

"I don't know, but—" Megan held her breath, wondering how much she should say. She decided against mentioning the clothes, since she didn't think anybody had given them a description of the man who had last been seen with their mother. "It looks like they've been here a little while, anyway. I think we should leave the room totally alone, but I wanted—you thought you might be able to find something in the diary," she said to Raquel. "Something that might make sense of everything."

"A map that might match one of Patrick's, here." Raquel opened the diary with trembling hands. "It won't match very well. These are Gigi Elsie's diaries, not Geepaw Patrick's. But he told her so many stories . . ." She turned pages with delicate fingers, her sisters and Megan all hovering over the diary and trying to restrain themselves from touching. "See, here. He talked all the time about the lakes, the big one and then the smaller one nearer to the druid's circle. She drew a picture from his descriptions." Raquel turned the book so the rest of them could see Elsie's sketches.

"That's not what it looks like, though," Megan said. The others frowned at her and she shook her head, tracing her finger in the air over the drawing. "This is a proper standing stone circle, with—actually there are more stones here than there are in the one I saw yesterday. There are only five up there, I think, and four of them are stacked up and leaning against the fifth. This is . . ." She trailed off, whirling her finger above the sketch again.

No one could call it Stonehenge-like, but the seven stones in the drawing were placed in a circle, with three of them standing upright, two broken, and the remaining two fallen over. "It doesn't look anything like this at all."

"This is . . ." Raquel turned the book around again, reading the pages. "This is how he described it from when he was a child. So it's been . . . over a hundred and twenty years, right? It could have changed?"

"It would be more surprising if it hadn't," Sondra said. "What else does it say?"

"I don't know. Nothing helpful." Raquel flipped through the pages, pausing at drawings. "More about treasure hunting when they were children. Oh. Oh! And about the evil—oh, it does say *earl*. I guess I didn't know what an earl was when I was little, so I decided it said *king*. It talks about the bad earl and . . . I don't remember any of this. It does talk about how the next earl tried to make things better, but he—Patrick—had decided to leave by then. He didn't want any part of his family's legacy."

"He wanted enough to be remembered that he told Elsie the stories, though," Sondra pointed out.

"But he wasn't the heir to the *land*," Raquel said in astonishment. "The bad earl left it to a cousin instead of the nephew who got the title, and the cousin said the new earl could work the land in—in Donny-gall?" She gave a quick, relieved smile as Megan nodded at her pronunciation, then went on. "And they . . . it looks like the cousin and his family, they were the ones who lived here in Leitrim, and none of the land ever went back to the earl's ownership. So . . ." She looked up, eyebrows furled. "So Anne Edgeworth . . ."

"Anne is the heir to the land," Megan said as the sisters tried to work through it. "You're the heirs to the title."

"And Anne just offered to leave the whole estate to us," Sondra finished. "Returning the title and the land to the same holders."

"Oh my god, could it *be* any more convoluted?" Jessie made a short, sharp upward motion with her hands, like she was throwing everything away, and knocked the diary out of Raquel's grip.

Everybody shrieked and lurched for the flying diary, and later Megan thought they couldn't have made more of a hash of it if they'd tried. Jessie, her hands already lifted, snatched at the little book and effectively punched it toward Sondra. Sondra screamed and her attempt at catching it turned into trying to keep it from smashing into her face. It flew higher and Raquel's hand shot upward, nearly catching it, but she misjudged slightly and hit the spine instead of catching it. The book flew toward the door as if it had sprouted wings, and cracked against the frame. Megan ducked, trying to grab it before it hit the floor, and poor little Thong, in a panic, threw herself into Megan's hands. Megan pulled her back just before the diary clobbered her in the head, and the diary splatted onto the dusty floor with an audible *crack*. Dip rolled onto his back and peed in the air again, making everyone scream, and Sondra, in a bid to save the book from a spray of dog urine, kicked it into the storage room. It spun across the floor, leaving a trail in the already-disturbed dust, and came to a whacking stop against one of the portrait frames.

The ensuing silence broke with Jessie's high-pitched giggle and turned to gales of whooping laughter that bordered on hysteria. "We couldn't have done that if we tried. Oh my god. Is the book all right?" She went forward to get it while Sondra said, "Is poor *Dip* all right?" and crouched to rub the puppy's ears while he made the most pathetic puppy-dog eyes imaginable at her. "Yeah," she said to him. "Don't worry about peeing on this house. It's old enough to have seen worse."

"Still, I'm sorry," Megan said weakly. "I'll go out to the car and get something to clean up with."

Sondra, rising, gave her an unexpectedly sympathetic smile. "Don't worry about it. If we were a little less controlled we'd probably be doing the same thing. This has been a difficult week."

"Guys," Jessie whispered. "Guys, um, look. Look, guys." She turned, displaying the diary, its spine now broken, and the aging cotton binding inside the front covers now split both at the glued top seam and down the middle.

Papers, the ink on them faded to almost the same colour as the folded sheets, slid from the split material, held in place by nothing more than Jessie's grip.

CHAPTER 20

Hairs rose on Megan's arms. She and the other two Williams sisters all took a step forward, as if the revealed paperwork had an irresistible pull, but she stopped to let the others go first. Jessie kept the book flat, not daring to do anything else, while Raquel—evidently the appointed diary-handler—cautiously pulled the papers free. Even Megan, a few steps behind the rest of them, could see that the handwriting on the outer sheet wasn't Gigi Elsie's, and it didn't take any of them more than one breath to guess it belonged to Patrick Edgeworth.

Sondra pulled a few papers from one of the emptier boxes and turned it over, making a table to rest the papers on. Raquel unfolded them reverently, and Megan crept closer to stand on her toes and look over the sisters' shoulders as they peered with their torches at century-old correspondence.

The inner sheets, except for along their creases, were remarkably creamy pale, with bold, browned handwriting scrawled across them. And they *were* correspondence: letters to home, addressed to Patrick's cousin, to his uncle, even to a sweetheart called Nancy. None of the letters had ever been sent, nor, it seemed, had even been intended to; the last of them said *If only I could send these* on its final line, and everyone skimming through them, even Megan, gave a soft, sad gasp, as if a fairy tale had come to an unexpected ending.

Raquel, without speaking, turned the diary to its back interior cover, touching the top seam. Like the front, it was glued down and bulky in the way that older, hand-bound books could often be. The front cover, though, had—now obviously—been modified to hold the letters. The sisters all looked at each other before Sondra said, testily, "Well, go on." Raquel slid a fingernail along the glue, breaking it, and after a few seconds, eased another small stack of folded pages free from the diary's back. Jessie whispered, "Shit!" as Raquel unfolded the pages, and Megan, biting her lower lip, was inclined to agree.

These were the maps Elsie had written about. Megan recognized the general lay of the Lough Rynn lands from having seen them online, with the grand house a centrepiece even in Patrick's sketches. Elsie's drawing of the druid altar inside the diary had clearly been inspired by seeing Patrick's, although his were rendered with the skill of a craftsman, and hers were amateur doodles by comparison. There were a dozen of the sketches, highlighting different parts of the grounds, including a huge, elegant garden that must, Megan thought, have long-since gone to ruin. It lay off to the left of the house, as they were facing it, and neither she nor the sisters had gone anywhere near it. But Patrick had written X-marks-the-spot-style X's at one corner of that garden and in various other locations, including the druid's altar, all around the grounds.

"They can't really be treasure," Sondra said in a kind of disbelief that asked to be corrected.

"No, they . . ." Raquel trailed off, obviously unsure of herself, and turned the maps, examining them. Then she spread them out, trying to make a whole picture of all the drawings. None of them were much larger than postcards, and their folds made the edges wing upward, so laying them flat seemed harder than it should be. Her sisters and Megan all cautiously put fingertips on their corners, flattening them to study the sketches. "There's too many for treasure."

"And there are these . . ." Jessie brushed her fingertips over squat circles drawn in the borders of several of the maps. "What are they? A key? There's something drawn on them." She moved her phone closer, squinting at the one nearest to her, then laughed. "There are faces and something that looks like runes. Didn't the old Irish use a runic written language? Ogham or something?" She said the word correctly, *OH-am*. "Maybe he found some. What?" she said irritably, at her sisters' glances of surprise. "I've got a degree in anthropology, you know. I learned some stuff in college."

"I don't think they made ogham coins, though," Megan said slowly. "The Vikings used runic coins. But I don't . . . that looks like a Roman numeral to me."

"Yeah, but that's different from the runes, see?" Jessie thrust a fingertip at the drawing she meant. "I don't know what any of them mean, but I'm pretty sure that's ogham writing. The numbers—oh. Oh!" She suddenly gathered the papers up, changing their order swiftly while her sisters made small, agonized sounds of protest at her apparent lack of care. Then she laid them out again, pointing triumphantly at the Roman numerals. "There! Look! Now they're in numerical order! That's got to mean something!"

"It means the whole landscape is a jumble." Sondra was clearly trying not to sound exasperated. "Before we had it laid out more like the grounds are actually shaped."

"Yeah, but who would make a treasure map easy to read?"

"Who would put a treasure map in the back of their daughter-in-law's diary?!"

"Gigi Elsie put them in here," Raquel said, clearly exasperated with her sisters. "I think that's pretty clear. She must have found them after Geepaw Patrick died and decided they were too precious to be thrown away, but also known he didn't want them shown around. She talks about hidden trea—" She laughed a little and shook her head. "About hidden treasures. That's what she meant. She was talking about these old papers of his, not *treasures*. I'd bet you anything."

"Well, what's all this for, then?" Jessie demanded. She gestured at the papers, but moved away with her sisters while they argued. Megan bent over them more closely, holding her phone up to the various sketches and trying to make sense of it all. The puppies, bored, tugged on their leashes, and she mumbled a promise that they'd go soon, but kept studying the papers until her eyes crossed from concentration. The drawings on the coins, particularly, looked familiar somehow, but she couldn't figure out where she'd seen them. She straightened away from the drawings, rubbing her eyes as Sondra said, "*I'm* certainly not staying in Ireland long enough to go dig up every one of those X's. I have a board meeting on Tuesday, Raq. I can't miss it."

"On *Tuesday*? Are we even going to have Mama *buried* by then?"

"We're going to have to," Sondra replied sharply. "My company is riding on this, Raquel."

"Oh, who cares about your stupid comp—"

"*I do!*" Sondra's bellow silenced her sisters and made Dip fall over again, although at least this time he didn't pee. "I realize," Sondra continued, frostily, once she'd gained everyone's attention, "that my life seems pathetic and rigid and uninteresting to you, Jessica. I'd love to tell you all the ways it isn't, but I don't think you'd even believe me. What I can tell you is that I will lose my job and everything else that I've managed to hold on to in the past two years if I am not back there on Tuesday to present at the board meeting. That may not matter to you, but it matters very much to me. It's all I've got left."

"You have us," Raquel whispered.

Sondra gave her a bitter, almost scathing look. "Do I? It's a nice sentiment, Raq, but when was the last time you weren't angry with me? When was the last time you listened to me, instead of just taking Mama's side?"

Guilt flushed Raquel's face. "You were just so hard on her, Sonny."

Sondra said, "Someone had to be," but without conviction, as if she knew it was an argument she'd lost long ago.

"Look," Jessie muttered, "if we've got to get Mama buried by Monday we'd better stop hanging around here trying to—whatever. Find treasure. We already found Mama's diary, for heaven's sake." The colour drained from her face as if she'd finally realized what that meant. "Wait. Jesus, Sonny. Megan found Mama's diary. Does that mean the person who killed her is living here in this house? We have to—to get out of here, or to—to—to *catch* them! We have to—"

Megan yelped, "Coins!" The Williamses turned to stare at her and she said, "*Coins*," again. "I thought of it when I was looking at them but I didn't even hear myself think it. The circles. The circles on the maps. They're drawings of coins. Old coins. Anne Edgeworth has a stack of old coins on her kitchen windowsill! I bet they're the key to the maps!"

All three sisters spasmed toward the door, then stopped as abruptly, their voices rising in a discordant argument—or maybe just questions—about what they should do. Go back to Anne's house, call the police, just get out of the house where a killer was apparently living, go upstairs and see if they could learn anything—

"No, we can't," Megan said to that one, loudly. "We can't disturb it any more than I already did. I shouldn't have even taken the diary, but I did. It seemed like a good idea at the time," she added defensively, although it wasn't the Williamses to whom she had to defend herself. Detective Bourke, on the other hand, would want to know what she'd been thinking. Her only justification went back to grade school, when she'd one day taken a pair of scissors and cut a large hole in her favourite shirt. Her outraged mother had demanded, repeatedly, to know *why* Megan had done that, and all she could say was it had seemed like a good idea at the time. Sometimes there just wasn't a better reason. In fact, Megan suspected that *it seemed like a good idea at the time* was the underlying reason for a lot of what people did, and that they generally learned to layer in more elaborate, if not more honest, explanations later.

"Should we put it back?" Raquel asked uncertainly. "We have all these papers out of it now but we could say we found them in the mess?"

"Oh, good," Sondra muttered. "Let's plan our story for lying to the police."

"I'll put it back," Megan said. "I took pictures of where I found it, so if I put it back, it's—"

"It's like we disturbed a crime scene, or whatever it is, and then put things back where we found them," Jessie said dryly. "But even if our fingerprints would show up on the diary, they'd all be there anyway—well, except Megan's—so if we just say we found the papers, maybe nobody will ask where and the diary can be where you found it as evidence or whatever."

"Here." Raquel offered Megan the damaged diary. "Go put it away and then we'll . . ."

"Call the police," Sondra finished.

"I already texted—" Megan's phone buzzed as she spoke and she took it out to check the incoming message from Paul, which said **DON'T TOUCH ANYTHING!!!**

Two second later the phone rang with his number coming up, and he opened with, "Did you touch anything? Don't touch anything. Are you still there? Get out," as Megan pressed the *speaker* button so everyone could hear. She widened her eyes at her clients, grimaced guiltily at the phone, and said, "We, um, okay, we'll—okay."

Bourke, suspiciously, said, "Okay *what*," while Megan took the phone off *speaker*, traded Raquel the dogs' leashes for the diary, and sort of half-ran, half-snuck back to the upstairs servants' bedrooms so she could put the book back where she'd found it. Why she snuck, she didn't know; it wasn't like either Bourke or the guy staying in the bedroom could see her, but sneaking felt important.

"Okay, we won't touch anything and we'll get out of the house. We found—we did find—some papers that— we don't know yet, but they might have some answers."

"Found them *where*? In that bedroom?"

Megan, face screwed up like a child trying very hard not to get caught in a lie, said, honestly if not exactly truthfully, "No, in the storage room." She slipped into the bedroom and put the closed diary back where she'd found it, tucking it down just enough that its square was visible, like it had been when she'd come in. Then she scurried back downstairs, suddenly very aware she was leaving a lot of footprints in the dust.

Bourke sounded ever so slightly mollified. "All right so. Don't touch anything else and don't go hunting down whatever you think those papers mean. I've called the local guards already and they'll be there soon. Go outside to meet them and *don't* go finding any more trouble."

"I do not find trouble," Megan said with as much dignity as she could muster as she got back to the sisters. She spun her finger at them and pointed down the hall, indicating they should leave. A little to her surprise, they did as she told them, and she fell in at their heels. "It keeps finding me."

"For the love of God, Megan . . ."

"Look, we're going outside and I'll call you again as soon as we know anything." Megan hung up, extremely aware she hadn't promised any of the things he'd asked for, and hurried down the stairs and outside after her clients.

CHAPTER 21

A priest and a hipster got out of their vehicles in the driveway as the Williams women left the house. Megan, in their wake, felt like she'd walked in on the beginning of a joke she couldn't find a punch line to. Jessie threw herself across the yellowed lawn into Reed's arms, babbling her astonishment at his coming for her, while he kissed her hair and looked puzzled. As the rest of the women drew closer, Megan could hear him saying, "I told you I'm here for you, babe, but you gotta keep me posted, Jess! How else can I be where you need me if you're back and forth all the time?"

The puppies sat down on Megan's feet, pinning her in place, and grumbled at the gathering, as if they regarded it as impeding their opportunity for a nap. Megan bent to rub their heads as Sondra approached the

priest, glancing once at her younger sister and Reed before sighing the sigh of a woman who had given up on
that fight for the time being. "Father Anthony? I'm Sondra Williams. These are my sisters, Raquel and . . ." Another sigh. "Jessie."

Jessie waved from within the circle of Reed's arms,
and Raquel, like Sondra, shook the priest's hand. "You've
spoken with Miss Edgeworth?" Sondra asked, and the
priest—in his sixties if he was a day, but compact and
well put-together, like he exercised vigorously—nodded
with a cheerfully bemused air.

"She's made it clear I'm to help you in every way I
can. It's your mother, is it? I'm sorry to hear of your loss.
And you'll be wanting to bury her here?"

"If we can arrange it very quickly," Sondra said wearily. "I have to be back in the States by Tuesday morning."

For a moment Megan thought the man might actually
allow himself a *faith and begorrah*, not that anyone in
Ireland ever said that unless—and not usually even then—
they were making fun of American ideas of Irishisms.
She had herself only once heard someone say an apparently totally sincere *top of the day to ye*, which was close
enough to *top of the morning* that she'd spent the rest of
the week laughing every time she thought about it. When
she'd related that story to Irish friends they'd been incredulous, even with the allowance that it had been said
on the first sunny day after a hurricane. However, Father
Anthony recovered himself with a shake of his head and a
brisk rub of his hands. "All right so. Will you be wanting
the whole ceremony, or will it be a smaller affair?"

The older sisters exchanged glances. "We're not Catholic, and nobody but us is even here," Raquel ventured.

"Probably smaller is better. Very small." Her eyes filled with tears and Sondra, for all her faults, put her arm around Raquel's shoulders.

"You'll be wanting to leave before Monday evening if you can," Father Anthony ventured. "I've Mass to deliver on the Sunday morning, but given that it's an emergency, we might make Sunday afternoon around half four?"

"Will they have released Mama's body?" Jessie whispered from within Reed's arms. All the sisters exchanged anguished glances and Megan lifted a finger, indicating she'd deal with it. She walked a few steps away, the puppies following to sit on her feet and grumble again, and called Detective Bourke.

"You've never found something out already," he said, and she shook her head like he could see her.

"No, they're trying to arrange funeral, uh, arrangements—" She winced at her own ineptitude with the language and heard Bourke's soft chuckle. "Yeah, I word real good. Anyway, they're wondering if Mrs. Williams's body can be released for a funeral at Lough Rynn on Sunday afternoon."

"There's nothing more to be done with the autopsy," Bourke said. "I don't see how that could be a problem. I'm glad they've got that sorted. How are they holding up?"

"As well as they can be. Thanks, Paul." Megan hung up and nodded at the others. "Sunday should be fine."

"We'll get it sorted so." The priest paused. "There's talk enough around Mohill about those who might be descendants of the old earls. If you wouldn't mind your own selves, there might be more people at your mother's funeral than you'd imagine."

The sisters exchanged startled glances, and Raquel

gave the priest a wet smile. "I think that might be kind of wonderful."

"Why don't we go over and invite Miss Edgeworth ourselves?" Jessie said suddenly. Reed, his arms still encircling her, peered at the top of her head.

"Who?"

"Our great-aunt, or something. The lady who owns all this land. She's the last of her family, except us."

Sondra, visibly trying to figure out the family relationship, said, "She's more of a distant cousin, I think," and Jessie rolled her eyes.

"Whatever. We should go invite her. And we can ask her about—"

"You have family," Reed said, dazed. "That's amazing. Could I meet her too?"

Jessie said, "Of course!" as Sondra said, "Absolutely not," as strongly. They stared at one another and Sondra said, "She's very old and didn't think much of having visitors, Jess. We don't need to invite somebody else along right now."

"No, no, yeah, I get that. It's cool, it's cool."

"Oh my god, though, Reed, you could stay here and protect the house. Somebody is living there and trashed the storage room! They had Gigi Elsie's diary!"

Reed paled behind his beard. "What?"

"No, it's okay, we found it and we're safe and you wouldn't believe what we found in it, old letters and what we think are maps and—" Jessie's excited burbling turned into tears without warning and it took her several seconds to recover enough to speak. "But whoever's living there, if they had the diary, they must be the one who killed Mama, so if you could just—the police are coming. If you could just stay and keep an eye on it until they get here? That would be the most wonderful thing anyone could ever do."

"Of course, babe." Reed looked shaken, but kissed Jessie's hair before giving her a tremulous smile and a nervous look at the house. "But I might stay out here, y'know? If that's cool."

"I think that's smart." Jessie sniffled, then smiled wetly at first Reed, then her sisters. "Okay. Okay, I think we should go talk to Anne, and then maybe I'll drive back to Dublin with you, okay, Reed? Okay, Sonny? Raq?"

Both of her older sisters nodded like they'd given in to the inevitable. Jessie's smile bloomed and they finally, under Megan's guidance, all got into the car to drive away.

Anne Edgeworth met them at her front door, framed in it like a gnome in a giant's house. "I suppose you're after coming back to tell me Maire Cahill's in hospital for treasure hunting on my own lands. Don't bother. I've heard it all." She stomped unceremoniously into the parlour and sat with a curmudgeonly *thump* as the younger women trailed in after her. Sondra and Raquel looked expectantly at Jessie, whom they evidently thought had the best chance of charming the old lady. She stared back at them a moment, then shrugged and turned her sweetest smile on Anne.

"No, we thought you'd have heard that already. We live in a big city," she said ruefully, "but even there it seems like everybody learns everyone else's business right away. It must be hard here sometimes, if you want a little privacy."

Anne sniffed. "Nobody bothers me if I don't want to

be bothered. What are you after, then, with your own beguiling eyes and the smile like my sister's?"

Jessie, caught, blushed and looked down. "We found some old letters from our Geepaw Patrick, and some—well, we wonder if they really are treasure maps. I know it'd be crazy, but . . ." She gestured to Raquel, who took the letters and the maps out of her purse and put them into Anne's gnarled hands. Silence fell while the old lady looked through them, lingering especially over one of the letters.

"I remember Nancy Dunne," she said eventually. "She seemed like an old woman when I first knew her, although I know now she wasn't yet fifty. She was a fair beauty still. They said she loved Patrick with all her heart, and that she never would marry after he disappeared. I thought it was romantic, when I was a wee lass my own self. The village thought it was sad, a girl like that wasting her life on the love of a dead man, but as I got older I thought she had more sense than any woman I'd ever known. Maybe she did love him that much, but what it meant for her was she was never shackled to any man, dying young of making the babies that the Church demanded of her. Between her and Patty I saw clear enough what would become of me if I married, and how I could live if I didn't. She died alone, but you'd never know it from the funeral mass. They came from all over the county to see the burial of sweet Nancy Dunne. Maybe they'll come to mine so. Let's see the maps, girl." She beckoned for them, then remembered they'd already been given to her, and shuffled the old papers around.

Unlike the other women, Anne Edgeworth had no problem with handling the delicate pages like they were newly made. She rearranged them, tapped them together, held them up to the light, turned them around, squinted at them and then at her distant family, then back to the maps. "It all looks like rubbish to me."

"There are coins drawn around the edges," Megan ventured. "I noticed you had some old coins in your collection. We wondered if there might be a correlation."

"There's one that me da said came from Patrick himself," Anne said without interest. "It's no good, though, all twisted and black. His carriage ran over it and bent it in half."

"I saw that one," Megan said hopefully. "May I get it?"

"Please yourself." Anne held the drawings up again, although the afternoon light was fading. "What were these pressed against?"

Megan, rising, glanced at the sisters and shook her head. "Nothing, why?"

"There's a bit of embossing so." Anne turned the paper so Megan could see what she meant, and light caught the edges of the faintest imaginable impression at its centre.

"Dang. Your eyesight is amazing, Miss Edgeworth."

Profound satisfaction settled in the lines around Anne Edgeworth's mouth. "So it is, for all that I'm eighty-nine years of age."

"There wasn't anything in the diary for them to be pressed against," Raquel said with conviction. "I would have noticed that when I was a kid, even if I didn't notice there was something weird about the bulky covers."

Sondra shook her head. "They weren't weird. Plenty of old clothbound books like that have really thick covers. I don't think it was something you had any reason to notice."

Surprised gratitude at absolution coloured Raquel's

cheeks. Jessie got up to look at the embossing on the page while Megan went to the kitchen to get the coin. By the time she came back, less than a minute later, all four Williams women were examining different sheets with their eyes and fingertips. "They've all got embossings," Raquel reported to Megan. "Really, really faint ones, right in the middles. I don't think they're accidental."

"Does the coin look like any of the ones on the edges?" Sondra handed Megan one of the maps and she turned the coin, trying to see its interior under the bent black grime.

Anne muttered, "For heaven's sakes," and got up with exaggerated stiffness to stump down the hall. She returned a moment later with silver polish and a rag, both of which she handed imperiously to Megan, who took them without complaint and set to polishing the coin.

A few swipes cleaned the grime away considerably. Megan scrubbed it with more enthusiasm, trying to get a good look at the image on its surface, and fumbled it with surprise. "I'm pretty sure this *is* a Viking coin."

"Really?" Jessie jolted to her side, trying to see, while the other women came over more slowly and made room for Anne.

"It's really old," Megan said with a fair degree of confidence. "It's not a perfect circle and the surface isn't polished the way modern coins are, and look at the back." She turned it so the outside of the bend faced the others. Letters, or shapes, she didn't recognize at all encircled the outer border, and the coin's centre had what looked like a hand-chiseled quarter-cross in it. Jessie curled her fingers around its outer edge, trying to get a sense of its circumference even though it was badly bent.

"Is this . . . it's about the same size as the emboss-ings," she said cautiously. "Isn't it?"

"Go get a hammer from the shed," Anne commanded the young woman, who jumped to do as she was told even as Sondra and Raquel exchanged horrified glances. "What?" Anne demanded. "It's my own coin, isn't it, and I'll do with it as I like, including smashing it flat again. Take it to the front stoop," she ordered Megan when Jessie came back with a hammer, and Megan, tempted to throw a salute, marched to do as she'd been told too. Everyone followed her, crowding into the doorway as she hammered the old coin flat again.

It unbent surprisingly easily, with only a few hard bangs taking the worst of the bend away. Even the etching on the reverse side didn't seem too badly damaged by Megan's efforts, and a man's profile could be easily seen on the face when they turned it over. Jessie ran to the par-lour, got the maps again, and held one of them up in front of the coin, trying to align it to the profile.

A shadow caught the light just right and the little gath-ering gasped collectively as coin and map etching lined up. Jessie whispered, "Holy shit!" and tried for another map. They had to turn the coin a little to make it line up.

Raquel vibrated with excitement. "He must have made those etchings before he ever even left Ireland. I can't be-lieve we can still see them. They're so faint."

"We'd never see them without the coin. Or at least we'd never know what they were. Maybe with digital en-hancement." Sondra passed a hand in front of herself as if brushing the idea away, like she knew they'd have never gone that far. "Do they all match?"

"You have to keep turning the coin," Jessie said, doing

that. "It must have shifted when he was making the etch-ings."

A cold thrill dropped through Megan. "No. No, give them to me, it's—they—" Excitement jumbled her words and she took the papers when they were handed to her, then shooed everyone back inside. "I need to—we have to—go, go!" Even Anne allowed herself to be herded, and the women all gathered around Megan again at a table in front of the parlour window. Megan shuffled the map pages into order, following the Roman numerals on the individual pages, then, starting with the bottom one, lifted it to the light so she could align the coin with it. She got it lined up, and, hands shaking, put it down carefully before doing the same thing with the next coin. She put it down too, still aligned to the coin's face rather than a tidy stack, and went through the whole pile that way, using the coin to orient them like a decoder ring. Before she'd got-ten halfway through, the Williamses were whispering with understanding, and when she'd finally finished, they all took half a step back like they were afraid of disturb-ing what she'd discovered.

Jessie hissed, "Take a picture, quick, take a picture," and in a flurry everyone but Anne did, ending with a col-lective sigh of relief that the work was recorded and any mistakes they made that undid the carefully stacked pa-pers would no longer be catastrophic. Only then did Jessie shiver and whisper, "It really is a map."

The dozen sheets, aligned to the coin and stacked in the right order, made a new picture of their own. The manor house lay in its centre, with the carefully sketched X's describing an elegant arch to the house's left, in the gardens, and the druid's altar off to the manor's right.

Lines from other parts of the original drawings came together to suggest a pathway between the two points, but something about the shadows at the druid's altar made Megan say, "A tunnel," suddenly. "There's no aboveground pathway there, is there? But there could be a tunnel."

Anne snorted. "We'd have long since found tunnels. Children and young people have been crawling around those stones for longer than I can remember."

"But they weren't always collapsed," Raquel said. "Patrick had a drawing from when he was a child, where they were all standing in a circle. Something could be hidden beneath them."

"Treasure hunters and archaeologists have poked at it for at least fifty years," Anne replied dismissively. "They'd have found an entrance if there was one. Go on yourself and try crawling under those stones, girl. See what you see."

"But Patrick used to bury things for his brothers, didn't you say?" Megan whispered. "What if he found his way into something and decided to hide it?"

"Why would he hide a treasure?" Anne demanded.

"Because of the evil earl," Raquel said. "He was afraid his whole family would be the same way. They were already rich. If they found some kind of real trove, he might have been afraid they'd hoard it all and never do anything decent again. Or maybe he thought he'd come back for it someday. Or maybe he took it all to America."

"We're not rich enough for that," Sondra muttered, and despite their nervous excitement, her sisters laughed. "But Anne says there've been treasure hunters all over those grounds for decades. They'd have found something."

"Would they?" Megan wondered. "Does anybody know how deep metal detectors detect metal?"

"No, but a woodchuck would chuck all the wood it could chuck if a woodchuck could chuck wood."

Raquel elbowed Jessie while Megan looked it up online and said, "Only a few feet deep at most, and wet ground apparently makes them work less well. Are there any—" She straightened hopefully, looking at Anne. "Are there any caves around here? Isn't there a lot of limestone?"

"It's Ireland," Anne said. "There's limestone everywhere, gell."

"If there's a cave—even just a natural hollow several feet down—digging a deep hole is *hard*," Megan said with the voice of experience. "But if there's a wee cave of some sort then filling an entrance to one might not be so hard. And then if you piled a bunch of rocks over it . . ."

"So you think the druid's altar is the entrance to a treasure cave?" Anne's thin white eyebrows rose, and when Megan nodded cautiously, she threw her hands up. "Well, what are you standing here for so? Go on! Go see!"

CHAPTER 22

"This feels like a French farce," Sondra said as they all climbed back into the car. "Everyone running in through one door and out through another until they all crash together in the middle. We've gone back and forth a dozen times already."

"Twice," Jessie said pedantically. "This is only the second time today. Oh, crap, we forgot to actually invite her to the funeral."

"There'll be time later." Raquel disappeared from Megan's view in the rearview mirror, bending to offer sleeping puppies her fingers to lick. They must not have awakened, because she sat up again and rubbed the heel of her hand over her forehead. "Even if there is treasure, who would have known that to come after Mama?"

"Flynn." Jessie spoke thinly. "I'd talked to him lots about the family and all your ridiculous ideas about the treasure from Geepaw Patrick's stories in the diary and that was his auntie out there with the metal detector, wasn't it?"

"Oh." Raquel's pitch fell with horror. "Oh, no. He wouldn't have hit her, would he? No. No. I'm sure he wouldn't. Besides, he didn't even know we were coming."

"He didn't know I was coming," Jessie said miserably. "I'd mentioned Mama was coming over. I'd even said . . . I'd said when, in case he wanted to meet her. I thought it would be nice for her to have a friend over here. She'd said I was silly when I told her, but you know Mama. She would be friends with somebody's pet rock. If Flynn . . . if he told her he was my friend . . ." Her voice had grown thicker with grief and guilt as she'd spoken, and finally choked into nothing while her sisters looked at her in distress.

"Why didn't you . . ." Sondra too, simply stopped mid-sentence, obviously all too aware that her own likely response would have been enough to keep Jessie from making that confession earlier. Raquel didn't ask any questions, just pressed her hands against her lips and stared unhappily at Jessie.

"I really didn't even think of it." Jessie's voice, raw with grief, broke on the words. "I know you won't believe me, but I didn't really think of it, not until Raq asked who knew. Flynn's . . . nice. We've chatted for ages. He couldn't . . . he couldn't . . ."

"Flynn wouldn't have any reason to stay in the Lough Rynn house," Megan pointed out carefully. "He lives here." She nodded at the village they were passing through on their way back to the grand old estate.

Gratitude and relief sprang to Jessie's face. "Oh my god, you're right. That wouldn't make any sense. Neither would attacking his aunt, but . . ." Her expression crumpled again. "But who, then? Who else even knew Mama was here?"

Megan sighed quietly. "I'm sorry, Jessie, but your mother wasn't very discreet. She came into our offices talking about being the countess of Leitrim and the estate she should inherit, and loads of people overheard and gossiped about it. Even if she didn't talk about treasure specifically, the fact that she was talking about this place like it was worth something might have gotten someone digging around for gossip, and then if they found out Maire Cahill was up here with a metal detector, like there might *be* treasure . . ."

She was certain Detective Bourke had imparted some of this to the sisters, but the slow shock settling into their faces suggested that if he had, none of it had really sunk in. Which made sense, really; they'd all been through a lot over the past few days, and what Megan had just told them was obviously difficult information to accept. Under the same circumstances, it might have bounced off Megan, too.

"You mean it could be anybody," Sondra finally said. "I mean, it really could be anybody. *God!* God, why couldn't she just keep her damn mouth shut? Why couldn't she just see a lick of sense for once in her damn life and realize that even fairy tales have dark sides!"

Raquel began, "Mama believed in the best of people," but Sondra overrode her with an unintelligible roar.

"Mama believed in every shyster and con man who came along, Raquel! She gave tens of thousands of dollars to frauds every year of her life! She got a second mortgage on her *house*, Raquel! She bought into a pyramid scheme that collapsed, because of course it did, and she couldn't pay the loans back! And even then you're damned right: she believed in the best of the scammer who sold her on it and said she was sure he didn't understand how risky it was for her! God bless that woman, I loved her, Raq, even if you don't think I did, but she didn't have the sense God gave a goose!"

"No, she couldn't—" Raquel stopped, dumbfounded. "She couldn't have done that. She never said anything about losing the house. She didn't lose the house."

"I paid her loans back, Raquel." Sondra lost the last vestiges of both anger and rigidity, slumping to stare out the window as they turned up the drive to the Lough Rynn house. "I paid back her loans. Trevor didn't want me to. That's why he left me. And it's why I have to be back for this meeting, because if I lose the company I'm so far in debt I'll never get out. So if Mama got herself killed by running her mouth, then God, I am sorry, I am so, *so* sorry, but honestly, Raq, I don't think I'm surprised. She never did a thing in her life without somebody having to bail her out, up to and including marrying Daddy. Oh, come on," she said wearily to her sisters' mystified faces. "Count the months, Raq. When did they get married?"

"September fifteenth," Raquel said promptly.

"And when's my birthday?"

"March ninth. Wh—oh. Oh my God. Oh my *God*."

Jessie, her voice high, said, "Was Daddy even your daddy?" and Sondra threw her hands up.

"In every way that mattered, he was. Whether he's my biological father I don't know. I can't believe you two never . . ." She sighed and closed her eyes. "Well, it doesn't matter now."

Raquel, fingers pressed against her mouth again, whispered, "Maybe Mama really *did* steal him from Peggy Ann Smithers," and put her face in her hands. Megan, feeling very much the interloper, but also glad for Sondra's sake that the truth had come out, parked the car and quietly got out to open the doors, first for Sondra. The oldest sister gave her a grim *well-the-cat's-out-of-the-bag* look as she got out, and Megan made some effort not to meet the other women's eyes as they too exited the car.

Tears streaked Jessie's face and she stumbled getting out, but Sondra caught her. A terrible understanding darkened the young woman's eyes, as if she'd realized, for the first time in her life, that Sondra had always been there to catch them when they fell. All of them, including their mother. Megan wasn't surprised when Jessie dissolved into tears and flung herself at Sondra for a hard hug. For once Raquel didn't join in the embrace, only stood a few steps to the side, watching with a shell-shocked gaze. After a while she said, "Where are the police?" and even Megan, who hadn't thought of that either, looked around for them.

"Where's *Reed*?" Jessie asked unhappily. "His car's not here. I was going to go back to Dublin with him." She got her phone and texted him, then smiled wanly when a response came back. "He went to get snacks for the drive back. That was nice of him."

"He's turned out all right," Sondra conceded. "It was nice of him to come all the way over here for you."

"Right?" Jessie's eyes welled up and she pushed her hand across them impatiently. "And I guess if we get married he'll bag himself an heiress after all. Should we go . . . I don't know. On a treasure hunt?"

"I have a crowbar in the boot, but not a shovel," Megan said. "But if there's much digging to do we're not going to get it done tonight anyway. The sun will set in about twenty minutes."

"I could really use the chance to shove heavy things around," Sondra muttered. Megan got the crowbar and Sondra stalked off while Megan let the dogs out. Jessie and Raquel hung back, walking ahead of Megan but well behind Sondra, whispering to each other about Sondra's revelations. Megan genuinely believed neither of them had had any idea of their mother's dangerous frivolity, but they were taking it surprisingly well. Maybe they had known on some level, and having it revealed actually did help explain how Cherise Williams had gotten herself killed on a miserable January afternoon in Dublin.

By the time they caught up with Sondra, she had levered the first of the stacked stones aside and was cranking the second one up to an angle where it, too, would fall to the side. Sweat and mist stuck her hair to her temples and curled it at her nape, but she almost snarled a refusal when Jessie edged forward to help. Instead of being hurt, Jessie just took a few steps back, watching with the rest of them as Sondra pushed the second stone on top of the first and stopped to decide what to do next.

She had two short piles of equal height now, making levying the third stone over onto the new pile more difficult. Jessie stepped up again, gesturing with her jaw. "Get it up on its side a little and we'll pick it up and move it."

"It weighs a ton."

"I bet it doesn't weigh more than a couple hundred pounds." Jessie smiled tightly and went around to one end of the stones while Raquel took the other. Megan, juggling leashes, felt guilty about not helping, but not guilty enough to actually help. Sondra had great form, using her leg strength to levy the stone, and her sisters helped crash it into place. The one standing stone suddenly shifted, pushing the flat stone on the ground up a little, and Sondra shoved the crowbar under it, taking the opportunity she'd been offered. The others had to lift that one considerably higher to get it onto the new pile they were creating, and the standing stone crashed over backward as they did. All three of them stood there panting and staring into the space they'd cleared until Jessie said, "Well, crap."

Megan came forward, dew turning to beads on her shoes, to look into the hole. Or depression, really: it wasn't deep enough to be considered a hole. And there was another stone inside it, with earth creeping over its edges, so that to remove it would take at least some actual digging. Sondra prodded at its sides with the crowbar, then pushed a hunk of grass out of the way, looking to see how deeply embedded the stone was. "Could be worse."

"Okay, but if you're going to dig that one out, do it from this side," Raquel said. "We need to flop it over to where you are instead of lifting it onto these other ones or my back will break."

Jessie said, "Wah-wah-wah," but neither she nor Sondra actually argued. She did say, "Should we move these other ones farther back so we have more room to work?" and after a long minute Sondra shook her head.

"No, we might want to put them back in place. We should, whether we find something or not. Let's not make more work for ourselves."

"I think trying to work around them *is* making more work for ourselves." Jessie shrugged, though, and when Sondra got tired of digging with a crowbar, took over. It didn't really take all that long to flop the buried stone out of its bed, but she let out a groaning laugh as it fell away. "Oh no. You've got to be kidding me."

"The good news is there were only seven stones in Patrick's drawings," Raquel said hopefully. "Maybe this is the last one."

"I hope so, because it's going to be a lot harder to get out." Sondra was right: It was full-on dark before they'd unearthed the final stone, the sisters taking turns working and holding phone torches so they could see what they were doing. They finally flopped it aside, though, and a shiver went down Megan's spine.

A hole about the width of a man's shoulders lay beneath the altar's site.

"We're not going in that in the dark." Sondra sounded like she hoped to be convinced.

"It's not going to be any less dark in there during the day," Jessie pointed out. "And don't you want to see what's down there?"

"Not that much!"

Jessie said, "I do!" and Megan, who felt the same way, didn't put in a vote, since she didn't belong to the family. Sondra still sent her a mute appeal for help, which would have been less effective in daylight. In the hard LED torchlight she looked quite pale and awful, like she was genuinely afraid. The dogs nosed their way forward and barked at the hole, which echoed dully enough to quell some of Jessie's enthusiasm. She looked at Raquel in hopes of finding a tiebreaker, but Raquel was frowning toward the distance.

"Weren't the police supposed to come? And where's

Reed? We've been digging for an hour. It doesn't take that long to get snacks."

"He's probably back at the house sitting in the car wondering where we are. I'll text him." Jessie wiped her hand on her jeans, trying to clean her fingers before using her phone. Megan, the only one of them who wasn't dirty, said, "Tell you what. I'll call Detective Bourke and see what happened to the guards out here, and then Jessie and I can go down the hole while you and Raquel keep watch, okay, Sondra?"

"I think that's a terrible plan, but I don't know why we dug it up tonight if we're not going down, so I suppose so."

"Reed says he came back and we weren't here so he went to get dinner." Jessie sounded confused, but shrugged. "I mean, the car was here, but whatever, I guess. He says he's on his way back now. I told him we're at the druid's altar. C'mon, let's go, Megan. I want to see what's down there."

"Hang on." Megan offered Sondra the leashes and she crouched to pet the dogs while Megan rang Bourke. He didn't pick up, and she left a message saying the gardaí hadn't shown up to secure the site and for him to call her back. As if that part needed saying, she thought as she hung up, but she'd said it anyway. "All right, let's try. It could be only three feet deep. It's too dark to tell."

Jessie got a branch from beneath one of the big oak trees and poked it as deeply into the hole as she could. "More than three feet," she said helpfully.

"It could be deep enough to break your neck climbing in," Sondra muttered. Jessie scowled, but then unwound one of her scarves. It turned out to be about ten feet long, much longer than Megan had expected. Jessie made a

cradle for her phone in the fringe at one end, and, satisfied it was secure, lowered it carefully into the hole. It
went down six or eight feet before reaching bottom, the
torchlight casting shadows on a tunnel entrance a couple
of feet high. A thrill of uncertainty shot through Megan's
gut and she accidentally let loose a nervous little laugh.

"Okay, I'm not sure I'm up for crawling half a kilometre through the dark to an uncertain destination . . ."

"It's not uncertain. We know it leads somewhere under
the garden."

"Maybe we should have started in the garden," Raquel
said. "We didn't even go look to see if we could find the
arch."

"If it's still there that means it's made of stone or concrete," Jessie said airily. "We'd never be able to break
through it. Okay, I'll go look at the tunnel and if it's im-
passable you can pull me back up and we'll do this another way."

"Tomorrow," Sondra said. "In the daylight."

Jessie, already sitting on her butt at the edge of the
hole, said, "Right. Tomorrow in the daylight. Whee!" She
slid down and landed on soft earth with what sounded
like a bone-rattling thump. Her muffled voice came up in
bits and pieces. "The tunnel opening down here is just
dirt. It's—" Megan peered down to watch her knock
pieces of it away. "It's pretty tall. Creeping height, not
crawling height. The air smells okay." She looked back
up at Megan, her face already smeared with muck. "Are
you up for it?"

Megan looked between the young woman smiling
hopefully up at her and Jessie's older sisters. Sondra rolled
her eyes expressively and spread her hands. "Might as
well."

"It shouldn't take too long," Jessie said happily. "We can mostly walk, and all we're really going to do is see if there's anything at the other end. We'll take pictures if there are. How long does it take to walk a kilometre?"

"About ten minutes. Under the circumstances let's assume it'll take that long to do half of one. If we're not back in half an hour, Sondra . . ." Megan had no good ideas as to what should be done if they weren't back, but Sondra nodded.

"Be careful."

"Absolutely." Regretting the future condition of her chauffeur's uniform, Megan sat on the edge of the hole and slid down after Jessie. For the space of a breath she fell, and in that time, considered this to be one of the stupidest things she'd ever done. Then she hit the soft earth with a thump and, safe and literally grounded, she thought maybe it wasn't so bad. Jessie and her torch were already several feet ahead of her, hunched in a tunnel about four feet tall but easily passable.

A few minutes later Megan decided that creeping through a limestone hollow had never been on her bucket list, and now that she was doing it, she was confident it wasn't something she'd ever *needed* to do in order to feel she'd lived a full and satisfying life. It was relatively easy going, though. The tunnel, while very dirty, was smoother than she expected. She supposed the little lake now behind them had, at some point in its history, been fed by the larger Lough Rynn somewhere ahead of them. "Can you imagine being a kid a hundred years ago crawling through this without a flashlight?"

Jessie said, "Oh my god," in genuine horror. "No, I didn't even think about that. Do you think he had an actual torch or something?"

"Probably. And also a more intrepid sense of adventure than I've got."

"He was only twenty-two when he left Ireland," Jessie said. "He was probably too young to think he could ever be in danger, when he was exploring this thing."

"The innocence of youth," Megan agreed, and they went quiet again, as if the weight of earth above them pressed them into silence. The tunnel widened and narrowed again a couple of times, then suddenly opened into a chamber that only earned that distinction by being twice as wide and slightly taller than anywhere they'd passed through before.

Moldering sacks and decaying wood spread across the floor, still half-visible beneath pellets of blackened silver and the gleam of pure, untarnished gold.

CHAPTER 23

Jessie Williams heaved like she might actually vomit with excitement. Megan, although sympathetic to the sentiment, said, "I swear to god if you throw up in here I'll rub your nose in it like a puppy," and Jessie gulped, then giggled through watering eyes.

"Legit. That would be the grossest thing ever. Oh my god, Megan. Oh my god. Is it real?"

"I think so." Megan couldn't quite get herself to move any closer to the piles of loot, which was unquestionably what lay in front of them. Most of it was lumped against the back wall—corner, if a roundish chamber could be said to have corners—with individual bits having rolled free as their containers rotted, or as intrepid small animals explored the little cave. Coins lay among the silver nuggets, and what gold she could see had been shaped into bracelets and torcs. She burped bile herself and put a rattling hand over her stomach, trying to calm it. Hot and cold kept running through her, breaking a sweat all over her body, then turning it icy. "Holy, um. Wow. I . . . Wow."

Jessie giggled again. "Yeah. Yeah. Oh my god." She finally nerved herself up and crept closer, kneeling near the outer edge of the hoard. "Oh my god. How could a *kid* find this and not tell anybody?" She started taking pictures before she even touched anything, which Megan thought was amazingly restrained.

"I don't know. Well. I guess it would sure be a great source of personal pocket money." She gave the same kind of high-pitched giggle Jessie was indulging in, and suddenly they were both wheezing with laughter at the idea of a short-pantsed Victorian tween passing off the occasional Viking coin as his allowance. "Oh my god. Oh my god." Megan finally wiped her eyes and came forward to crouch beside Jessie, passing her hands over the lumps of silver and gold without touching it. "There must be twenty pounds of this stuff here. What's it *doing* here? This is—" Megan sat hard, breath suddenly coming in short gasps. "Jessie, this is . . . I drive people around Ireland all the time and I've learned a lot of the stories about treasure finds here. This has got to be one of the biggest finds ever. This is—we better not touch it. We're supposed to call the authorities. I'll call Paul as soon as we're back aboveground."

"But it's our land!"

"It's Anne Edgeworth's land," Megan said dryly. "Which means she'll probably get half of whatever valuation the government puts on it to pay out to the treasure finders, which is you and your family."

"And you!"

"I—if that's what you decide, that would be . . ." Megan shook her head. "The point is this is a national treasure. It doesn't matter if it's your land or not. Take—we'll just take . . . pictures." She couldn't blame Jessie in the least when the younger woman picked up one of the gold bracelets and slid it on her wrist, then hefted its weight in astonishment.

"It weighs a ton," Jessie whispered reverently. "Wow. Try it on." She took a selfie with the bracelet on display before offering it to Megan, who wasn't quite good enough a person to say no. For the next several minutes they traded items, trying them on, taking pictures, and giggling like idiots, until Megan suddenly cried, "Oh no, we said we'd be back in half an hour! We'd better run!"

"Can't I take just one?" Jessie pouted when Megan pointed imperiously to the hoard, but she put everything back. Megan took a few more pictures of the whole thing, then followed Jessie back out the tunnel, both of them chattering with excitement and not really listening to the other as they hurried back. Part of Megan wanted to turn back and go sit with the ridiculous trove they'd found, as if it would somehow disappear if not watched. Up ahead of her Jessie yelled, "I'm back, help me up!" to her sisters. Megan caught up to squat, put Jessie on her shoulders, and stand with a dramatic grunt, lifting Jessie as someone's hand came down to pull her from the surface. Jessie shrieked, "Reed!" gleefully as she rose. "Reed, Raq, Sonny, you won't believe what we found!"

"Treasure?" Reed asked with a chuckle.

Jessie squealed, "Yes! Help Megan up, we'll show you the pictures! Where are Raq and Sonny?"

"They went to use the woods as a toilet."

"*Sonny* did that?" Jessie laughed and obviously started

showing Reed pictures anyway, because no one offered a hand as Megan looked up. She rolled her eyes, put her back against one side of the entrance hole, and tested the distance to the other side with her feet. She'd never get her jacket clean, but she could climb the walls herself if she had to. Reed was up there gasping over the photos while Jessie giggled happily, and Megan, faintly exasperated, dug a handhole into the dirt, seeing if it would hold her. It collapsed as soon as she put weight on it, which was what she expected from earth she could dig a hole into with her hands anyway.

"Hey, hello?" Megan shone her torch upward, trying to get their attention.

"Sorry, Megan!" Jessie appeared at the top, smile sparkling. "Can you use a braid of my scarves to help climb up with or should I find rocks or something to drop down for you to boost yourself up on?"

"The scarves should work." Megan smiled and Jessie disappeared, the ends of her scarves flying above the hole as she took them off and started braiding them. The shadows from Megan's upward-facing phone torch made a fascinating pattern against the dark sky before a weirdly familiar hollow *thunk* sounded, the dull noise of flesh hitting flesh. The scarves fell as Jessie gave a short cry of pain, and a moment later Reed appeared above the hole, his teeth bared in a furious smile. He held a bowie knife in one hand, its short blade bouncing torchlight around. Megan went cold to her core, her body feeling thick and stupid even as she abruptly understood, on some level, exactly what had been going on for the past few days.

"So now you're going to go back in there and bring out as much of that treasure as you can carry," he said, almost conversationally. "When you've brought it all, we'll see whether I help you out or not. If you don't, I'm going to start by killing this stupid, needy, won't-shut-up bitch, and then her sisters, and then your goddamn dogs."

Megan croaked, "What?" and bent to get her phone, shining its torchlight more toward Reed, like she could understand him better if she could see him more clearly. She said, "What?" again, trying to sound genuinely stupid and using it to cover the action of activating her phone's voice recorder.

"I said go get the fucking treasure, Megan, or I'm going to kill everybody and your dogs. *Jesus*, why are women so stupid? Fucking Jessie, mouthing off about her family's estate since forever, like there was something important on it, and her stupid Irish boyfriend telling me all about his crazy aunt who goes treasure hunting. Jesus Christ. Go get the gold."

"Okay." Megan spread her free hand, her voice hoarse. "Irish boyfr—Flynn? What does Flynn have to do with anything?"

Reed stared at her like she was a fool, which Megan, her frozen shock starting to thaw, thought might have some merit. "I hacked Jess's genealogy account to see who she was cheating on me with. I found Flynn," he sneered the name, "and read all his messages about his aunt treasure hunting on Jessie's estate. So I flew the fuck over here to check it out, and then it turns out her stupid mother was coming here too, and I couldn't let her get in my way."

Megan, softly, said, "Oh my god," and took a step back like she was afraid, before whispering, "Do you . . . I could carry more with a bag. It'd be faster. Do you have a backpack?"

Reed curled his lip. "In the car, but like I'm going to

leave you alone to make a phone call while I'm getting it. Why would you want me to hurry anyway?"

"Because I'm in a pit ten feet deep and I won't get out until I've done what you wanted? It's gonna take more than one trip anyway, and I don't want to be down here any longer than I have to be." Megan's heartbeat nearly drowned out her words in her own hearing, adrenaline and fear crashing through her. "What if I throw my phone up there so I can't call while you're gone? You can give it back to me for the light when you get back."

"Yeah. Yeah, okay." Reed sounded dubious but satisfied at the idea. "Throw it up here."

Megan turned the voice recorder and the torch both off, made sure the phone was locked to her fingerprint, and tossed it up to him. It soared up in an easy arc and he snatched it from the air on the first try, then threw it aside. His voice was mocking as he said, "Don't go anywhere."

"Not likely." Megan waited a full minute for his footsteps to fade, then scrambled to brace her back against one side of the tunnel and her feet against the other. It would be easier with another ten inches of width to scrunch into; as it was, she had to put a lot of weight on her toes to squeeze upward, but she reached the top in less than five minutes and flopped herself onto the stones, gasping for breath.

Her eyes had adjusted to a darkness barely brightened by a crescent moon while she'd climbed, and she could see well enough to find Jessie's unconscious form slumped a few feet away from the deconstructed druid's altar. Megan checked the young woman over very quickly—she had a massive bruise coming up on her jaw, but didn't seem otherwise hurt—and bet on youth and vitality overcoming any potential unseen injuries. She found her own phone, sent a text that said only **911** to Paul Bourke, and dragged Jessie off the ground and into a fireman's carry. Hauling a dead weight from the ground to over her shoulders wasn't Megan's favourite thing to do, but she really wanted to get Jessie well away from Reed's return. She followed the already-trampled path back toward the house, then cut away into the woods far enough away from the altar that she hoped Reed wouldn't notice. Her whole body buzzed with endorphins as she found a tree to deposit Jessie under and whisper, "Hey. Hey, Jess, can you wake up? Jessie?"

Jessie came awake with a gasp and Megan whispered, "Shh, shh, it's Megan, you're safe. He's back at the car. I'm going to go find your sisters. Don't go anywhere and don't use your phone, he'll see the screen glow. I already texted for help, okay? You hear me? You understand?"

"Yeah." Jessie shivered, tears in her eyes, but she nodded. "Come back for me."

"Don't worry. I will. You just stay here, stay quiet, stay brave. Okay? Can you do that?" At the younger woman's nod, Megan smiled, kissed her forehead, and sprang up to run, quietly, back to the druid's altar. The grass immediately around it was flattened from them working and walking around earlier, but there were no signs of bloodshed, no stains of purple-black under the thin moonlight. Megan's chest hammered with relief. She didn't think Reed had killed the older sisters—his knife had been clean, and if he'd had a syringe of air to pump them full of, he probably wouldn't have bothered showing off with the blade. Or, at least, Megan wouldn't have, in his position. She would have waited until she, Megan, was out of the hole, killed *her* with the syringe, and gone in for the treasure herself. Either Reed wasn't that clever, or she had a wider criminal streak than she'd previously imagined.

There were trails in the grass where bodies had clearly been dragged to the side. Megan followed them and found Raquel and Sondra, both conscious but gagged and bound with, Megan saw in dismay, the dogs' leashes. She pulled their gags out and Sondra said, "The puppies ran away as soon as they were off their leashes."

A shock of relief much stronger than she'd expected knocked Megan back a moment. She let out a shaky breath, nodded, and whispered, "Jessie's safe. He clobbered her, but I got him to go look for a bag to put the treasure in and got her to safety," as she untied them. "He killed your mother. I'm sorry."

"*How?*" Raquel kept her voice quiet, but the single word resounded as a plaintive cry anyway. "He didn't get to Dublin until after Jessie and Sonny did!"

"He'd been here for days. Maybe weeks. Jessie said she hadn't heard from him since Christmas, right? He must—ah, dang it! He must have been the person staying in the house. And we left him to guard it!"

"No wonder the police didn't show up." Sondra rubbed her wrists as Megan released them. "Or rather, they probably did, but he would have cleared everything out and they wouldn't have found anything, so they probably left again. Dammit!"

"And he knew what Mama looked like, so sneaking up on her—she wouldn't even have been suspicious if she saw him. She'd just have been delighted to see someone she knew," Raquel whispered. "And the diary, he knew about the diary, Jessie would have told him all about it all. Oh no. Oh no."

"You two stay put," Megan half-asked, half-ordered.

"Do you have your phones? I texted Detective Bourke for help but if someone doesn't show up soon, you should try again. Wait as long as you can stand, though. I don't want Reed to see the phones glowing. You'd be surprised how easy they are to see in a dark night, and if I'm gonna go deal with him I'd rather he didn't have any idea I was coming."

"You're going to deal with him? By yourself?"

Megan gave Sondra a tight smile. "I mostly drove and was a medic in the military, but they taught us how to do a few other things too." Even in the dim moonlight, Sondra visibly paled and nodded. Megan nodded back. "Keep an eye out for the dogs, would you? But don't call them. It's too quiet out here and he'll hear you."

"You'll come back for us?" Raquel whispered, just like Jessie had done. Megan pulled a reassuring smile for her, even knowing it would barely be seen in the darkness.

"Absolutely. Give me twenty minutes." She rose, then paused. "We found a treasure, by the way. A huge one. That's what Reed was after."

"He wanted an heiress all along," Sondra said bitterly, but for once, Raquel was the more cynical.

"He never wanted Jessie at all, just her kingdom."

"Well, he's not going to get any of it." Megan stalked back toward the druid's altar, taking a long way around the clearing and moving carefully between trees to keep cover even in the darkness. One enormous tree stretched directly over the altar, its big branches reaching down to nearly touch its one standing stone. Megan, keeping an eye on the path Reed would return on, shimmied up the tree and tucked herself behind its main trunk, just beside the broad V that split the reaching branch over the altar.

Her heartbeat had slowed and her thoughts were calm before Reed, carrying his hiking pack, approached again. Sometimes the moments before a fight could be like that: clear and calm, instead of raging with adrenaline, although the heightened sharpness of her mind meant she *was* still pumped high on natural chemicals, just not feeling the effect of them as strongly. She saw him realize Jessie was no longer lumped on the ground, and despite her night vision being disrupted by his torch, she clearly saw panic descending on his features. He ran closer to the altar, to where he'd left Jessie and then, foolishly, spun away from the altar, and the tree, to scan the nearby woods.

Megan launched herself out of the tree and crashed into his shoulders so hard she kept rolling when they hit the ground. She slammed her elbow into his temple before he could recover, and he made a faint sound of groggy confusion that indicated she'd stunned him. It wouldn't last. Megan came to her feet, yanked the empty backpack off him, and hog-tied him with the dogs' leashes before even checking for a pulse. She disarmed him, taking the knife first, then patting him down thoroughly to see if he had any other weaponry before walking several steps away and sitting down on the fallen stones with a *whoof*. Her shoulders and jaw were already starting to ache from the impact of tackling him, although she knew it wouldn't really begin to hurt until the excitement wore off. After about ten deep breaths, she shouted, "Okay, it's safe now. I've got him tied up, you can come out!"

A flurry of small white bodies rushed at her immediately, licking and whining and wiggling as they made sure Megan was all right. The Williams sisters appeared more slowly, but once they saw each other they ran forward, crashing into one another and falling to the ground in a sobbing, relieved heap. Megan rubbed the puppies thoroughly and got up—stiffly, as it turned out—to find her phone. Its glass was cracked, but it had otherwise survived unscathed, and she was just about to call Detective Bourke when a flare of police lights cut through the woods. She stood there, the phone at her ear, watching the lights come closer, then stop.

A moment later, Paul Bourke, flanked by a handful of other officers, all of whom were carrying torches, came through the woods at a run. Bourke slowed as he recognized her, tucking away a gun she'd never seen him unholster before, and raised a hand to slow the other officers as he took in the scene—the trussed-up Reed, the weeping sisters, the hopping puppies—around her, and finally met her eyes. "We really have to stop meeting like this."

Megan sat hard on the fallen stones and laughed until the tears came. "Yeah," she said eventually, wiping her eyes. "Yeah, we probably should, but it doesn't look promising, does it? It keeps happening. We got the bad guy. I think I managed to record most of his confession. And there's a massive Viking treasure down the hole behind me. Did I miss anything?" she asked the Williamses, who looked between her and Paul with a kind of conniving interest.

"No," Sondra said. "No, I don't think you did. I think we'd better try to get this all over with, Detective. We still have a lot to do before the funeral."

CHAPTER 24

The funeral was, as Father Anthony predicted, attended by nearly the entire population of Mohill, as well as Father Nicholas from St. Michan's and, to Megan's amused surprise, Peter the tour guide. Anne Edgeworth and Maire Cahill, the latter's head still bandaged from the wound Reed had dealt her, effectively presided, which none of the Williams sisters seemed to object to. The older two sisters didn't even object to Flynn's presence at Jessie's side. And on Megan's side of things, Jelena, frowning with worry over the entire mess Megan had gotten herself into—she'd heard about it all over coffee and cinnamon rolls that morning—drove up on her own to be there for Megan, which Megan thought was an exceptionally nice gesture.

Even Orla, so relieved to be cleared of any association with Cherise Williams's death that she came up from

Dublin for the funeral, had the decency to look upset over the whole mess. She went so far as to mutter, "Thanks," at Megan, without any clarification on what the thanks were for.

Megan, pleased, accepted them for what they were worth, and, as the funeral wrapped up, walked a little distance away from the crowd to put a call through to a landline in Texas. A few rings later, an older woman's voice picked up with, "Hello?"

"Hey, Mom, it's Megan."

"Megan!" Astonishment filled her mother's voice. "Is everything all right, honey? It's awfully early to be calling."

"Yeah, I know. Everything's fine." Megan closed her eyes, grateful for the concern in her mother's voice. "Work's been a little crazy and I just wanted to say hi."

"I heard from Gabriela Silva," Cate Malone said rather sternly. "Another death, Megan? You know I didn't like you joining the military, but I did think driving a limousine would be safer."

Megan laughed quietly. "Dang, the Texas gossip wheel does its work fast."

"I have to get my information from outside sources because my daughter only calls on major holidays and my birthday."

"Well, I'm calling now and it's neither. And it is safer, Mom. Nobody's shooting at me or anything."

"Still, you could come home," her mom said hopefully. "Jerry Hodges moved back recently. You used to like him."

"When I was twelve." Megan laughed again. "No, I think I'm good, Mom."

"Yes, but you could be good at home with me and

Jerry and a couple of babies if you squeezed them out really fast."

"See, this is why I only call on holidays, Mom."

Her mother sighed heavily. "All right, fine. It's not that I want grandchildren, you understand. It's just a genetic imperative to carry on. I simply don't want the line to die out."

"Fortunately Aunt Carol has three kids who all have children of their own. I think your genetic contribution to the future is safe for the time being."

"A quarter of it," her mom said morosely. "It's not the same."

Megan pursed her lips. "I only have half your genes anyway, so any potential kids of mine would be a quarter of yours, which is what Carol's kids have anyway. I think her grandkids must be like a twelfth of your genes or something?"

"You're not helping, Megan."

Megan smiled. "I love you, Mom. How's Dad?"

"I love you too, honey. Your father has manicured the backyard within an inch of its life and was eyeing my zinnias. I had to send him to the golf course before he became completely demented. I'm not sure retirement agrees with him. Are you sure you're all right?"

"Yeah. I just wanted to say hi before I had to get back to work."

"Okay. If you call me again and it's not a major holiday I promise not to mention grandchildren."

"I may never call on a holiday again!" Megan said her goodbyes and hung up, smiling and shaking her head. As she put her phone away, Paul Bourke walked a crisply uniformed woman in her late fifties over to Megan, and pleaded with his gaze for her to be on her best behaviour.

"Megan, this is my captain, Ruth Long. Captain, this is Megan Malone."

Megan offered her hand and an apologetic smile. "It's a pleasure to meet you, Captain. I'm sorry for being a trouble magnet."

"I'm sure you are." Captain Long examined Megan with a gimlet eye before letting go an exasperated breath. "You don't *look* like trouble. Have you ever considered giving up driving, to let the gardaí have a moment's peace?"

"In my defense, ma'am, most of Dublin's crime doesn't centre around me. I don't know how I keep ending up involved in these things."

"Well, I'd like you to stop." Long gave Megan a sharp nod, Bourke a less sharp one, and walked off to offer her condolences to the Williamses. Megan watched her go, then squinted at Bourke.

"She does know it doesn't work that way, right? Unless she's got a leprechaun on hand to ask a wish of, in which case I assume she'd spend it on something better than keeping me out of trouble."

Bourke glanced in the general direction of the car park. "You're the one with the leprechaun on your dashboard. Maybe you should ask it for a wish. And Captain Long is used to the world falling into line the way she expects it to, so she might think it works that way. I, however," he said with a long-suffering sigh, "have already asked you repeatedly to stop getting in trouble and it hasn't worked yet, so I haven't much faith for the future. How's the treasure hunt coming?"

"Oh, I don't know. They say it'll be weeks, probably months, before there's any kind of full assessment, and longer than that before they decide what the finder's fee is. Apparently it really is one of the best of its kind, though. I'd thought there were loads of big Viking treasures in Ireland, but I guess this is almost unique. They said it's worth millions, even though if you melted it down the silver, especially, wouldn't really be all that special. Silver costs a lot less than I thought it did."

"Gold costs more, though. Who's going to get the finder's fee?"

"The Williamses. Anne apparently really has called her lawyer in and amended her will, thanks to that DNA test you ran. That was nice of you," Megan added. Bourke shrugged it off, albeit with a smile. "So they're keeping the whole fee in the family. Sondra wants to put the money into the estate, try to turn it into a luxury hotel. I don't think they'll get that much money out of it, but they can probably get some help from the government, and having the treasure site as part of the gardens will be a draw. And I don't know how much Anne Edgeworth is worth even without a Viking treasure."

"More than most of us will ever be." Bourke slid his hands into his overcoat's pockets, exhaling a steamy breath into the cold air, and nodded toward the mourning Williams sisters. "I wouldn't want to be giving you the idea I approved, but you've done well by them, Megan. They were lucky to have you."

"You'd have figured it out, if Reed hadn't straight-up confessed to me after assaulting all of them. Faster, if I hadn't accidentally let the killer go clear out his hideaway and tell the local gardaí that it was all a wild-goose chase."

"But you'd taken pictures to prove it had all been there, even if we hadn't found it all in his boot. Stupid," Bourke said absently. "He should have dumped it in the lake so. Even so, I left Dublin as soon as I got your text about the room being used in the house. I was almost here when you sent the 911—it's 999 here, Megan—but I still didn't get here in time to do anything but the formal arrest. We really do have to stop meeting like that."

"It's not like I mean for us to!"

Bourke chuckled. "I know. All right so, I've got to head out. I was supposed to pick Niamh up at the airport, but I've left her to fend for herself so I could come to the funeral."

"I'm sure she understands."

"She does so. I hear you're driving us to the premiere tomorrow night."

"I am," Megan said, pleased. "I'm looking forward to seeing you all dolled up."

"You've seen me 'all dolled up' before." Bourke made vague air quotes around the objectionable phrase, and Megan laughed.

"I have, which is why I'm looking forward to seeing it again. She was trying to talk me into dressing up too, but I keep telling her a chauffeur's job is to be invisible."

"I'm terrified." Paul made a face at the confession, but Megan smiled.

"All you have to do is hang around and look handsome and slightly uncomfortable while they fawn on her. It'll be grand so."

"I can do the uncomfortable part well enough. See you tomorrow."

Megan called, "Safe home," after him, then stood aside and waited for the crowds to clear before finally approaching the sisters. "Ready to drive back to Dublin?"

"I just arranged to fly home tonight. Would you mind dropping me off at the airport first?" Sondra looked shattered, her usually precise posture sagging. Jessie, whose jaw sported a dramatic, fist-sized bruise, had an arm around Sondra's waist, helping support her. Flynn stood a few feet back, looking like a hopeful third wheel while Raquel shook a few last hands, giving everyone their thanks. She too looked wrecked when she joined her sisters.

"Of course," Megan told Sondra. "What about you two, when are you leaving?"

"Tuesday morning," Raquel said. "There's some more paperwork we need to deal with tomorrow, but it looks like we can leave after that."

"I'll help," Flynn volunteered clumsily, and flushed when everyone looked his way. "With whatever I can. Must be some good to being local." He shrank in on himself as he spoke, becoming increasingly mortified, but Jessie gave him a smile that seemed to help restore his confidence.

"That'd be really nice of you," she murmured to Flynn, and he brightened considerably.

Raquel, shaking her head with a faint smile, said, "Thank you for all *your* help, Megan. I don't know how we would have gotten through this without you."

Megan exclaimed, "Oh good! I can introduce you to Niamh!" before she'd quite heard everything else Raquel said. "Oh. Oh, well. Thank you. I'm glad I was able to help. I'm glad you're all okay."

"Not just okay. Heiresses," Raquel said with a rueful smile, but Jessie was bouncing up and down beside her, rattling Sondra's teeth.

"Niamh? Niamh O'Sullivan? Really? You'd introduce us?"

"She's coming into town tomorrow. We can go out for

a quick coffee," Megan promised, then glanced around. "Are you ready to go, or would you like a little time alone with your mother?"

All three of them looked toward the grave, then heaved a sigh as one. "I think we can go," Sondra said quietly. "We think we'll come back this summer to visit. Maybe we'll see you again?"

Megan, smiling, gestured them toward the car. "I look forward to the future."

AUTHOR'S NOTE

I mostly try not to take liberties with actual Irish geography and sites while writing the Dublin Driver books, but I have made very bold with one location in *Death of an Irish Mummy*: the Lough Rynn house exists in the real world not as an encroaching ruin, but as an actual luxury castle-hotel.

The story of the missing heir, however, is absolutely true, although the family name has been changed for the purposes of this book. In the early twentieth century, the last remaining heir to the earldom left Ireland (presumably fleeing to America under an assumed name), and despite great effort and cost on the part of the last earl, was never found. A writer really couldn't ask for a better story premise than that!

DEATH ON THE GREEN
A Dublin Driver Mystery
By
Catie Murphy

As an American in Dublin, limo driver Megan Malone will need the luck of the Irish to avoid a head-on collision—with a killer . . .

Life has been nonstop excitement for American Army veteran Megan Malone ever since she moved to Ireland and became a driver for Dublin's Leprechaun Limousine Service. She's solved a murder and adopted two lovable Jack Russell puppies. Currently, she's driving world-class champion golfer Martin Walsh, and he's invited her to join him while he plays in a tournament at a prestigious Irish locale. Unfortunately, there's a surprise waiting for her on the course—a body floating in a water hazard.

Everyone loved golfer Lou MacDonald, yet he clearly teed off someone enough to be murdered. Martin seems to be the only one with a motive. However, he also has an alibi: Megan and hundreds of his fans were watching him play. Now, with a clubhouse at a historical lodge full of secrets and a dashing Irish detective by her side, Megan must hurry to uncover the links to the truth before the real killer takes a swing at someone else . . .

Look for **DEATH ON THE GREEN,** *on sale now!*

Connect with U s

Visit us online at
KensingtonBooks.com
to read more from your favorite authors, see books
by series, view reading group guides, and more.

for sneak peeks, chances to win books and prize packs,
and to share your thoughts with other readers.

facebook.com/kensingtonpublishing
twitter.com/kensingtonbooks

Tell us what you think!

To share your thoughts, submit a review,
or sign up for our eNewsletters, please visit:
KensingtonBooks.com/TellUs.

Grab These Cozy Mysteries
from
Kensington Books

Available Wherever Books Are Sold!

All available as e-books, too!

Visit our website at **www.kensingtonbooks.com**